Tears filled Jill's [...] [...] ross the wood. Gage [...] pre-sented all that had gone wrong in her life.

"You kept it," she murmured. She hadn't expected him to, couldn't imagine seeing it constantly without reliving that awful day.

"I kept it." Gage wrapped his arms around her. "It's part of me," he said softly in her ear. "Just as you are part of me."

She should resist, but she didn't. Instead she curled herself into Gage's embrace. Hot tears spilled down her face. She'd cried so many times over the past two years, but these tears were different. Till now, she'd always shed them alone.

"I love you, Jill," Gage said tenderly. "I want us to be together, and I'm willing to wait for as long as it takes. Because there will never be anyone else for me. Ever…"

Dear Reader,

I don't think I have to tell you that our lives are composed of triumphs and tragedies. We live for the triumphs, but somehow it is the tragedies that mold us. They define us, not only in our own minds but in the minds and hearts of others.

Jill Manning and Gage Engler experienced happy triumphs, successful careers, a loving marriage and the birth of a perfect little boy. But the tragedy in their life, the death of that adorable child, molded their relationship ever after. No two people handle grief or guilt the same way. This is especially true of these two devoted parents. How they rediscover each other and the love that creates new life is the heart of my story. First, however, they must come to grips with serious matters of trust.

I've set this adventure in the fabled town of Tombstone, Arizona, a quiet little place today, but one filled with a violent history. There's no reenactment of the legendary gunfight at the O.K. Corral in the pages that follow, but I hope you find the modern people who live there and the contemporary problems they must face intriguing and satisfying.

I enjoy hearing from readers. You can write me at P.O. Box 61511, San Angelo, TX 76906, or you can visit me on my Web site: www.kncasper.com.

K.N. *Casper*

The Toy Box

K.N. Casper

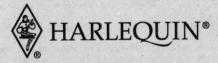

HARLEQUIN®

TORONTO • NEW YORK • LONDON
AMSTERDAM • PARIS • SYDNEY • HAMBURG
STOCKHOLM • ATHENS • TOKYO • MILAN • MADRID
PRAGUE • WARSAW • BUDAPEST • AUCKLAND

ISBN 0-373-71213-8

THE TOY BOX

Copyright © 2004 by Kenneth Casper.

This edition published by arrangement with Harlequin Books S.A.

www.eHarlequin.com

Printed in U.S.A.

This book is dedicated to the memory of Jim Walton,
whose generosity and insight inspired many writers
and who left us all richer for having known him

Books by K.N. Casper

HARLEQUIN SUPERROMANCE

Don't miss any of our special offers. Write to us at the
following address for information on our newest releases.

Harlequin Reader Service
U.S.: 3010 Walden Ave., P.O. Box 1325, Buffalo, NY 14269
Canadian: P.O. Box 609, Fort Erie, Ont. L2A 5X3

CHAPTER ONE

"YOU ASKED TO BE transferred to Tombstone. Why?" Brent Williams sat behind a ragged sea of papers and folders, his arms crossed over a prodigious belly. "The terrorist cell you busted up in San Diego last month was vital to national security. Tombstone is small potatoes by comparison. And you've asked to be assigned there alone, as a helicopter pilot." His eyes narrowed. "What gives, Engler?"

"Two reasons." Gage assumed a relaxed posture in the chair facing his boss. "Doug Vogel's a friend of mine. We flew together in Virginia. I don't think the crash last month was his fault."

Williams nodded. "We suspect the accident may have been sabotage."

"Yet you're willing to dump the blame on him?" Gage worked his jaw. "He may end up in a wheelchair for the rest of his life, and you'll let him sit there, burdened with guilt for his branch chief's death and his own helplessness? The man deserves better than that."

"I don't like it any more than you do," Brent fired back, "but our best forensics team was unable to find any evidence of mechanical malfunction or the fuel contamination he claimed. The agency felt it best to officially close the case."

Gage drew in a breath. The "agency" meant a bunch of bureaucrats who liked to tie things up in nice, neat packages.

"I worked with Vogel for three years and learned to respect him as a man and as an aviator. Instead of ending his career with this black mark on his record, he should be receiving honors. I'd like a stab at setting the record straight."

"Very noble." Williams removed a roll of antacid tablets from his middle desk drawer and popped one into his mouth. "And the second reason?"

"I've been monitoring the situation out there." Actually he'd been following the goings-on in the small southwestern post since long before the crash. "Intelligence reports indicate narcotics traffic and the movement of terrorist weapons through the Tombstone corridor have grown significantly over the past twelve months, and we're hearing more and more rumblings of an Al Qaeda connection."

The corridor or gap was one of the routes traditionally used by cocaine and marijuana smugglers from Central and South America. More recently, however, Middle Eastern terrorists had been finding their way to Mexican shores for infiltration across the porous American border.

"I want to look into the situation out there firsthand," Gage continued. "Robbins's death and the loss of the command pilot smells to me of more than a drug-war casualty or revenge for a bust. My gut tells me something else is going on."

The executive director of Customs and Border Protection stroked his chin. "I'm approving your request to investigate, Engler, but not for the reasons you've given."

Gage frowned. He'd been prepared for rejection, but…an alternate mission?

"You're right," Williams went on. "Something is going on at the Tombstone station. We suspect a mole in the outfit and right now Jill Manning tops the list of suspects. Taking over as the new senior pilot should give you good cover to find out how involved she is."

"Jill…Manning?"

"The new branch chief," Williams explained, apparently taking Gage's stammer for unfamiliarity with the name rather than shock.

"Don't worry about the Al Qaeda connection. Other people are delving into that. Or Vogel's record. That'll be corrected in due course. What I want you to concentrate on is Manning's possible involvement in the drug trade. Since she arrived at the Tombstone station, major narcotics busts have steadily decreased at the same time her personal confiscation rate has gone up, almost geometrically."

"Robbins gave her excellent performance reports."

Williams agreed. "Yeah, well, he indicated to me that his next one wouldn't be nearly as glowing. Let's face it, she had the most to gain by his death."

Gage felt as if someone had just hit him in the solar plexus and sucked all the wind out of him. Being set up against the very woman he wanted to protect hadn't been part of his plan. Finding out she was under suspicion for murdering her boss was even more devastating.

"Yet you appointed her as acting branch chief," he pointed out.

The executive director nodded. "Over several more senior candidates." ·

"Why, if you think she might be mixed up with what's going sour out there?"

"Because she was far and away the best qualified. Her record isn't just clean, it sparkles."

You had to love bureaucracy, Gage thought. It promoted people it didn't trust, mostly because it didn't have the intestinal fortitude to confront them.

"You report Monday," Williams said. "I'll give her a call later today to let her know you're coming."

I'm sure she'll be thrilled.

JILL MANNING NEVER expected to be intimidated by a desk, but even after three weeks the battleship size of this one made her feel like an imposter playing a role. Except she was the branch chief now, the boss, a goal she'd set a long time ago. She wasn't about to let a piece of furniture stand in her way.

The desk, of course, was a minor obstacle. Getting selected for the position over the heads of several of her co-workers added another dimension to the challenge. Most of them had received the news philosophically. A few, though, notably Pratt Dixon, had not been as sanguine. The irony was that Dixon wouldn't even have been considered for the post if the myriad government agencies involved in national security hadn't been brought into the new Department of Homeland Security. Dixon had been the local head of the old Immigration and Naturalization Service. Under the alphabet-soup reorganization he'd been resubordinated to the new Bureau of Customs and Border Protection. He still maintained a separate office south of town, but he'd lost his autonomy and now worked for Jill, a woman ten years his junior.

A tap on the door had her looking up from the daily activity reports she received every morning from each of the sections under her supervision.

"Good morning, Jill. I have that analysis you asked for."

Victor Reyes, the chief of Intelligence, was average in height, swarthy and on the hefty side. He was also smart, even-tempered and thorough. She felt lucky to have him on her team. He'd been at the Tombstone Customs office more than twenty years but hadn't applied for the number-one position, claiming he was in his comfort zone and had no desire to be promoted to his level of incompetence.

She picked up her coffee mug as he closed the door. "What did you find?"

He shook his head. "I wish I could tell you your theory was brilliant." He smiled and took the seat across from her.

"But you can't."

After two years of working on the smuggling problem in the corridor, Jill believed she'd discovered a pattern in the activities of the two major gangs. Her office would receive word that one group, say the Black Hand, was planning to move a large shipment of cocaine through the area. Customs would focus its resources against them, find considerably less than expected, only to learn later that the Green Turtle had gotten a major cache of assault weapons through during that period.

Were the two gangs working in cahoots, coordinating their activities, or could they be monitoring each other and taking advantage of the opposition's vulnerabilities?

"I've cross-referenced our human resource reports with communications intercepts." Reyes handed her a thick folder of papers. "With one exception, I found no commonalities, and that one is probably a fluke. Both groups refer to a man by the name of José García."

Jill sighed. "José García. That's the Spanish equivalent of John Smith." Her command of the language was functional, if not particularly fluent. "Chances are it's a cover name rather than a real person."

Victor nodded.

She took a sip of her coffee, which was cooling fast, and flipped through the pages. "What else?"

"I've reviewed methods of operation to see if there are any common denominators, like means of transportation, routes, the types of diversions used. Again, nothing you can hang your hat on." He shook his head in frustration. "Where did you get the idea they might be linked? We've been keeping close tabs on these groups for a long time and have never seen anything to indicate a tie between them."

"Mack mentioned it," she said, referring to Mack Robbins, her predecessor. She didn't bother to point out that she was the one who had initiated the discussion, based on little more than a gut feeling. The last thing she needed was word spreading that she was operating on female intuition. She'd been surprised when he hadn't rejected her hypothesis out of hand. The two of them had locked horns several times over strategy. In this case, though, he had acknowledged that hunches sometimes paid off and promised to explore her theory.

Unfortunately he died in a helicopter crash before he got a chance.

Reyes ran his fingers through his straight black hair. "If the Green Turtle were an ordinary group of arms merchants, I might buy it, but they've got a political agenda that abhors the use of narcotics."

"Still," Jill said, "politics has been known to make strange bedfellows. The Green Turtle wouldn't be the first terrorist organization to ally itself with the very people it holds in contempt."

"The enemy of my enemy is my friend." He rose to his feet. "I'll keep an eye peeled for leads that might show promise. Do you want me to check with head-quarters to see if they have anything?"

She considered the question a moment. "Let's come up with something more convincing than José García first."

He chuckled. "Probably wise. If they'd discovered a link or hints of one, I'm sure they would have alerted us."

"Thanks. And, Victor, I'd appreciate it if you'd keep this between you and me."

The phone rang. His mission accomplished, Reyes nodded and left the office.

Jill lifted the receiver. Brent Williams was calling. He'd phoned her the past three Fridays, ever since he'd appointed her as branch chief. He'd contacted Mack pe-riodically, as well, but she suspected the senior officer was keeping especially close tabs on her. She tried to convince herself he'd do the same with any new branch chief, but she couldn't shake the nagging suspicion she was receiving exceptional scrutiny. Perhaps that wasn't unreasonable. Her appointment was only temporary; at thirty-two she was young for the job and, of course, she was a *woman*.

"A new pilot?" She repeated Brent's words. "Good." Doug Vogel's slot had been vacant now for six long weeks. "Who is it?"

"Gage Engler. Good man. Excellent record…" The rest of his words slid by without making an impression.

Gage.

Did her boss know they'd once been married? Maybe not. She'd been a Customs agent, he a Coast Guard aviator. Two independent agencies. Though they'd worked closely together, their personnel files were in separate offices, and since she'd always used her maiden name at work, there would be no reason for the new Department of Homeland Security to associate them.

"One of the best chopper pilots we have," Williams said. "I think you'll be pleased with him."

Pleased? No, not pleased. She'd hoped when she'd divorced him in Florida two years ago that she'd never see him again, which was why she'd transferred to Tombstone. Suddenly her stomach contracted.

Gage. The father of her child.

Images flashed before her. A white crib. A bright mobile floating above it. Bottles and lotions. Soft baby-blue blankets. For a moment she thought she caught the scent of talcum and experienced the sensation of an infant suckling her nipple, his tiny hand pressed against her breast. In her mind, his blue eyes were open, studying her, contented.

Her throat tightened and burned. She struggled to get the words out. "When is he arriving?"

"Monday."

She had two days to figure out how she was going

to deal with the man she loved…used to love. The man responsible for her son's death.

"WE'RE MOVING, SON." Gage knelt at the wooden chest, opened the lid and began removing the children's books he'd stored inside. He'd been collecting them for months, each a little more advanced than the previous. At almost two, Rickie would have already taken his first baby steps. Now he'd be climbing where he shouldn't and getting into mischief. Kids did that, boys especially. Gage could almost hear his son laughing, banging toys, practicing his increasing vocabulary, making a racket in general. Little boys did that, too.

Gage had spent occasional evenings reading the books out loud. *I'll huff and I'll puff and I'll blow your house down.* Anyone hearing him would have thought he was out of his mind, fallen into senility, second childhood. But for him, grieving involved sitting in an easy chair, pretending his son was tucked in his lap looking up at him with adoring eyes, then following daddy's finger as he moved it along the simple words and pointed to the colorful pictures. *The first bowl of porridge was too hot. The second was too cold. But the third bowl was just right, and she ate it all up.*

Once he'd lightened the toy box, he covered it with blankets and tied it securely with rope, making it easier to carry downstairs by himself.

"We're going to see Mommy," he said, his voice no more than a whisper. "I know she misses you, too."

CHAPTER TWO

SATURDAY MORNING, Gage walked up the concrete path to the steel-and-glass rehabilitation facility in Tucson. A motorized wheelchair passed him going in the other direction. Its occupant was a middle-aged man missing his right arm and left leg. Gage experienced a ripple of discomfort as he returned the man's friendly greeting and then marched forward. The building's doors opened when he reached them and an elderly woman, wearing a volunteer badge, welcomed him with a Polident smile.

"Mr. Vogel is in 308," she informed him. "Let me see…yes, he should be back from therapy. You can go right up."

The first thing Gage saw when he entered the room was the metal frame over the bed holding a trapeze. On the one occasion he'd been able to visit Doug in the hospital in Phoenix, shortly after the accident, his friend had been heavily medicated with tubes and wires attached to him. At least they were gone.

"Now here's a surprise," the patient said, his voice chipper. "I haven't even had time to give you my forwarding address."

"You can run but you cannot hide." Gage had learned of the move when he'd called the hospital the evening before.

Doug elevated his bed farther with the push of a button. "Not running much right now. Thanks for coming." He extended his left hand. The right arm was in a blue cast.

Gage hoped his eyes didn't betray the sadness he felt. His friend was a big, physically fit man—or had been. He looked weak and vulnerable now against the white sheets. Only his smile of greeting harked back to the stalwart image Gage had of him.

"How are you feeling?" He had spoken with his old friend on the phone a couple of times a week since the crash and had sent get-well cards, mostly of the humorous variety, but this was their first real face-to-face conversation in almost five years.

"I'm alive," Doug said, "even if I'm not kicking. Does your appearance mean you got the assignment we talked about?"

"Since it looks like you'll be vacationing here for a while, the powers that be decided you needed a replacement in Tombstone. Only the best would do, so they sent me."

Doug chuckled. "I'm honored. Pull up a chair."

Gage glanced around. Beside a commode seat was a wheelchair with a gel-filled cushion. In the far corner he found a brown metal-frame armchair that he dragged over.

Using a remote, Doug clicked off the mumbling television mounted on the wall and smiled. "I can't tell you how happy I am to see you, old buddy."

They'd gotten along like brothers when they were stationed together in Virginia, then career assignments had separated them.

"How are things going, really?" Gage asked.

"They tell me to be patient. As if I had much choice."

In addition to several broken bones, Vogel had suffered a contusion of the spinal cord, which had left him paralyzed from the waist down. Since the cord hadn't actually been severed, there was a chance he would recover, but at this point the doctors weren't able to say to what extent or when. It could take up to a year for them to know and several more years of physical therapy before he could walk. Even then, he might never regain full mobility or be able to fly again.

"I'm sorry," Gage said, surprised when he heard the thickness in his own voice.

"Hey—" the guy in the bed checked him with a smile "—it could be worse."

Gage pictured the man who'd lost two limbs. Yeah, it could be worse, but somehow that seemed small consolation. What would he do, he wondered, if he were the one stuck in a bed, faced with the possibility of spending the rest of his life in a wheelchair? The thought was terrifying.

"And things will get better." Doug sounded as if he really believed it.

Gage looked around the room. A couple of potted plants. The cards he'd sent and a few others. Doug had no family, which meant he probably spent most of his time here alone. "Had many visitors?"

"A few, now and then."

"No special lady in your life?"

Doug had never been the marrying type, but he hadn't been celibate, either.

"No, thank heavens. I'd hate to burden a woman with this." He waved his good hand over the bed linens. "I'm not much of a man right now."

Gage wanted to weep for his friend. This was no time to be alone. Of course, in the face of tragedy some people didn't stick. Being abandoned by someone you were counting on would have been worse.

"You're going to be fine, as good as new," he said, and hoped it was true.

Doug shrugged his good shoulder. "Things change. Life goes on." So he did have doubts and fears. "But let's not talk about me. How have you been?"

Gage gave him a thumbnail sketch of the terrorist network he'd just helped bust. The other man showed the expected professional interest in the operational aspects of the case and asked plenty of questions. When Doug asked about his visitor's private life, Gage recounted his assignment to Florida and his transfer to San Diego three years later.

"Jill ever talk about me...about us?" he couldn't help asking.

Doug shook his head. "She recognized my name from the list of people you invited to your wedding, so she knew we were friends." He had sent a gift but couldn't attend the ceremony because of a classified assignment he'd been on at the time. "She said the two of you had split but didn't explain or mention the baby. She even asked me not to tell anyone that she'd ever been married."

That stung. Yet Gage hadn't told anyone on the west coast about his failed marriage or the child they'd buried, either.

"She'll make a good branch chief," Doug went on, "but she's got a real challenge ahead. I'm glad you can be there with her."

"I'm not sure she'll feel the same way." Gage didn't

want to dwell on what would happen when she found out about his clandestine mission. He was tempted to tell his friend but decided to wait. They were reestablishing their connection. He didn't want to spoil it by admitting he'd taken on the role of snoop for Internal Affairs.

Restless, he got up and began pacing. "What's going on out there, Doug? You're too good a pilot to crash your chopper. You told the investigators you experienced engine problems."

Doug's face muscles tightened at the implication that his explanation might be an excuse for his own incompetence.

"I flew with you enough to trust your judgment without question," Gage told him, "and I spent enough time with you out of the cockpit to know you don't lie."

Doug's smile was wan. "Thanks, I needed that."

In an uncharacteristic gesture, Gage moved forward and covered his friend's good hand sympathetically. For just a moment the unique bond only men can share formed between them, and in that instant Gage understood the fear and uncertainty his friend was experiencing but would never voice.

"You suspected fuel contamination," Gage said a second later, withdrawing his hand, "but the investigators found no evidence to substantiate it, either at the accident site or the depot where the aircraft was topped off."

"Whatever was added was probably destroyed in the explosion and fire."

Which made it a perfect weapon. "You think it was sabotage?"

Doug nodded. "Especially since nothing was found

anywhere else. Bad fuel wouldn't be isolated to one aircraft."

"I assume you suggested this to the inspectors?"

"Of course, but they called it pure speculation on my part. In other words, an excuse."

"That's not fair."

Again the man in the bed gave a lopsided shrug. "But it's logical."

"You don't sound bitter." In his position, Gage would be furious.

"I told you, life goes on. Trust me on this. In the past six weeks I've been through it all. Anger, guilt, depression, self-loathing. Now it's time for me to accept reality and move forward. To hell with official reports. My conscience is clear."

Brave words, and Gage was convinced his friend wanted to believe them, even if deep inside he didn't.

"Any idea who did it or why?"

"It could have been a random act, I suppose. Someone wanting to make trouble. God knows, there are enough crazies out there these days. In this case, though, I think the bad guys had a specific victim in mind."

"You?"

"Nah," Doug said with a laugh. "I don't even have a jealous wife trying to get rid of me, and none of the loose women in my harem are the possessive types."

"So you think they were out to get Mack Robbins? I never met him. What was he like?"

After taking a sip of water, Doug leaned back into his pillows. "Smart, opinionated and ambitious. He wasn't the friendliest guy in the world, not what you would call a people person, and he didn't tolerate fools lightly."

"Was there a particular fool he was having trouble with?"

"Since the creation of Homeland Security, a lot of people have resented not faring better in the reorganization, but the person who comes immediately to mind is Pratt Dixon. He used to be the local Immigration honcho and was pretty much his own boss. Now he's subordinate to the branch chief. He and Mack had a couple of shouting matches about how things were being handled. Pratt's convinced he should have gotten the top job. Jill would be well advised to watch her back."

I'll do it for her, Gage vowed. "Anyone else? Maybe someone who had a personal grudge against Robbins, a hothead who might act first and think later?"

"Believe me, I've wondered." Doug pursed his lips. "Ruben Ortiz is the only one I can think of in that category. He's a highway patrolman and his fiancée is going to be your copilot. Definitely the volatile, jealous type, which is understandable as far as Nita Gomez is concerned. Wait till you meet her, Gage. An absolute knockout."

"Are you suggesting Robbins may have been fooling around with her?"

"No. Mack was straight-arrow when it came to women, especially those he worked with. But he did make Ruben persona non grata for a while a few months ago when Ruben got verbally abusive with Nita on the flight line. He wanted her to go somewhere with him and she refused."

"Do you think this guy could or would tamper with the fuel?"

Doug's rejection of the idea was immediate. "Ruben is one of those people who flares up and cools down almost as quickly. The next day he went to Mack and apologized, probably at Nita's behest. Mack was the one more inclined to hold a grudge. Ruben hangs around the maintenance area enough to have the opportunity, but he didn't do it. First of all, he would never do anything that might put Nita in jeopardy. Second, Ruben had nothing against me. If he wanted to kill Mack, he would have confronted him face-to-face with a loaded gun."

"Who else might have had a motive to kill Mack?"

"I honestly don't know. Something was bothering him, though."

Gage tilted his head. "What makes you think that?"

"A feeling more than anything he said. He seemed preoccupied that last morning, less talkative than usual. Distant, as if he had something weighing heavily on his mind."

"You don't know what it was?"

"No idea."

"Family troubles?" Gage shifted in his seat.

"Possibly. He'd been divorced for several years and his ex-wife was constantly bugging him about money she claimed he owed her."

"Did he?"

"Probably. Mack liked to gamble."

"Did he have a serious problem?"

"It was the reason for their divorce."

Gage decided he'd have to check that out.

"He told me, though, that he'd taken the pledge, sort of like Alcoholics Anonymous, I guess. Went to regular meetings."

"Sounds like you knew him pretty well."

"I wouldn't call us close friends, but we did get together sometimes over a beer in the evening. Speaking of which," Doug added, "if you come back for another visit, do you think you could smuggle me in a six-pack?"

"Sir, I'm in the business of preventing smuggling." Gage chuckled. "I'll do my best." He also promised himself he would be back often. "You said Mack didn't tolerate fools lightly. Does that mean he had high regard for all the people who worked for him?"

Amusement lit Doug's eyes. "More like he respected their limitations. He didn't ask me to give him intelligence analysis, for example, or expect Victor Reyes to develop operational plans."

"And if someone did offer suggestions outside their areas of expertise?"

"He listened, then tended to ignore them."

"Sounds close-minded," said Gage.

"You could say that."

"How did he and Jill get along?"

"Initially, very well. But everyone could see their philosophies on the drug war differed widely. Mack had his eye on the commissioner's job one day, and he was convinced the way to get there was with big, high-profile raids that garnered him a lot of positive publicity. The trouble was, his success rate was falling. He hadn't had a major bust in over a year. Jill, on the other hand, was concentrating on the low-level stuff and her statistics were steadily climbing, eclipsing his. He never came out and said it, but I had the feeling Mack suspected her of undermining him."

"Was she?"

With a wave of his good hand, Doug dismissed the

notion. "She was doing her job and doing it well. Mack was getting paranoid at the end, convinced someone was sabotaging him."

"Maybe he was right."

MONDAY MORNING, the armed guard on duty notified Jill when the new helicopter pilot presented himself at the compound entrance for admission. She stood at the bank of monitors in the security office and gave the order to admit him, then watched as the electronic gate slid aside and a Jeep Wrangler advanced through it. Gage had always gone for sporty vehicles rather than conventional cars.

Two years seemed like twenty, yet the first sight of him as he extended his long legs outside the SUV erased time. The image on the back-and-white screen was grainy, but that didn't make any difference. Gage Engler hadn't changed. He was still tall and lanky. His tailored white shirt accentuated the breadth of his shoulders and the narrow firmness of his waist. Nor did his mirrored sunglasses prevent her from picturing his hazel eyes with their sea-green flecks. He'd grown a mustache. Involuntarily, she touched her own upper lip, as if feeling it brush against her skin.

He slammed the Jeep door, glanced toward the fleet of official and personal vehicles parked nearby, then scrutinized the hangar on the west side of the compound. Turning, he approached the main building, not walking fast but rather moving with the easy stride of an athlete, sure of his place in the world. Her world now, she reminded herself. He was on her turf, and she would do well to make sure he understood that.

She resented his coming here. Why couldn't he leave

her alone? Hadn't he done enough? Every day, she was reminded of her loss in one way or another. There was no escaping it. The sight of a mother with her toddler in the supermarket. A baby seat in the back of a car. The playground at McDonald's. Gage had robbed her of all the future memories she'd stored up, of bathing Rickie at night, the touch of his satiny-soft skin, the feel of his tiny fingers curled around her thumb, the sound of him giggling when she tickled his ribs.

Why was Gage here? She would have thought he'd want to escape reminders of his son, too, but being in each other's presence, how could they think of anything else? Why was he torturing them both this way? There was no going back. A small white coffin would always lay between them.

She closed her eyes and willed away the tears that came with the burning in her throat, but the pain in her heart wasn't as obedient.

The sound of the buzzer at the front entrance snapped her out of her reverie, the same one she'd been in all weekend.

"Mr. Engler is here," the guard announced over the intercom.

Jill drew in a deep breath and let it out slowly. "Show him to my office."

CHAPTER THREE

SHE LOOKED GOOD, Gage decided, better than good. The southwest desert had highlighted her brown hair with golden tints and given her smooth complexion a glowing radiance. The combination brought out the green in her eyes, the rose color of her lips. Enticing lips. Desire warmed his blood, surged through his veins. It had been two years. Two long years.

Her new job could be responsible for the hint of fatigue he saw in the shadows of her face, but he was vain enough to suspect the telephone call Friday announcing his impending arrival might have kept her sleepless over the weekend. Vain but not proud. The last thing he wanted was to cause her more pain. He could never make up for the past; the question was whether they had any chance of a future together again. He hoped so. Life was empty without her.

He'd checked out her address after arriving in Tombstone on Saturday afternoon in hopes of catching a glimpse of her, but she hadn't appeared. He'd been tempted to knock on her door, to watch her reaction when she saw him, but decided it wouldn't be a smart move. Better to meet on neutral ground first, where they'd be forced to control their emotions, to give them both a chance to get used to each other.

She greeted him now with a plastic smile and a formally extended hand.

"Welcome aboard, Mr. Engler." She met his eyes with suspicion, as if she were afraid of what he might say or do—like lean over and kiss her.

He realized her polite words were for the benefit of the secretary watching them. He was inclined to prolong the handshake, to enjoy the feel of her skin—it had been such a long time—but he followed her lead by breaking off almost immediately. "I'm glad to be here."

At a nod from Jill, the secretary closed the office door, giving them privacy.

He hesitated a moment, trying to measure her mood. "Congratulations on your promotion," he said.

Her movements stiff, she took her place behind the desk. He didn't miss the vulnerability in her eyes or the way she compressed her lips into a thin line the moment she faced him.

"We need to talk," she said after perching herself on the edge of her seat, her hands folded on the glass-topped desk. "You need to remember that the personal ties between us have been severed."

Right, he thought. *Keep telling yourself that.*

"I've worked hard to get where I am. I don't want you to do anything to jeopardize my—"

He sat down across from her. "I'm very proud of you."

The compliment caused her to miss a beat. In that split second he glimpsed joy, then the shield went back up, locked in place. Too late, though. The spark between them still snapped when they made eye contact, which was probably why she avoided it now.

"Does headquarters know...that—"

"We were once married?" he finished for her. She'd always hated it when he did that. "I don't think so."

"You haven't told anyone?"

He shook his head, not sure if she was pleased or disappointed.

"Why not?"

"Because it's nobody's business." Watching her, he realized she was holding herself in by sheer force of will. Her knuckles were white, her chin set. Did she want to rant at him, call him a baby-killer, as she had the night she demanded a divorce? "As you said, our ties have been severed. We're two independent adults, unlinked by any legal bonds."

She flinched at his choice of words, as if they were an indictment. In a sense they were, but not of her. He was the one who had failed.

"Why are you here, Gage?" She hadn't changed. Still blunt and to the point, especially when she felt threatened.

Should he tell her he'd sought the job because he wanted to be close to her, because for his own sanity he needed to make sure she was safe, because he was determined to try one more time to win her back? Should he admit he was here to spy on her? The temptation to confess ate at him, like acid in his stomach.

"You have a vacancy for helicopter pilots," he said. "That's what I do, fly choppers. It's a job I love, just like you love yours."

It had been twenty-four months, three weeks and two days since they'd last seen each other, but all those empty nights disappeared as they sat studying each other. Some things hadn't changed. He could still read the thoughts running through her mind. Some of them, at least. Beneath the cool—no, cold—facade, was she as lonely as he was? For all her success, was something vital missing in her life, as it was from his? He needed to know. He came here fully aware they couldn't bring Rickie back, but he'd hoped they might be able to re-kindle the love that had given him life. Seeing the anger in her eyes, he realized he might have miscalculated. For her, time hadn't brought healing, but a hardening of the scars.

"As long as we understand each other—" she began.

"We both suffered an unbearable loss when Rickie died. If I could go back and do things differently, I would." He paused, surprised at how hard it was to express these feelings out loud. He wanted to say he would give his life to bring his son back, but he wasn't sure he could force the words past the lump in his throat.

She remained still, except for her measured breathing. The space between them thickened, a miasma that made it impossible for them to touch each other. He'd ripped open an old wound by just being here, made it bleed. Maybe this assignment had been a mistake.

"What's past is past," she said. He heard despair in her voice. "There's no going back, Gage. I expect you to do your job, nothing more."

"You're the boss," he said.

HE CHARMED EVERYONE, as Jill had known he would. Her secretary stood at her desk, preening her mousy-brown hair as if Gage were a royal prince holding out a glass slipper. Victor Reyes, the intelligence officer, treated him like a long-lost pal—or son. The other staff members in the building—the agents, analysts, data technicians, planners, computer geeks and admin clerks—were equally enthralled by his quick wit and easy manner.

Jill used to admire Gage's rapport with people, but today it irritated the hell out of her. She knew why. He made her feel unsure of herself. He had the charisma of a born leader, the type of person who could walk into a room and instantly take charge, and she was just insecure enough in her new job to worry about him doing just that.

She'd wondered all weekend if she would be affected by his presence. That wasn't precisely true. She'd worried about how much she'd be affected. Now she knew. She was afraid of him. Not in the physical sense. In some ways he was the most gentle man she'd ever met, with the possible exception of her father.

The two most important men in her life had let her down in the most fundamental ways. She'd long ago forgiven her father, but she could never forgive Gage for what he had done. He'd taken from her the reason to go home at night, the joy of planning a future and dreaming of happiness. He'd cheated her of hope and robbed her of a reason to live.

She wouldn't let him dominate her life again. She wouldn't go to bed at night thinking about him and wake up with him still on her mind. She'd gotten past all that. This past weekend after the announcement of his arrival didn't count. Nor did the tears she'd shed. For old times' sake. For the good times.

She had new goals now, new ideas, new sources of satisfaction, and Gage Engler didn't play a role in any of them.

Dammit.

Damn him.

They exited the administration building by the side door and walked into the bright May sun to the hangar a hundred yards away. Jill's insides were mush as she marched beside the man she'd once promised to cherish for the rest of her life. During his exchanges with various members of her staff, she'd learned he'd come from San Diego, where he'd been stationed the past two years. That was something she would have asked any other newcomer but hadn't gotten around to asking him. She'd been too preoccupied with memories and fears to perform her duties in a professional manner.

That would change, she vowed. He was a helicopter pilot who worked for her. Her role now was to introduce him to his flight crew, return to her office and lose herself in the mounds of paper on her desk, the intimidating desk that suddenly beckoned like a haven.

Stepping into the cavernous hangar, she was grateful for its cool shade and was almost able to convince herself it was the desert sun making her uncomfortable and sweaty. Three Blackhawk helicopters were parked side by side, their rotor blades drooping in the morning light. Chief mechanic Paco Moreno was on a ladder servicing the bird on the right. Two men and a woman in flight suits were standing by the one on the left. Jill steered Gage toward them. They turned at her approach and ceased their conversation. Jill introduced Nita Gomez. She and Nita had hit it off the first time they'd met two years ago. They were the only females in the organization not performing administrative duties and were both single. Since becoming branch chief, Jill had had little free time to spend with her friend. She missed their get-togethers, the girl talk, the undemanding companionship that allowed her to relax and, for a little while, forget.

Five-four and barely a hundred pounds, Nita had large black eyes, short, curly, ebony hair and a smooth olive complexion.

"Nita is your copilot," Jill explained.

Gage seemed to hold Nita's hand a moment too long and smiled at her more than a professional introduction warranted.

"Is this your first time in Arizona?" she asked while shooting Jill a raised eyebrow that said, *What a hunk.*

"I've driven the northern route through Phoenix but never been this far south. I'm sort of a coastal animal. Spent most of my time in Virginia, Florida, Louisiana and California. You have a lot more beach here, but the water seems a little shallow."

She chuckled. "Wait till it rains."

"What's your background?" he asked.

"Air Force."

"Special Ops?"

She smiled. "Yep."

"Why'd you leave it?"

She shrugged. "It was great, but I wanted something closer to home."

"You're from around here then?"

"Born and raised in Bisbee, just over the hill, so to speak."

The sharp point of jealousy at his easy manner prodded Jill. Clearly, Gage was settling in very well with his new crew. She excused herself and retreated to her office.

BEFORE HE'D LEFT HEADQUARTERS, Gage had made contact with Sid Regis, the research specialist he'd worked with on other investigations. If you wanted to know anything about a suspect—the amount his grandmother had in her checking account on the day of his birth, for example—Sid was the guy who could find it. In this case, Gage's inquiry wasn't nearly as arcane.

"I need to know everything you can find on Jill Manning," he'd told the tall, skinny computer expert, "especially for the past two years. Where she's been, who she hangs out with, her financial and medical history, the men in her life, everything."

"You got it. Am I looking for anything in particular?"

"Not right now. I'll let you know after I get there. And, Sid, what you find out…I don't want it going anywhere. This is between you and me."

Confidentiality was standard procedure. The hesitation in Sid's reply indicated he was wondering why it was even being mentioned. "Sure, Gage. Whatever you say."

Monday evening, the guy had called Gage. "I understand now why you wanted this kept under wraps. You didn't mention she used to be your wife."

Gage had known Sid would find out; he'd just wondered how long it would take him. "You realize that if word gets out, I'd be pulled off this job."

"No one will hear it from me," Sid had assured him.

"Thanks. I appreciate that. Come up with anything yet?"

"Nothing you probably don't already know. Her father was a cop, killed in the line of duty. Good academic record. I'll check on financial and police records next, then start getting into the good stuff. Sorry about your kid. I didn't realize—"

"Thanks. You can understand why we don't want this broadcast. How easy was the information to find?"

"For me, a piece of cake. But since she never took your name, I wouldn't worry about anyone else stumbling on it. The only information in your personnel files is that you both passed your five-year background checks. Nobody gets to see the details unless they have a reason to look."

Gage had always been a little uneasy about her never wanting to be known as Mrs. Engler. Now he was glad she hadn't. Sort of.

OVER THE NEXT WEEK he occupied himself with getting to know his flight crews and aircraft better. Two pilots had been off duty the day he'd arrived and two more were on leave.

"We're authorized four choppers, eight pilots and fourteen flight mechanics," Nita had briefed him. "Our standard crew on operational missions is two pilots and one flight mechanic who doubles as an observer, plus whatever ground forces we might carry. Occasionally we're called upon to perform taxi service for visitors or VIPs. In those cases, we might fly with just one pilot and no mechanic."

In spite of his urge to seek Jill out and spend time with her, Gage kept his distance. The one mandatory meeting, when they couldn't avoid each other, was the morning "stand up." Staff members briefed the branch chief on the status of current projects and plans, and Gage reported on the availability of aircraft and flight crews.

The expanded Customs and Immigration enforcement mission now included border patrol and transportation security, as well as animal and plant health control. Centralizing these functions was logical and would no doubt prove more efficient in the long run. Short term, however, it laid a heavy burden on branch chiefs, whose backgrounds were usually narrower and whose staff were still struggling with the administrative chaos of reorganization as well as institutional issues of trust.

Gage was impressed by the way Jill handled these sessions. She sorted through details, caught discrepancies, directed further coordination and still managed to find occasional bits of humor. She awarded praise where it was due and focused on solutions when things went awry. Though she'd been in charge barely a month, it was clear that most people accepted—and liked—her.

One exception was the immigration officer, Pratt Dixon. Gage suspected cynicism was a natural bent of his personality, but his sarcasm at these meetings seemed pointed at his boss. A few of the people around him snickered nervously at his snide comments, but most of them ignored him, a few showing disapproval.

At the second Tuesday's staff briefing, Jill asked Gage the status of their request for a replacement aircraft.

"Per your instructions, I contacted headquarters. They say it'll be at least two months before one is available. I told them that wasn't good enough, that we're flying multiple missions daily and paying overtime to perform scheduled maintenance at night instead of rotating aircraft. I asked them to take another look at their resources and see if they couldn't accelerate the schedule."

"Do you seriously think it'll do any good?" Dixon asked.

Gage shrugged. "All I know is that not speaking up won't get us anywhere. I'll continue to call every so often to rattle their cages."

Jill nodded. "Just don't alienate them."

"I'll be the soul of diplomacy," he promised, and got a chuckle from the group.

"WE HAVE A MAJOR DRUG shipment coming through," Reyes announced that afternoon at a few minutes past five. Most of the day staff had already gone home.

Jill shoved the papers on her desk to the side and straightened. "How big?"

"Five hundred keys of coke."

She drew a breath. A key was a kilo, equivalent to two point two pounds. Eleven hundred pounds of cocaine had a street value of nearly fifty million dollars. The existing record bust in the area was just over eight hundred pounds.

She exhaled. "Are you sure?"

Reyes nodded. "This information has an A-1 rating. Everything adds up. Informers report a two-truck convoy in Mexico will be moving north toward Nogales. Communications intercepts confirm it."

"How are they planning to hide it?"

The usual method was to have a false partition in a vehicle or container. With modern X-ray equipment, however, even those carefully crafted secret compartments could be detected.

"They're packaging and commingling it with a legitimate shipment of prescription medications coming from the pharmaceutical plant in Hermosilla."

Several American drug companies had relocated

their manufacturing facilities south of the border to take advantage of lower overhead costs.

"The Black Hand has apparently infiltrated the trucking company," Reyes continued. "They'll replace part of the legitimate cargo with their stuff, using the original containers, and bring it in that way."

The ploy could work. Jill dragged a hand through her hair. If the contraband was vacuum sealed, placed in approved cartons and completely surrounded by legitimate cargo, search dogs wouldn't be able to sniff it out, and a random inspection of boxes wasn't likely to go deep enough to uncover anything.

"When is this supposed to happen?" she asked.

"Dawn tomorrow."

She glanced at the clock on the wall. Less than ten hours to coordinate a plan and get all the components in place. They had operated on much shorter lead times.

Her pulse racing, she picked up the phone to activate their special task force.

CHAPTER FOUR

GAGE FELT RIGHT at home in the buzz that surrounded a special mission. The atmosphere in the briefing room was restive, on edge, with the keen excitement of high adventure.

"This could be another red herring," Pratt Dixon called from the sidelines where he was standing with several others.

Gage watched Jill. Judging from her expression, the thought had also crossed her mind.

"Last go-round we had a single source of intelligence. This time we have multiple sources," Reyes reminded everyone. "For example, we know from satellite imagery that the vehicles in the reports are positioned where our informants say they are. I'd expect some discrepancy if this was a setup."

"Still sounds too pat," Dixon insisted.

Gage recognized the game he was playing—harp on the negative. Dixon was the type of malcontent who took healthy skepticism and turned it into a disease. "I haven't heard anything on the street," the immigration officer declared.

"We have reliable contacts in Mexico," Reyes assured him. "But we're not depending on them exclusively." His tone became patronizing, as if he were explaining something for the hundredth time to a slow-witted child. "Human intelligence assets are by nature secondhand—someone reporting what they want us to hear. Wiretaps and communications intercepts, however, constitute a primary source of information because we're listening to them talk to each other. Can they deceive us? Sure. Have they in the past? Occasionally. But they usually end up confusing themselves, too."

"I still don't like it," Dixon said. Clearly the two men didn't much care for each other. "I've got people on both sides of the border and I've heard squat about this."

"If your snitches alone had the complete picture," Reyes observed, "I'm sure you would have passed the information on, and this war on drugs would already have been won."

"Even if this is a setup," said Fritz Bradley, the border patrol chief, "I don't see how we can afford to ignore it."

"What's the plan?" Gage asked Jill, putting an end to the debate and redirecting everyone's attention to her and the mission objective.

"They'll be subject to the normal Customs inspection at the border. Unless the K-9s catch something, we won't dig any deeper than usual." She turned to Gage. "I'll fly with you and establish an airborne command post. We don't know where the drop-off point is. When we determine that, I'll contact the highway patrol to move in and secure the area."

"What communications will we be using?" Dixon asked.

Anyone could monitor their regular radios, but not

using them would be a dead giveaway that they were up to something. She held up a copy of one of the papers she had distributed. "As you can see, we've superimposed the road names and numbers around Fort Huachuca onto our area."

"This is amateurish," Dixon said.

Jill sucked in her cheeks. "Do you have a better idea? If you do, perhaps you'd care to share it with us."

The room turned graveyard silent. Finally, Dixon clucked his tongue and reexamined the sheet. "I guess it'll work if we minimize chatter," he grumbled without looking up.

"Keeping one's mouth shut is always a good idea," Gage observed.

Dixon raised his head and glared at him.

"We expect them to approach the border at five tomorrow morning," Reyes reiterated. "If things go according to schedule, they should be in our neighborhood between seven and eight."

"You have your assignments," Jill announced. "The duty officer in the tower will be handling communications from this end. If you run into problems, contact him ASAP via your cell phones, not your radios."

Digital cell phones could not be intercepted.

"Go home, everybody, and get what rest you can," Jill said. "We have an early day tomorrow." A murmur ensued as people rose to leave. Over the babble and shuffling of feet and chairs, she called, "Mr. Dixon, hang around for a minute. I need to talk to you."

"I've got work to do," he protested.

Chatter subsided as people waited for Jill's response. If she let him brush her off, her authority would be compromised. "The thing you have to do right now," she said, "is comply with my request."

Everyone stared first at her, then at him.

He twisted his lips and let out a deep sigh of impatience. "Okay, but then I have to go."

Gage was among the last to leave the room. He tarried in the hallway until everyone else had disappeared, then stepped into the projection booth behind the podium. Leaving the light off in the cramped audio-visual space allowed him to make out shadowy forms on the bright side of the opaque screen. There was also a spy hole for the AV operator to monitor what was transpiring on the other side. Gage activated the intercom switch so he could hear, as well.

JILL BRACED HERSELF for what she had to do.

"Close the door," she said from her position near the podium.

Dixon eyed her. She was closer to it than he was. Working his jaw, he strolled over and shut the door, none too gently, then slumped on one hip and faced her.

"Mr. Dixon, we have a problem, one that either you will fix or I'll fix for you. Your attitude over the past month has been unacceptable."

He started to say something, but she pressed on. Engaging in dialogue would grant him equal status, and she couldn't afford that. "I don't care what you think of me personally, but I will not allow you to show disrespect for my position. I am the chief of this branch. You work for me, whether you like it or not." She raised her hand to forestall another interruption.

"I'm giving you a pass tonight, but if you ever speak to me again in that tone and manner you used during this briefing, I'll take appropriate disciplinary action against you. There is a common public misconception that government employees cannot be fired. Don't fall for that urban legend. More than a thousand civil servants are terminated for just cause every year. If you don't want to be one of them, you had better change your approach, because I assure you, I know how the system works and I'll use it."

"Is that a threat?"

"As I said, this evening is a freebie, but I'm putting you on notice. I expect you to perform your role tomorrow with great skill and efficiency. If, however, you do anything to jeopardize the mission or if you continue to make comments that affect the morale of this branch, I'll have your ass. Is that plain enough?"

"You'll screw up tomorrow," Dixon said. "Then we'll see whose ass is in a sling."

"Just make sure you're not the cause of the screwup. I'm going to do my best tomorrow. I hope you do the same. Good night, Mr. Dixon."

He narrowed his eyes, then left.

Jill's heart was pounding. The contempt she'd seen in Dixon's eyes had nearly paralyzed her, but she followed the advice her father had given her when she was a little girl. "A bully is only a bully until you stand up to him." Now she had to see if her gambit had worked. Would Dixon reconsider his position and cooperate with her, or had she hardened his hostility into determined hatred?

GAGE WAITED AN EXTRA minute after Jill left the conference room before stepping out into the hallway. Then he nearly tripped over her. She'd bent down to pick up some papers she'd dropped and glared up at him now with wide eyes. The flash of fear he saw startled him. This wasn't what he'd expected from the confident woman who'd just faced down a hostile subordinate.

"What are you doing here?" she demanded. Snagging the last sheet from the floor, she rose to her feet, her attention riveted on him.

"Are you all right?"

"I asked you a question." The papers rustled in her trembling hands. "You were listening in."

"I just wanted to make sure—"

She closed her eyes, took an unsteady breath and opened them again. "I should have informed Williams the minute he told me he was sending you—"

"Why didn't you?"

"If I didn't need you for this operation, I'd call him tonight. Tomorrow, when this is over, I will."

He hoped the threat was hollow, that it was a panicky reaction to being taken by surprise.

"It'll cost you," he said. In addition to losing a pilot, she'd be admitting a weakness in her ability to lead.

She gazed at him. "It already has." She walked away.

JILL SLEPT LITTLE that night. Her mind should have been on the myriad details covered in the evening's planning session. The adage that, if something could go wrong, it would, always seemed to apply to operations of this magnitude. Taking command of other leaders was another tricky proposition, and being new in the senior role added a further challenge. Tomorrow's mission would be her first big bust. Success would prove her bona fides with her subordinates, as well as headquarters, while a botched operation would undermine her chances of being permanently assigned as the branch chief.

She'd told the former branch chief she thought there might be a mole in the outfit. Nothing that had happened since his death persuaded her otherwise, but she was no closer to discovering who it was.

Maybe these concerns were the underlying cause of her restlessness, but what occupied her conscious thoughts were the events that followed the team briefing: her encounter with Dixon and her discovery that Gage had been snooping on her.

Dixon might pose a serious problem. Malcontents always did, especially when they had friends in high places. As an immigration official, he also wielded considerable local influence. But was he the spy? She wouldn't allow herself to be intimidated by Dixon in any case. She'd follow through on her threat if he didn't change his attitude.

What about Gage? He was far more troubling. If she'd caught any other member of her staff eavesdropping on her, she would conclude he was the traitor, but Gage had just arrived. Besides, if there was one thing she could be certain of, it was his professional integrity. He would never compromise national security.

Did he think she wasn't up to the job? He claimed he was proud of her. She didn't want to admit how good that made her feel, convincing herself instead that she would be just as pleased at being praised by anyone with experience in the business.

When she'd been a little girl, her ambition had been to follow in her father's footsteps. He'd been a cop on the beat in a Virginia suburb of Washington, D.C., at the time. She'd loved seeing him in uniform and the certainty of being safe when he was with her. Later he rose to detective and rarely wore the uniform, but she never forgot he was a policeman, someone sworn to "protect and serve." He was killed in the line of duty when she was a junior in college. He had been all she had. She'd never known her mother, who'd died giving her birth. In Jill's mind, family always meant her and her dad.

For a year or so after his death, she'd abandoned the goal of entering law enforcement, not out of fear but disillusionment. Her father had been a good man, a conscientious, dedicated cop. His bleeding to death in a dirty alley had meant there was no justice, no purpose to his profession. No matter how hard he'd worked, no matter how honorably he'd served, the bad guys won. Rather than try to fight those evil forces, she'd chosen to withdraw.

Then, when she was just finishing graduate school, young, handsome Coast Guard Lieutenant Gage Engler came to the university as part of a recruitment team for the Customs Service. Until then, she'd never given much thought to the close working relationship between the two agencies, a government team effort that had a long, successful history. He'd looked dashing in his white uniform. His forceful, masculine presence had impressed her enough that she'd had trouble following his words. When, at the end of the canned spiel, he'd smiled and invited her to the new Starbucks for a cup of coffee, she'd been hooked.

She'd signed up and he'd disappeared. They hadn't seen each other for another two years. By then she'd completed the seventeen-week academy in Glencoe, Georgia, and survived her initial rookie assignment; he'd transferred to the Customs Service and received advanced training as a chopper pilot. When they'd found themselves assigned to the same Customs house in Norfolk, it was clear the attraction between them was still there. A year later they'd married and were jointly assigned to Florida.

They were both ecstatic when she became pregnant the following year. Then Gage asked if she was planning to resign from the Customs Service to become a full-time mother, and she became incensed. As it turned out he wasn't quite the male chauvinist pre-feminist she'd supposed. He was inquiring, not demanding, he explained, offering her a choice, not an ultimatum. She appreciated his concern for her and their baby's safety and in the end they'd compromised. In addition to her maternity leave, she'd requested and was granted an extended leave of absence, which ended, of course, when Rickie died.

Gage no doubt expected her to be grateful that he was here now to protect her. It probably never occurred to him that he was insulting her. She wasn't a rookie anymore. Being selected for branch chief over her peers attested to that. He ought to have confidence in her ability to get the job done. And yet a little part of her was gratified that he still cared—which irritated her all the more.

Impulsively she'd said today she would ask for his transfer. The trouble was she'd lose face if she did, which he no doubt knew. First, she'd have to tell her boss she hadn't been up-front with him about her past relationship with Gage. Second, she'd be admitting she couldn't handle her personal life. Gage would be reassigned, but she'd end up being the big loser. The only solution was to hang tough.

Nevertheless, she decided with a vicious grin, there was no reason she couldn't let him dangle for a while.

WHEN GAGE ARRIVED at the compound at a quarter to four in the morning, Jill's Ford Taurus was already there. This would be her first big operation, and he was excited for her.

By four-fifteen, thirty team members had assembled in the briefing room, some still half asleep, several clearly psyched, most simply quiet. All but a few were sucking down caffeine in the form of hot coffee or cold cola.

"We might have a small change in plans," Jill announced. "Our latest intelligence suggests the point of entry might not be Nogales, as originally reported, but Douglas."

A buzz resonated throughout the room, accompanied by raised eyebrows.

"Why the switch?" Dixon called out. His tone this morning was inquisitive rather than confrontational, but the challenge was still there. "Are they on to us?"

Good question. Gage wondered the same thing.

"Douglas doesn't usually process this company's shipments," a woman on the other side of the room pointed out.

"Could this be a diversion?" another agent asked. "Maybe the real shipment will be going through Naco, while we're focusing on Douglas and Nogales. We don't have the resources to cover all three at the same time."

"We'll monitor those stations by air for any suspicious activity," Jill replied. "We should still have time to redirect our efforts if we need to."

"This last-minute change might be to foil hijackers on our side of the border," Reyes said. "Drug dealers have to contend with each other as well as with us."

"As for processing at the border," Jill said, "I think they're counting on their paperwork being in perfect order. Nogales is bigger, but it's also busier. Either way, they'll get through, which is all they care about."

"I wish they'd told us this yesterday," a sleepy male voice muttered. "I could have stayed in bed a few more hours."

"This way Betty-Sue can finally get some rest," his buddy called out.

"Hey, a man's got to do what a man's got to do," came the roguish reply.

Everyone laughed, while Jill distributed new one-time chatter sheets. They briefly discussed contingencies.

"Now let's go get the bad guys," she said, dismissing them.

Gage and the other pilots reported to the flight line, where their helicopters were fueled and ready.

One minute before scheduled take off, Jill appeared at the door of Zero-Seven, Gage's aircraft. She was wearing a blue flight suit similar to his and a white helmet. Earlier she'd greeted him politely but impersonally. Immediately after liftoff, she positioned herself between him and Nita and peered out the window at the rugged landscape slipping by beneath them.

"Looks like they got through," she commented twenty minutes later. Two eighteen-wheelers bearing the pharmaceutical company logo had just exited the Douglas checkpoint and were moving north on Highway 80.

"Let's see if this snake has a head and a tail," Gage said.

They shadowed it from a distance for several minutes. Cars sped past the slower, massive rigs and kept going.

"Appears they're on their own," Nita observed.

"We'll have to see if they pick up any fellow travelers along the way," said Gage. Point and rear guards were sometimes used when contraband was being moved, especially shipments this large.

The two tractor-trailers proceeded through Nita's hometown of Bisbee, entered the Mule Pass tunnel and exited the other end a few minutes later. Six miles south of Tombstone, the lead truck turned left onto a dirt road. The chase was on.

CHAPTER FIVE

JILL'S PULSE WAS UP as she consulted the chart in her hand. "They're headed for the old Ellis ranch."

"Nobody's lived on that place for years," Nita said over the intercom.

"I bet it has a big barn, though," Gage said. He climbed to three thousand feet. At that altitude no one on the ground would pay much attention to them.

"Quonsets," Nita corrected him. "You see a lot of them around here."

Jill caught herself staring at Gage's gloved hands as he maneuvered the helicopter for a different view of the activity below. Snapping out of her trance, she used her binoculars to study the world below. When everyone was in place, she instructed him to call in.

He keyed his mike. "Control, this is Zero-Seven. We have a fender-bender on Highway 80, six miles north of Fort Huachuca. Request assistance."

"Roger, Zero-Seven. Help's on the way."

Even if the truckers were monitoring the radio and were quick enough to figure out they were being pursued, it was too late for them to turn back. The narrow road afforded the lumbering rigs no maneuverability. Their only option was to keep moving forward. Gage watched as highway patrol cars began to block off the road behind them.

Jill called the duty officer on the secure link. "Check the latest satellite imagery and tell me what buildings are on the Ellis ranch. Also, see if you can find any indications of recent activity there."

"I see ruins of a small stone house," he reported a minute later, "and three, large, open-ended Quonsets in good condition, each big enough to conceal a tractor-trailer. The most recent pictures show several closed vehicles parked nearby."

"This has to be the drop-off point," Jill told the others.

The atmosphere in the cockpit was tense, but Jill also sensed an underlying confidence on the part of both Nita and Gage. Had they been facing each other, she would have smiled at him, she was feeling that good. Regardless of the strain in their private lives, they worked well together, a smooth team. Maybe that was the way it had to be. Two separate worlds.

Twenty minutes later she issued the order for all units to move in.

Highway and border patrol vehicles streamed into the compound, their lights flashing. Jill's heart was pounding as she put on her flak vest and watched the Special Response Team surround the cavernous structures. While the second helicopter flew cover, Gage landed in a cloud of dust in front of the row of round-topped shelters. Jill jumped out as soon as the noisy, vibrating aircraft touched the ground. Armed government forces formed a phalanx around her. As ordered, Gage lifted off at once to look for any threatening activity. Jill barely gave the departing chopper a glance, but for a fleeting moment she experienced a tug of abandonment. There was no time for sentimental emotions, however.

At her direction, the Special Response Team leader gave the signal. "Go."

The events that followed were almost anticlimactic. The young Hispanic males unloading the cargo offered no resistance and surrendered without a fight. Several sentries who had been guarding the trucks and overseeing the operation tightened their grips on their AK-47s but seemed to change their minds the moment they realized they were outnumbered and outgunned.

Within an hour, eight men were arrested and bussed to the jail in Tombstone. K-9s helped in the long and tedious work of separating the legal from the illegal cargo. Jill had to work at suppressing a smile of satisfaction. Reyes's intelligence reports had been on the mark. By the end of the day, they'd uncovered five hundred kilos of raw cocaine.

Jill Manning, Tombstone branch chief, was on a drug-free high.

THE ANNUAL Memorial Day picnic at Victor Reyes's hacienda was a tradition going back more than a decade. This year the timing was perfect, just a day after the Customs station's biggest single raid ever against the Black Hand cocaine cartel. Everybody was in an jubilant mood.

After filling a plastic cup from the iced keg under a ramada, Gage wandered over to the big, smoky grill, where his host was basting chicken pieces and pork ribs with tangy barbecue sauce.

"Welcome to *La Hacienda Dolosa*," Reyes said, a broad smile on his face.

"You have a beautiful place here." The land was high, rolling desert, stark in its beauty and treacherous for the unwary. "I have to ask you, though, why it's named *dolosa*. Doesn't that mean deceitful?"

"Ah, you speak Spanish. Actually, I didn't name it. It came to us from my wife's side of the family. Do you know how Tombstone got its name, Gage?"

"I've heard a couple of versions," he said. "What's the straight poop?"

Reyes smiled. "Back in 1877, a miner by the name of Edward Schiefflin came here from California, liked what he saw, geologically speaking, and decided to dig. This was Apache country back then, and they were on the warpath, as much against each other as the white man. When he went to Fort Huachuca to establish his grubstake, the soldiers warned him the only thing he'd find here would be his tombstone. A month later he struck silver and the rush was on. Soon Ed Schiefflin's tombstone was known simply as Tombstone. It's had its boons and busts over the years, but it's still here, the town too tough to die."

Gage chuckled. "And the *dolosa* part?"

Victor painted a rack of ribs and turned them on the steel-mesh grill, then took a generous swallow of beer from his insulated mug.

"My wife's family has owned this land for over two hundred years. They gave it to us as a wedding present. When silver was discovered, Selinda's great-grandfather, still a young man, came up, fought off the Indians and a few white men, and staked several claims. Unfortunately, they all turned out to be flashes in the pan. In a letter to his family, he described the land as *dolosa,* deceitful, and that soon became the name of the hacienda he built."

"Colorful," Gage remarked. "How big is the place?"

"It was once much larger. Now it's only a couple thousand acres."

"What do you do with it?"

"Run a few head of cattle, sheep and goats, but it's more for fun than profit. Ah, here she is now." His dark eyes warmed. "Selinda, dear, this is Gage Engler, the new helicopter pilot I was telling you about."

Victor's wife was a beautiful woman of about fifty with a shock of gray in her long, jet-black hair. Two things were immediately obvious: she was charming and her husband adored her.

"Señora Reyes, you have a beautiful home."

She extended her hand. "That's very kind of you. I'm so glad you could all come. We don't have people out nearly enough. I understand you had a very successful mission yesterday."

"I was glad to do my part," Gage said. "But I think Chief Manning deserves the real credit."

"Victor tells me she's doing very well as branch chief. I will have to give her my personal congratulations. Do enjoy yourself, Mr. Engler—"

"Gage, please."

Did he detect a slight sadness in her smile? "Gage. If you'll excuse me, I have some things I must attend to in the kitchen."

After she left, Gage asked Victor if they had any children.

"A son in Europe studying music. At least, I hope he's studying. Our daughter is married to a physician in Massachusetts."

They started toward a field where people were organizing a softball game.

"Last year we lost our other son," Victor confessed. "Francisco was nineteen."

A shiver, like a cold spike, ran down Gage's spine. "I'm very sorry."

Losing Rickie, who'd been only six weeks old, had been the greatest tragedy Gage had ever experienced. How much more terrible it must be to lose a child after raising him to manhood. To have all those memories and dreams cut short. "Was it from an illness?"

Victor's jaw flexed. "He was killed, murdered, here on the hacienda."

Gage stopped and stared at the man. "How? Why?"

"We believe it was drug dealers, or possibly arms smugglers. Cisco rode the fence line regularly. One night he didn't come home, but I didn't realize it, didn't even question it when he wasn't at breakfast. Figured he was either sleeping in or had gotten an early start. One of our workers found him later. He had been dead several hours, shot to death. Selinda…my wife, has never been quite the same since."

"Did they catch the people who did it?"

Reyes shook his head. "The killers were almost certainly from the other side of the border. I'm sure you know how difficult it can be when a crime involves more than one jurisdiction." He paused. "Do you have any children, Gage?"

It was a question he hated. There was only one reply he could give, yet he felt as if he were abandoning his son by denying his existence. "No."

They resumed walking toward the revelers who were noisily taking their positions on the playing field, their merriment sounding sacrilegious in the face of death.

"Some people have asked why I didn't apply for the branch chief position after Robbins was killed," Reyes went on. "It was a temptation, and perhaps I would have been selected, but I decided I could keep my ear closer to the ground in my current position as an intelligence officer. Yesterday went well. A good start for Jill. I'm glad. I'll continue to do everything I can to support her."

"At the same time you hunt for your son's killer," Gage observed.

"Can a father do otherwise?" He offered a feeble smile. "Don't worry. I'm not planning a vendetta. The only way to prevent more senseless killing is to live by the law, imperfect though we may find it, not by vigilante justice. Even if personal vengeance is very appealing at times."

"I admire your self-discipline," Gage said. "You've made a hard choice but an honorable one."

"What is a man without honor?" Reyes pulled himself out of his melancholy the moment Nita approached him with a plastic cup of beer.

"The smell of whatever you're cooking is driving me crazy."

Reyes chuckled. "You'll have to be patient, young lady. Fine food can't be rushed. The meat won't be ready for another half hour."

"What did you think of yesterday's mission?" she asked Gage when Reyes returned to the barbecue.

"Impressive."

"We've confiscated more marijuana and cocaine in the weeks since Jill's been in charge than we did the previous six months."

"Why is that?"

"She has a knack for team building. Too bad we didn't catch any of their leaders."

"Maybe during interrogation we'll get some names," Gage suggested.

"Don't count on it," said Fritz. The head of the local border patrol was drinking soda from a can. "They undoubtedly work through intermediaries. Besides, spending time in prison is often preferable to what would happen to them and their families if they squealed."

"Is this the most successful raid you've conducted?" Gage asked, though he already knew it was.

"By far," Nita said.

"Where's Jill?" He hadn't seen her since their flight the previous day had landed.

"Said she'd be a here a little later," Nita told him. "Needed to make a few phone calls."

To request his transfer? He suspected not. He was a thorn in her side, but she had too much to lose professionally by exposing him…them. Still, she'd surprised him before. "What made this raid different from others?"

"The openness of our planning session, when everyone could contribute," Bradley said, echoing Nita's sentiment. "People feel like they're part of a team now, rather than robots taking orders. Mack Robbins wasn't real big on consensus. He took briefings, listened to comments, but he tended to make unilateral decisions, then issue orders."

This confirmed what Doug had said. The crack of a bat and the cheering of the crowd drew Nita to the softball field, leaving Gage alone with Bradley at a table loaded with snacks.

Gage dipped a corn tortilla chip in fiery-hot green salsa. "Jill seems to be off to a good start."

Fritz opted for a carrot and the spinach dip. He crunched the raw vegetable. "Maybe it was just a matter of better coordination, but something about yesterday doesn't feel right."

"Because we didn't get any of the big guys?"

"I would have been even more surprised if we had. No, things went too easily. I've never known a drug raid to go down without at least one big glitch."

Gage scooped up more salsa. "Beginner's luck?"

The older man chuckled. "If it is, let's hope it holds."

The gurgling sound of a diesel engine had them turning. A Dodge Ram came to a halt, the passenger door opened and Jill climbed down from the high club-cab. She was wearing snug jeans, a Western-cut red shirt and boots that would make her right at home on the rodeo circuit. Her black cowboy hat added to the image. The ballgame halted between innings.

Victor Reyes went to the passenger side of the truck and greeted her, then escorted her to the assembled crowd.

"We broke a record yesterday," he announced to everyone. He turned to Jill. "Since you've taken over, we've doubled last year's narcotics confiscation rate and turned in the biggest bust the Tombstone station's ever had. Here's to a job well done." He raised his beer mug in a toast. Jill grinned as people hooted their agreement.

For a lingering moment she caught Gage's eye and he glimpsed smug satisfaction. For just an instant the warmth of her gaze said she was also happy he was there to share her victory.

Only after she had passed by did he notice the driver of the big truck. The man was slightly shorter than

Gage, maybe six feet, broad-shouldered and lean-muscled. Nita ran up to him and kissed him on the cheek. So this was Ruben Ortiz, the fiancé Doug Vogel had mentioned.

Gage caught up with Jill a few minutes later at the beer keg.

"Why did you come with Ortiz?"

Jill squinted up at him as she finished pouring herself a cup, and he realized the question made him sound jealous. Well, maybe he was, just a little. She had every right to tell him it was none of his business, and for a moment he could almost see the words forming on her lips. They'd worked well together yesterday, their efforts seamless. He'd hoped that smooth rapport might carry over into their personal lives.

"My car wouldn't start," she said instead. "I didn't want to take an official vehicle to a party."

"You should have said something. I could have brought you."

She sipped the foamy brew, leaving a white mustache, which she licked away with the tip of her tongue. His heart skipped a beat. "I'm quite capable of taking care of myself, Gage." On a less hostile note, she added, "I didn't know the battery was dead until I got into the car. No sweat. I was able to catch a ride with Ruben."

He was about to offer to drive her home when Nita and her boyfriend approached them. Ruben Ortiz was handsome enough that even other men noticed. He had a smooth, olive-toned complexion, high, wide cheekbones, a strong jaw and a cleft chin. When he removed his sunglasses before shaking hands, Gage noticed he had blue eyes, very unusual for someone whose heritage was clearly Hispanic with a conspicuous Native American influence. The striking combination was the stuff of movie stars.

"Ruben's with the highway patrol," Nita explained.

"Were you involved in what went down yesterday?" Gage asked.

"I set up the roadblock at the intersection of 80 and 92. Where are you going?" Ruben asked Nita when she started to walk away.

"I need to talk to Pratt. He said yesterday he knew someone who would sell me handmade Indian jewelry at a discount. My sister has been searching for a squash blossom bracelet. I thought I'd get her one for her birthday."

"The guy's trouble. Stay away from him."

"Oh, for heaven's sake," she protested, "I'm just going to talk to him about jewelry."

"I still don't like it."

"Well, excuse me, but I don't recall asking your permission. Get a grip, Rube."

"Don't call me that. I'm not some country bumpkin."

"Well then, stop acting like one. And don't tell me who I can or cannot talk to." She strode away, her head held high.

Ruben followed her with his eyes. Anger flared behind his tight-lipped glare, but Gage saw hunger, as well. He sympathized with the young guy, knowing what it was like to want to hold a particular woman and never let her go.

"Why do you say Dixon's trouble?" he asked.

Ruben filled a plastic cup. "He has a reputation for shaking down illegals—"

"For money? They can't have much."

Ruben snorted. "Money from the men, favors from the women."

"Have there been complaints filed against him?"

The highway patrolman gave a sarcastic chuckle. "Who's going to squeal on the honcho, and to who?"

"He has a local boss now."

Ruben shook his head. "Nothing's changed. He's still *the man.*"

Gage decided to watch Pratt Dixon more closely. The guy seemed to have undergone a metamorphosis overnight. No longer sulky or hot-tempered, he was playing the consummate team member—at least on the softball field. Chameleons were lizards, and lizards could be dangerous.

Reyes called everyone to eat a few minutes later. Gage observed his copilot and her boyfriend. The tension between them now was strictly of the sexual variety. They were making eyes at each other like a couple of moonstruck teenagers. Gage envied them.

CHAPTER SIX

THE SUN HAD BEEN DOWN for over an hour when people began leaving the hacienda. Reyes had a rule that guests at his parties had to surrender the keys to their vehicles upon arrival. He returned them only when he was satisfied they were able to drive safely or had designated drivers. No one objected. Only occasionally were keys withheld.

Jill looked around. "Where's Ruben?"

"He left a little while ago," Gage told her.

She clucked her tongue in disappointment. "He was supposed to drive me home."

"I told him I'd do it."

Her temper flared then subsided into a slow burn. He was taking over, presuming her acquiescence. What was even more infuriating was that at some level she was pleased. She'd told him their association on a personal level was over, but it was more complicated than that. As angry as she was with his presence here and his eavesdropping, having him around felt somehow reassuring. Or maybe it was the satisfaction of being able to prove she could do her job in spite of him.

"That was presumptuous," she snapped.

"Nita wanted to go with him," he explained. "She

came with Kim, and Kim was taking Ray home. Victor didn't think Ray should be driving."

"He has a hard time stopping at one sometimes," she said.

"So this works out for all of us." Gage placed his hand on the small of her back to guide her to his Jeep.

Dammit, she was supposed to put up more of a fight than this. Sitting next to him...alone...in a car...at night...wasn't a good idea. But of course he'd engineered it so she had little choice. "You should have asked me first," she told him.

"You were deep in conversation with Bradley," he said. "Come on. I won't bite. I promise."

She was about to say he'd made other promises, too, promises he hadn't kept, but she caught herself in time. No use dredging up ancient history. Besides, she'd gone back on her threat to report him to Williams. She hadn't told him yet, but he knew, and it put her at a disadvantage. She sighed.

He walked her to the passenger side of the four-wheel-drive SUV and opened the door. Without thinking, she took his hand when he offered it to help her onto the high seat. The feel of his rough palm, the warmth of his grasp, did unwelcome, pleasant things. For a few seconds she ceased to be an independent person, the branch head of an important governmental agency involved in fighting crime and terrorism. In those fleeting moments, she was a woman being touched by a man.

She muttered deprecations to herself as he swung around the front of the vehicle and opened the driver's side door. Staring straight ahead, she refused to look at him when he climbed in beside her. It wasn't until they were pulling through the iron gate of the adobe wall surrounding the house that she dared glance over at his profile, at the silhouette of his chiseled features against the backdrop of the starry, moonlit night. Something silky and vibrant stirred inside her, something she didn't want to feel, yet cherished with a hunger that left her pulse racing.

They rode in silence for several minutes, the only sounds within the vehicle coming from the police scanner mounted under the dashboard. Mostly static and occasional service checks.

"You did well yesterday," he said. "You shouldn't have any trouble getting the branch chief position permanently."

The note of approval he injected into the compliment pleased her, but, she reminded herself, she didn't need and wasn't seeking his blessing. He was stating the obvious; she wasn't about to thank him for telling the truth.

"We'll see," she murmured, mindful that nothing was certain. Not life. Not love.

The silence between them stretched on, not the comfortable tranquility shared by two people content in each other's company, but the tense awareness of forbidden association, like two teenagers who knew their parents wouldn't approve of their being together.

They came within sight of the small town. Though filled with tourists by day, Tombstone was true to its name at night—dead. A few streetlamps twinkled, but not a living soul wandered the wooden sidewalks or dusty streets. No bars or honky-tonks broke the gothic stillness. It was as if the place were in hibernation, awaiting the sunrise to bring it back to life.

Jill started to give him directions.

"I know where you live."

She shouldn't have been surprised. There weren't many options in a place that had only about twelve hundred permanent residents. Her apartment house was on the southwestern edge of the legendary town, a nondescript two-story building that resembled a motel more than anybody's home. He pulled up in the parking lot and turned off the engine. That meant he intended to stay for a while. How long? She certainly wasn't going to invite him in.

"No need to get out." She opened her door, but before she had both feet on the ground, he was by her side. "Thanks for the lift."

"My pleasure."

She walked toward the outside staircase that would take her to her four-room apartment. He trailed along beside her.

"I said, you don't have to come with me."

"I heard you."

Annoyed, uneasy, unsure of herself, she kept marching, hoping he would take the hint. He didn't, of course. He followed her up the narrow stairs, his boots tolling dully on the metal steps behind her.

Her heart fluttered. From irritation. From anticipation. He had no right to expect anything from her. And she expected nothing from him. She didn't want him here, near her, watching her, pulling at her in ways she'd almost succeeded in forgetting. She didn't need him reminding her of what they had once had, the way he made her feel inside. Cherished, desired, loved. They were divorced, no longer married, no longer emotionally involved. That was the way she liked it, the way to remain.

She managed to reach her door without tripping over her feet or whirling around and snapping at him. Unnerved by his closeness, she dug into her jeans' pocket for her keys, selected the right one, then fumbled when she tried to insert it into the lock.

Gage rested his hand on her shoulder. His touch was warm and firm, the way she remembered him caressing her so many times in the past. She decided to let him take the key from her and open the door. Then she'd say good-night and slip quickly inside.

But he didn't reach for the key. He put his other arm around her, drew her to him and brought his mouth down to hers before she was fully aware of what was happening. His lips covered hers. Her heart soared. It was all so familiar, so perfect. This was where she was meant to be. The feel, the scent, the taste of him, incited awareness of her need for him with a suddenness that robbed her of her very breath. His mustache tickled. His tongue began to part her lips. She was about to fall under its intoxicating spell when some remnant of reason or anger or pride reasserted control.

With the force of anger and a whimper of erotic frustration, she pushed out of his embrace with a sharp jab on his chest. He dropped his arms, gave her the space she demanded, but not an inch more.

"No," she snarled in a low, constricted voice. After all, she didn't want to wake the neighbors. "You have no right— I told you—" Her mind was running on empty. She couldn't find the words she was looking for or the air to pronounce them. Why was he tormenting her this way? Why did she want him to?

The low-wattage light on the balcony was enough for her to glimpse the hunger in his eyes.

"I want you to go." The words quavered. Her whole body was trembling.

His gaze never left her. "Good night, Jill."

He turned and bounded down the stairs, then looked up at her. "Pleasant dreams, sweetheart."

"Has she caught on yet?" the man asked.

His larger companion shook his head. "No, and she's not going to."

"Robbins did."

"He was beginning to, but thanks to you, he never got that far. Otherwise he would have reported up the chain and we wouldn't be sitting here drinking good beer and expensive cognac, and puffing these fine Cuban cigars."

The smaller man sucked on his stogie and started coughing. He didn't really like cigars, but he felt obligated to accept one when it was offered. "How can you be so sure he didn't talk to someone at headquarters? Maybe they're just waiting for the right moment to pounce."

The Black Hand leader blew a perfect smoke ring into the still night air. He hated dealing with mental midgets, but this particular genius was the right guy in the right place, so there wasn't much choice. For now, at least. Eventually he'd pose a threat, either because of some hidden strength or his obvious weaknesses. When—not if—that happened, he'd just have to be disposed of.

"There's no reason for them to wait," he explained. "If they knew what was going on, they'd come in guns blazing."

"That's what I'm afraid of."

The boss crooked an eyebrow. "Getting cold feet?"

His hireling looked suddenly frightened. "No, of course not. I didn't mean that."

The big man smiled, as if it were all a very funny joke. "Just checking. Relax. Everything's going to be fine."

"What about this new guy?"

"Engler? What about him?" He shrugged. "He's a helicopter pilot."

"He's been asking a lot of questions about Robbins and Vogel."

"Normal curiosity."

"He stopped by to see Vogel at the rehab center in Tucson before he arrived here."

The kingpin examined the gray-ash tip of his cigar. "How do you know that?"

"A friend of mine's a nurse there. She was on duty when he came in, said they greeted each other like old friends."

"They probably are." The senior man sipped his cognac. "There aren't that many aviators in Customs. I imagine everybody knows everybody else, at least by name."

"Suppose Vogel tells him—"

"Tells him what?" the boss snapped. "He doesn't know anything. If he had proof of what happened, they wouldn't have closed the investigation. If you'd done your job right, he wouldn't even be alive."

His beer-drinking subordinate stared straight ahead, clearly disturbed at the reminder that he'd killed one man and crippled another. "But if they get talking, maybe Engler will figure out what really happened and who did it."

Something to consider. "Relax. The investigators examined everything with a fine-tooth comb and didn't find diddly. Everything's under control."

"I don't want to have to do that again."

The man was a wimp. "You probably won't have to," his superior informed him. "But if it's necessary, you'll do as you're told. You like the money, don't you?"

"I ain't complaining," the other man said without much enthusiasm.

"After what you've done, there's no backing out. I hope you understand that."

"Hey, I'm cool. Okay?"

"Make sure you stay that way. I wouldn't want anything to happen to you or members of your family."

Sweat broke out on the little man's forehead. "No need to make threats."

"Just a friendly reminder."

"Yeah." His companion sighed. "I get the message."

"You brought up a good point, though. I'll check on this guy Engler, see what his background is, where he's been."

"I need to get back," the other man said, getting up.

"Hang on a minute. I want you to pass on some information. Jill Manning did real well with the last tip. Let's see how well she does with this one."

"But...you're not—"

"Now listen carefully."

GAGE REMOVED THE precut pieces of trim he'd packed separately from the toy box. They weren't fancy. He didn't want any sharp angles on the chest. This molding would round the edges and corners. All they needed was some sanding, then he could clamp them in place while the glue dried. Like the box itself, they were fine-grained hardwood that would withstand a lot of little-boy battering. He should have put them on a long time ago, but after Rickie died he hadn't had the heart to finish the job. What was the point?

He's almost destroyed the box after the funeral, seeing it as an instrument of evil, too much like a coffin. Of course, that was ridiculous. It was an inanimate object, having no moral value. But it was also a reminder of what he had lost. His friends would have said he was a masochist to keep it, if they had known he had. Even Jill didn't know. This was his private memorial to the son who would never grow up, never mature into a man, make love to a woman, produce children and grandchildren. A life not lived.

He sat on his balcony in the dark and rubbed the fine-grit sandpaper over the wooden strips. The stars twinkled in the black-velvet sky. The night air was still, warm and dry. He thought about Jill and the kiss he'd given her. The one she'd almost given back. Was she lying in bed now, curled up contentedly, recollecting the successful day she'd had? Was she thinking of him?

He put down the piece of molding and took up another, feeling very lonely.

"I SEE YOU GOT THIS morning's Terrorist Watch Advisory." Dixon pointed to the piece of paper on top of the stack in the middle of her desk. "Apparently the Green Turtle is targeting Fort Huachuca."

The post was the home of the Army Intelligence Center, where soldiers were trained in vital intelligence skills. The southern tip of the installation came within ten miles of the Mexican border.

Jill twisted her mouth as she finished reading the bulletin. "Attack a military target? That would be foolhardy, wouldn't it?"

Reyes, sitting across from her, took a copy of the bulletin out of the folder he'd brought with him and scanned the page. "It doesn't make any difference to them whether they succeed or fail. Their purpose is to show the world no one is safe, even American armed forces in garrison at home."

"Ideally," Dixon said, "they'd like to create a large number of casualties, destroy multimillion-dollar facilities and seriously degrade our operational capabilities."

"Prove the impotence of our sophisticated intelligence efforts," Jill contributed.

"Even if they fail, they will have demonstrated their suicidal boldness in fighting us." Dixon crossed his arms. "After all, the whole idea of terrorism is to demoralize, convince the opposition that they're helpless to fight back."

"It would be a mistake," she insisted. "Pearl Harbor didn't demoralize America, it galvanized it. So did 9/11. Both resulted in declarations of war."

"Exactly." Reyes tugged on his ear. "On the other hand, terrorism is a long-term strategy. Its goal is to wear down the opposition. And, unlike conventional war, it's cheap."

"We have to assume this threat is real," Jill said, directing their attention to the matter at hand. "That puts us, if not in the line of fire, definitely on the front lines of defense. Pratt, see if you can set up a meeting with army officials at the fort to discuss how we can best help each other. Defense within their perimeter is their responsibility, and we don't want to even appear to be infringing on their turf. But let's see if there's anything more we can do to improve our mutual support. The first defense against terrorism is good intelligence. Victor, you're going to be a major player in this."

Reyes nodded.

"If an attack comes, I want to be sure we did everything in our power to prevent it."

After they left, Jill leaned back in her chair and reread the terrorism advisory. Like many such warnings, it was broad-brush and vague on details, including dates. That wouldn't prevent critics, using 20/20 hindsight, from pointing fingers at specific words and phrases in an effort to find scapegoats.

Under the list of items to be on the lookout for were large quantities of ammonium-nitrate fertilizer, especially in association with diesel fuel, C-3 and C-4 plastique explosives, and shoulder-mounted, surface-to-air missiles or components thereof, as well as grenades and grenade launchers.

Dammit, she couldn't allow this to happen on her watch.

THE FOLLOWING DAY Dixon tapped on Jill's office door and stepped inside. "I just received a report that the Green Turtle will be moving a consignment of C-3 through here tomorrow."

Plastique. A terrorist weapon.

Jill studied the man standing in front of her. His change in attitude since her unofficial counseling session and the drug bust had been so dramatic she was worried. He hadn't apologized for his unprofessional behavior. Maybe if he had, this transformation would feel less insincere. Instead, it was as if he'd flipped a switch.

"You're sure?"

"I got it from a reliable source."

She picked up the phone and asked her intelligence officer to come to her office. When he did, she had Dixon give a rundown of the information he'd received.

Reyes listened, then stroked his chin. "The day after tomorrow, you say. I'll do a file search, but I can tell you now I haven't seen anything to corroborate this."

"Your source said it was being shipped on motorcycles?" Jill asked.

"Not much room to hide anything on a bike," Reyes noted.

"They know in cases like this we're more inclined to tear the carrier apart than the cargo," Dixon explained, "especially if the first items we inspect are clean."

Victor turned to Jill. "What do you want to do?"

"Unfortunately, I don't have much choice when it comes to terrorist threats."

GAGE HAD SERIOUS misgivings when he was brought late into the operation. Smugglers were ingenious at devising subterfuges, but this setup seemed unlikely. Getting the C-3 into and out of the motorcycles would be almost as difficult as finding it.

He was tempted to visit Jill that evening to offer to act as a sounding board for ideas on the upcoming mission, but he had already raised his concerns at the task force meeting she'd called. She would regard any further intrusion on his part to be meddling in her domain. She had no real option but to follow through on the report, no matter how implausible. If the mission failed, launching himself into see-I-told-you-so mode later wouldn't garner him any points. On the other hand, if it succeeded, she'd consider his second thoughts an attempt to undermine her confidence. It was a no-win situation he would do well to stay out of.

The raid the next day was indeed a failure. The assembled cycles proved innocent. The shipping company registered a formal protest with the government over the delay in meeting the contracted delivery date. The manufacturer sued for damages and the expenses incurred in having to reassemble one hundred and fifty brand-new machines. Jill wouldn't be held personally responsible for the fiasco, since she was acting as a government official in good faith, but too many such incidents would have a negative impact on her career.

"What happened?" Gage asked Bradley when it was all over and they'd retired to a small tavern not far from where Gage lived.

The border patrol chief shrugged. "Dixon thought he had a tiger by the tail. He puts too much stock in his snitches." Informants were crucial, but like eyewitnesses to a crime, they were also unreliable. People tended to interpret what they saw and heard, sometimes consciously, sometimes unaware they were bringing prejudices to their reports. And if they have an agenda…"

"You think Jill jumped the gun? Smuggling explosives in motorcycles didn't seem very credible to me."

"If we'd had more time, we could have investigated further and maybe spared her the embarrassment."

Bradley crunched a pretzel. "Under the circumstances…better to err on the side of caution."

"A costly mistake, don't you think?"

"She'll survive." Bradley sipped his ginger ale.

"Was it a setup?" And was Dixon the mole Gage was looking for?

The older man pursed his lips, as if the same thought had crossed his mind. "Dixon may be the victim of his own methods."

"What do you mean?"

"He's the aggressive type. Been known to…browbeat illegals to get what he wants."

"Intimidation?" Ruben Ortiz had mentioned shakedowns.

Bradley rotated his glass. "Maybe. No one has officially complained about him that I know of, and nobody's ever gotten hurt, but that's his reputation."

Gage began to peel the label off his sweaty beer bottle.

"Let's not forget, too," his companion went on, "most of the people he depends on are illegal immigrants, so they've already broken the law by coming here. That makes them criminals, regardless of what you think about the conditions they're fleeing."

It was a legal and a moral conundrum Gage didn't consider himself smart enough to resolve; a game that seemed to have no winners. What he could do was check a little more deeply into Pratt Dixon's background.

CHAPTER SEVEN

THE PROSECUTING ATTORNEY elected to proceed with a preliminary hearing to bind over the drug smugglers for trial instead of convening a grand jury. It was quicker and easier since the judge alone made the decision, rather than a group of unpredictable individuals. It was also a calculated risk. Grand jury testimony was given in secret and the accused did not have the right to have an attorney present, whereas a preliminary hearing was public and the accused could be represented by counsel, who could also cross-examine witnesses.

The hearing required the branch chief and the other agents involved in the arrest to be available to testify. Since Gage had already cultivated an alliance with Jill's secretary, he knew when her boss would be going into town and called scant minutes before Jill walked out the door.

"I thought I'd check to see if you needed a ride to the courthouse."

"I have an official car for that," she reminded him.

"Oh, well, in that case, would you mind giving me a lift?" he asked. "It's such a waste to take two vehicles. Besides, I think it appropriate that you have a chauffeur this morning."

She snorted. "I'm perfectly capable of driving my-self."

"No argument there, and if you want to sit behind the wheel, that's fine with me. You're in charge."

There was a pregnant pause on the line, then a starchy, "I'll drive."

"Thanks," he said in his most friendly and casual manner.

She wasn't thrilled at the prospect of his company, he mused. Was it because she didn't enjoy it or because she was afraid she might? She'd pulled away from his kiss too late the night of the party…only after she'd melted, or started to. After she realized she wasn't supposed to be enjoying it.

THE COURTROOM was packed with relatives of the accused, as well as reporters and ordinary spectators. Debbie Sanchez, the prosecutor presenting the government's case, was busy flipping through papers but raised her head to acknowledge Jill when she and Gage took seats behind the rail. Debbie appeared distracted, but then again, this was a big case for her.

A minute later a man walked down the aisle, passed unopposed through the swinging gate and took his position at the defendant's table. He wasn't the public defender who had been present at the arraignment, and based on the cut of his suit, he wasn't a struggling attorney, either.

Jill leaned over the rail. "Who is he?"

"J. Clanston Parks," Debbie said.

No wonder she wasn't smiling. Parks was one of the biggest names in criminal defense, a man known for getting celebrities off in cases that seemed doomed.

Two questions came to Gage's mind. Why was Parks interested in defending these nobodies? And who was paying him? This ragtag bunch couldn't afford a high-priced mouthpiece.

The courtroom over which Judge Lester Keeling presided was old-fashioned, with bare wood floors, dark-paneled walls and slow-moving ceiling fans. His Honor was diminutive and appeared almost lost in his billowing black robe. From the moment he spoke, however, there was no question that he was in charge.

The clerk read the charges against the accused.

"How do your clients plead, Counselor?"

"Your Honor, I move that the charges against my clients be dismissed—"

"On what basis?" Debbie demanded.

"Your Honor, my clients were arrested without their Miranda rights being read and explained to them. English is a foreign language to them. They were not read their rights in Spanish, nor were they given Spanish-speaking legal assistance as required by law. Any statements they made are therefore inadmissible."

"That's absurd. They had their rights read to them in English and in Spanish at the time of their arrests," Debbie countered, "and I have multiple witnesses to verify it. Furthermore, their arrests were not based on anything they said. The presence of counsel is, therefore, moot. They were taken into custody and charged based on the presence of illegal substances found in their possession. Reference Mitchell v—"

"That's another problem, Your Honor," Parks cut in. "My clients were apprehended on private property and the vehicles they were driving subjected to illegal search and seizure, since the Customs and police forces had no warrant to search the premises."

"Your Honor, as you've explained at many previous hearings and trials, Customs has legal search authority independent of a search warrant."

"The government must still be able to articulate a reasonable cause." Parks glared at her. "What was it?"

"Mr. Parks," Judge Keeling said in a stiff voice, "you are in my courtroom. I ask the questions here."

"My apologies, Your Honor."

"Ms. Sanchez, what was the basis for the search?"

"We had reliable information that the convoy was transporting large quantities of illegal substances."

"Your Honor," Parks said in an ingratiating manner, "the actions of the Customs Service clearly violate my clients' right to be protected from unreasonable search and seizure, as guaranteed by the fourth amendment to the Constitution. The government claims they had intelligence that this convoy was carrying illegal substances before the trucks crossed the border from Mexico into this country. They had the information before the trucks arrived at the Customs stations at Douglas, Arizona, at which location they performed a thorough—and I might add, perfectly legal—search. They found nothing. They allowed the trucks to proceed into U.S. territory. Then, twenty miles up the road, the highway patrol claims the truckers committed a minor traffic violation—to wit, failing to signal their turn in sufficient time. Did the highway patrol stop the convoy then and there? No, Your Honor. They allowed it to continue for another three miles. Only when the convoy stopped of its own volition was it intercepted and Customs agents brought in to search it once more."

"I must point out, Your Honor," Debbie said with confidence, "that we seized nearly five hundred kilos of high-grade cocaine."

"By means of an illegal search," Parks said. "It constitutes fruit of the poisoned tree. The search was illegal, consequently the evidence seized cannot be used in a court of law against my clients. They were not aware of the true nature of the cargo. I move, therefore, that the charges against them be dismissed for lack of evidence."

"That's ridiculous," Debbie snarled. "We have fifty million dollars' worth of evidence."

"Not if it was seized in violation of the law."

"Is what Mr. Parks has stated correct?" Judge Keeling asked.

"Essentially, but—"

"You had information that illegal substances were being smuggled in these vehicles before they crossed the border?"

"This is not the first time we've—"

"And the Customs Service inspected the shipment and found nothing?"

Gage had been watching the proceeding with interest and satisfaction to this point. The government's attorney was prepared, competent and aggressive. But the judge's hostile tone in asking his questions was now giving Gage a queasy feeling in the pit of his stomach.

"We did not perform a thorough search as my esteemed colleague claims, Your Honor, but a standard one," Debbie replied.

"Even though you had what you considered reliable information that they were carrying contraband?"

"We were after bigger fish. Your Honor, it has been standard practice to trail suspects—"

"Is it also true that these vehicles were not stopped at the time of their purported traffic violation but allowed to continue for several miles?"

"The road was very narrow. There was no room to stop—"

"When you did finally come in contact with them," Keeling asked, his face becoming red with obvious anger, "did any of the clients do or say anything to indicate they were carrying something they shouldn't be?"

"They were beginning to unload their cargo."

"My question, Ms. Sanchez, was if they did or said anything to give the highway patrol probable cause to call in the Customs Service and proceed with another search. Answer my question."

"Unloading their cargo in a remote location was in itself suspicious, Your Honor." Frustration seemed to overwhelm her. "They were in the middle of nowhere, for God's sake."

"Watch your language in my courtroom, Counselor," the judge said.

"They were concerned that their cargo was shifting," Parks interjected, "and were looking for a safe and convenient place to rearrange it."

"What about the five hundred kilos of illegal narcotics?" Debbie shot back.

"Ms. Sanchez, I've already advised Mr. Parks that I ask the questions here, and now I'm warning you. Unless you abide by the rules of this court, I'll hold you in contempt. Is that clear?"

"Yes, Your Honor. Sorry." She took a deep breath.

Gage looked over at Jill sitting beside him. The tension in her features as she took in the proceedings told him she could see what was coming. The case was falling apart, her case, the one that should be her finest achievement. Not because the evidence was weak or because of anything she had done or failed to do. It was all going down the tubes because some crazy judge was being intimidated by a high-priced shyster. It wasn't fair, Gage wanted to tell her, but she already knew that.

"Your Honor, if I may." Parks removed the horn-rimmed reading glasses he'd had perched on the tip of his nose. "No one is denying that the illegal substances exist. But as the prosecuting attorney has pointed out, my clients did and said nothing to indicate their awareness of their presence. And since the search was illegally conducted, there is no evidence against them. I request, therefore, that the charges be dismissed."

"Your Honor, this is outrageous."

Judge Keeling appeared to be both uncomfortable and furious. "Why did the government wait until they were twenty miles beyond the border to conduct a detailed search, if they had information of contraband beforehand?"

"As I stated, Your Honor, we were hoping to catch their higher-level contacts in this operation."

"Did you?"

"No."

Keeling closed his eyes briefly and shook his head, his jaw set. "Defense counsel's motion is granted," he said, none too happily.

Gage was furious. He'd been in the courtroom often

enough to know their case was solid. Not a single one of Park's objections had merit, yet this incompetent judge was letting drug smugglers go free. It was outrageous. Worse, it was an affront to Jill, who had led one of the best coordinated raids against a major narcotics shipment along the southern border. He wanted to cry out for her, to challenge and fight.

Keeling was raising his gavel when Jill rose from her seat behind the rail. Gage could feel the tension emanating from her. He had an urge to get up, sweep her into his arms and soothe her with promises that everything would be all right.

"Your Honor, may I address the court?"

"Who are you?"

"Jill Manning, branch chief of the Tombstone office of Customs and Border Protection." When he didn't tell her to sit down, she continued. "Dismissing the charges against these individuals establishes a very disturbing precedent. It is accepted practice to grant Customs agents broad discretion on how they follow up on leads involving smuggled contraband, especially illegal narcotics—"

"Ms. Manning, the end does not justify the means, nor does it trump the United States Constitution. You're new at your job, I understand, but that's no excuse for violating the civil rights of persons in this country, whether they are citizens or not."

She stood there, speechless, and seemed to realize nothing she said was going to make any difference. Still, she held her head up, unintimidated. Gage was proud of her.

"The charges are dismissed," Keeling continued, his red face reflecting the anger in his voice. "The defendants are hereby released from custody." He slammed down his gavel.

The room exploded with cheers from family members.

Judge Keeling pounded his gavel and demanded order. When it wasn't forthcoming, he ordered the bailiff to clear the courtroom. He then stepped down from the bench and disappeared into his chambers.

Jill remained standing among the chaos. A minute passed as people clapped each other on the back. J. Clanston Parks picked up the attaché case he hadn't even opened, walked down the center aisle and disappeared through the double doors.

Gage stood up beside Jill and had to resist the impulse to touch her, to wrap his arm around her waist and comfort her. "I think we were just sandbagged."

GAGE TOOK THE WHEEL for the drive back to the station. He could feel Jill's helplessness. She needed to get the anger out of her system, he reasoned, but first she needed a friend. He reached over and placed his hand over hers. When she didn't pull away, he plied his fingers with hers.

"I'm sorry," he said. "That travesty back there should never have happened. Our case was solid. We did everything by the book. Don't blame yourself."

"I know you're right." She tightened her hold on his hand.

It was their first real connection and it sent a punch of adrenaline surging through him. Be patient, he told himself. It's a beginning. Don't push too hard, too fast.

"Dismissing the charges doesn't make sense," she said. "I don't understand Keeling. He knows we have

Customs search authority. What the hell is he thinking? Is the man becoming senile?"

"Senile maybe. More like someone got to him."

She was only half listening. "Debbie Sanchez says she'll appeal Keeling's action and request the charges be reinstated."

"Not much chance of that happening."

"Keeling's always been a good judge. If he's suddenly on the take or his mind is slipping, we need to get him off the bench as soon as possible."

"Removing a judge isn't easy."

She nodded. "Which raises another issue. Why was J. Cranston Parks there? The guy could have been on O.J.'s dream team. What does he care about a bunch of truck drivers and narcotics mules? Even if they pooled all their resources, they probably couldn't have come up with enough cash to buy one hour of his time."

"Maybe he's taking the case pro bono," Gage said, though he didn't believe it.

Jill shook her head. "The courtroom would have been packed with reporters. The only reason people like Parks contribute their services free is to get publicity that's more valuable than their hourly rates."

That left but one alternative. The judge was on the take.

GAGE ENTERED HIS office, closed the door and called Sid on his cell phone. He'd already received several background reports from the computer research specialist.

"I need information on the judicial record and personal life of Lester Keeling, the district judge here in Tombstone."

"Looking for anything in particular?" Sid asked. Gage could picture the rail-thin researcher munching on a doughnut as he scribbled a note to himself on a food-stained pad.

"He made a ruling today, threw a major narcotics case out of court. I want to know how often this happens. Are there any indications of corruption in his background?"

"Spell the name."

Gage complied. "Also, J. Clanston Parks defended the smugglers. See if you can find out who's paying him. There must be someone big involved for him to make a personal appearance on a dinky little case like this. Anything on the other names I gave you?"

"Your fellow aviators all look clean." Sid gave a brief rundown of the seven, two of whom Gage had yet to meet. "Ditto half the flight mechanics on your list." He gave their names. All were in their early twenties and unmarried, so their histories were short and relatively easy to investigate. "I haven't had time to review the records of the others yet. Give me a few more days."

"What have you been able to dig up about Mack Robbins?"

"Poor choice of words." Sid snickered.

Gage groaned at his inadvertent pun.

"Robbins had a gambling problem, all right," Sid went on. "Ended up losing his house and car. The only thing that made him stop was when the loan sharks threatened his kids."

"I heard he took the pledge. How did he finally get the sharks off his back?"

"He didn't. He was still forking over a chunk of change every month when he died."

Was it possible the mob had decided to cut its losses? Unlikely. Despite movie legends, loan sharks didn't rub out people who owed them money. What was the point? They couldn't collect from dead men. The exception was when a person's unfortunate demise was used as an example to others.

"Anything else?"

"You asked for background on Victor Reyes."

"What about him?"

"Nothing sinister. Just that the hacienda comes from his wife's side of the family. Apparently she's old money."

"He gave me the lowdown shortly after I got here. Goes back to the days of the Tombstone silver rush over a hundred years ago. Her family comes from Mexico City, or did."

"Still does," Sid said.

"What's Reyes's personal background?"

"I guess the politically correct term would be 'humbler.' His father was a common laborer, barely literate in Spanish, spoke no English, but he managed to support the family at the subsistence level. He was killed in an industrial accident, leaving behind his wife, Victor and his seven brothers and sisters. Momma Reyes had no marketable skills, so fortunes went downhill from there. Five years later, when Victor was nine, she remarried. Papa *numero dos* had been in and out of jail a dozen times. Small stuff mostly. Disorderly conduct, public intoxication, petty theft. Was about to be picked up for grand theft auto when he decided they all needed an extended vacation in Mexico. Victor came back to the U.S. when he was seventeen, finished high school in Texas and got a scholarship to a private college. That's where he met Selinda Peralta-Rodriquez. They married right after graduation."

"The American dream. Any problems?"

"Nope, not until…" Sid said. "Not until last year when his younger son was killed."

"Reyes told me about that, too," Gage said. "The hacienda sits on the border. They have to monitor it constantly. Cisco must have come up against a bunch of drug smugglers while he was riding patrol on horseback one night. His body wasn't found till the next day."

"Did he tell you the kid had been shot in the back of the head?"

"Executed?" This was even uglier than Gage had realized. No wonder Reyes had rededicated himself to fighting the drug trade.

After hanging up, Gage reviewed the day's flight bulletins and reread the terrorist watch advisories. He was scheduled to fly patrol with Nita and a mechanic this afternoon. The routine surveillance mission would give him a chance to check out the Reyes's hacienda more closely. He'd flown over it before but hadn't realized the land belonged to their intelligence chief.

One thing he discovered an hour later that Reyes hadn't mentioned was the caliche pit on the south end of the place, a great yawning white slash at the base of an eroded mesa. A few pieces of heavy equipment were scattered around a small wooden shack, but there were no signs of human activity. Apparently the excavation didn't operate full time.

As they continued along the border, Nita pointed out the spot where Victor's son had been found, several miles to the east. Gage saw no evidence that the four-foot-high, barbed-wire fence had been broken, but infiltrators were good at covering their tracks, sometimes tunneling under obstacles rather than going over them.

After completing their flight debrief, Gage finished the day's paperwork and sat ruminating. She'd resisted him when he kissed her after the party at the hacienda, but he'd sensed she was fighting herself more than him. He'd given her space. She'd loosened up after the fiasco of the preliminary hearing this morning. Now it was time to take the next step.

Be careful, he cautioned himself. Push too hard and she'll push back.

What they needed was some quality time together… In private would be nice, but he didn't suppose that was going to happen, not yet. Where could they go that would be public and private? He smiled, got out the phone book and made a call. When everything was arranged, he left the hangar, crossed the wide parking lot and entered the Customs building.

"Boss-lady in?" he asked.

Kim smiled up at him. "Shall I tell her you're here?"

"Let me surprise her."

The pert secretary ran her tongue across her teeth. "I'm not sure that's a good idea. For me, that is. I'm supposed to vet her callers, give her a warning of—"

Former husbands on the prowl?

"I'm not exactly a stranger," he said with what he hoped was a beguiling smile. What would people's reactions be when they found out he and Jill used to be man and wife? "I work for her."

Kim shook her head, but she couldn't suppress a smile. "If I get fired, it'll be your fault, and you'll have to support me for the rest of my life."

"It'd almost be worth it to barge in there, ranting and raving. Except I'd get fired, too, and we'd both end up trying to live on cactus."

"Yuck."

"Actually it's quite good fried. With plenty of jalapeño, of course."

"I think I'll pass." She laughed. "Go on in, but be polite."

He winked and stepped through the doorway. Jill was sitting at her desk, a piece of paper in her hands. The frown on her face said it all. She wasn't happy and for good reason. Her day in court had been rotten.

"Let me take you away from all of this," he said, and tilted his head to one side in a come-hither manner.

She raised her eyebrows. "To eat cactus? Are you sure Kim won't object to a threesome?"

He chuckled. Maybe things weren't as bad as he thought. "Does that mean you're going to fire us?"

She awarded him a patronizing smile. "Helicopter pilots are a dime a dozen, but good secretaries are a true rarity. I think I'll keep her."

He almost asked, *And me?* "It's nearly four. Why don't you quit early today? I'd like to take you somewhere."

He expected her to argue, to demand to know what he was talking about, to warn him that she wasn't in the mood to play his games. But she didn't do any of those things. Out of pure fatigue? Or because she really was interested in spending time with him? The notion stimulated him, put fire in his blood. Or maybe it was nerves. She felt something for him, something positive, but they still had issues to settle, and he couldn't be sure they'd ever be resolved. She'd had two years to come to terms with Rickie's death. But two years of grieving couldn't cure a lifetime of regret. He hadn't forgiven himself. How could he expect her to forgive him?

"Go home and change. I'll meet you at your place in an hour. Oh," he said as he headed for the door, "wear boots."

"What?"

"We're going horseback riding." He dashed out before she had a chance to question him further.

CHAPTER EIGHT

JILL KNEW she was making a mistake the moment she walked out of the office. She could still change her mind. It was, after all, a woman's prerogative. But she also realized she wouldn't. She could tell herself the attraction was the horseback riding, something she hadn't done in years, but on that score she knew better, as well.

She wasted no time on the niceties of hanging up her clothes or tossing them in the hamper. Like a rebellious teenager, she dropped them where she shed them and scurried into her closet to find appropriate replacements. Not the gray cotton sweatpants she wore around the house at night or on her rare days off, or her new pair of stone-washed black denims. She opted for comfortably used jeans that struck just the right note for an evening in the saddle.

From the looks of him, Gage hadn't been indulging in beer and pretzels in the two years since they'd separated. If anything, he appeared more muscular, but then he'd always taken care of himself. A well-disciplined man—except on one very important occasion, but she wasn't about to go there, not even in her thoughts. The problem was: how did she *not* think about something? Like the body of the man who'd made love to her? Like the sensation of his skin in contact with hers? Like the feeling of being special whenever she was with him.

By establishing distance. That's what she'd done when she'd transferred to Tombstone. It had worked, for the most part. Until he'd turned up again like a bad penny.

As she tucked in her shirttail and buttoned her pants, she had to ask herself why she was doing this. It was bad enough that he'd come back into her professional life and she had to see him every morning at the staff briefing. Socializing with him only compounded the problem. Yet here she was fluttering around, getting ready for him, when she should be doing just about anything else.

She heard footsteps on the metal stairs outside and glanced at her bedside clock. He was early, but then that had always been his way. And she'd been perpetually late. Well, not this time.

GAGE WAS SURPRISED to find Jill ready when she answered the door. As meticulous and organized as she was in her work, she had never been a slave to social punctuality. Her shiny brown hair was pulled back in a ponytail, but it spilled over the tops of her ears, exposing small teardrop earrings. She'd also applied a darker shade of lipstick than she wore on the job. When she greeted him, her green eyes danced with the kind of anticipation he hadn't seen since his arrival here. In her left hand she held the same black cowboy hat she'd worn at the party at the Reyes's hacienda. Jauntily, she plopped it onto her head.

"I wasn't sure I wanted to do this," she admitted, locking her door behind her. "But the more I thought about it, the more I liked the idea."

"Good." Downstairs, he opened the passenger door of his Jeep for her, then walked around the front of the vehicle and climbed in behind the wheel. He felt a kind of adolescent excitement with her sitting beside him, especially when he caught her familiar scent. He nearly dropped the key before putting it in the ignition.

"I haven't ridden in a long time. How about you?" she asked.

Their second meeting had been on a bridle path in Virginia, after she'd graduated from the academy. They'd ridden many times over the year he'd courted her and vowed they'd continue to do it after they were married. But conflicting work schedules had soon gotten the best of both of them.

"Actually, the last time was with you," he replied.

She seemed to weigh his words but said nothing.

"I called Earl's Livery Stable and reserved two of his finest steeds, but I haven't had a chance to check them out, so we may be disappointed."

IN FACT, THEIR MOUNTS were quite acceptable quarter horses. Earl, a burly black man of indistinct age with a ready smile, had pointed to the trails outlined on a wall map. Since this was their initial excursion, he'd recommended a route that took about an hour at a moderate pace but also had a dogleg that would allow them to return earlier if they felt so inclined.

Sunset was about an hour and a half away. They rode a narrow rambling trail to the east that wove between eroded buttes and gently rolling hills. The ground beneath the horses's hooves was coarse taupe, broken only by gray rocks. On his first day here, Gage had picked up a brochure on the natural history of the desert, so he recognized the spindly brown ocotillo tipped with tiny red blooms and the feathery gray-green of salt cedar. This was rugged, unforgiving desert, the kind that bleached bones.

He had let Jill take the lead, content to watch the rhythmic sway of her hips in the Western saddle, to indulge his eyes with the smooth curl of her tight-fitting jeans. Eventually the path widened and he was able to ride by her side. He considered striking up a conversation but changed his mind. There would be plenty of time for talk later. For the moment he was content to simply be with her, to feel her unwinding beside him.

Half an hour passed in companionable silence.

"Why are you here?" she finally asked.

It wasn't the opening he'd expected or wanted. "To fly helicopters."

She slanted him a doubting expression, then kicked her horse into a lope and pulled out in front of him.

"Nice going," he muttered. Why didn't he just say because he wanted to be with her? She might object that she didn't want him here, but at least she would be able to respect his honesty. Instead he'd equivocated.

She turned west onto the path that would bring them back to the livery stable.

"Let's stop a minute and enjoy the scenery," he suggested.

The sun was low now, casting long shadows, the sky ahead of them ablaze with an iridescent glow. Mauve and charcoal, pink and powder blue, gold and silver, all woven into a patchwork of stripes and folds. The desert's gift would subtly change for another hour or more, constantly rich, always filled with fading promises.

They dismounted and tied their horses loosely to a

stunted cedar, then settled against a table rock nearby and watched the light play out its slow-motion kaleidoscope of color.

He ran the tip of a finger along the clean sweep of her hair under her hat. She tensed for a second, then relented in a way that said she was only tolerating the physical contact. He could feel the tremor of her muscles beneath his fingers.

"What's happened to us, Jill? You used to welcome my touch."

She gazed straight ahead at the simmering horizon. "You know what happened."

The mournful tone, the note of desolation in it, twisted in his gut. "I loved Rickie more than I can ever express," he said. "You must know that."

She bit her lip but said nothing. Maybe that was a positive sign. There had been a time when she would have exploded at him, cursed him for killing their baby.

How often had he relived that day, replayed its dreadful events and asked himself if she was right, if he was responsible for the loss of that delicate sweet life?

Rickie had been running a slight fever that morning. Jill had been in a panic until Gage had called their pediatrician. The doctor had asked a few questions and dismissed the situation as not serious. Children often ran low-grade fevers for no apparent reason. It could have been something as simple as mild indigestion, or perhaps he was fighting off germs. Battling bacteria and viruses one at a time was how infants built up their immune systems.

"Monitor his temperature," the doctor had said, "and if it goes over 101, bring him in."

Jill had been scheduled to go to lunch and shopping with friends, her first girls' day out since before Rickie had been born. She'd wanted to cancel the date, but Gage had talked her into keeping it.

"It'll do you good to get away for a few hours. Don't worry," he'd assured her. "I'll check his temperature every half hour. If it reaches 101, I'll take him to the emergency room."

"Call me," she'd insisted. "I'll carry the cell phone."

"I promise." He'd kissed her on the lips and sent her off.

While Rickie slept, Gage went to the workshop in the garage to do more work on the toy box he was building for his son. He took the baby monitor with him so he could hear if Rickie awoke.

When next he looked up, almost an hour and a half had zipped by. Not a peep out of the nursery, but he hurried to check on the boy nevertheless.

Rickie's face was mottled. Gage touched his forehead. The infant was burning up. Frantic, Gage put his son in his car seat and raced to the garage just as Jill was being dropped off by her best friend, a good hour earlier than expected. The moment Gage told her of the fever, she became frenzied, touching Rickie, snapping questions.

"What's his temperature?"

"I don't know. I haven't taken it."

"What was it the last time you did?"

"We've got to go. Get in the car," he'd insisted, hoping she wouldn't notice he hadn't answered her. But as she examined the baby, she continued to barrage him with questions. When she realized he hadn't been in the nursery since she'd left, she grew nearly hysterical.

Gage drove to the hospital like a madman. Jill's harangue alternated between accusations of neglect and screams of terror at the way he was weaving in and out of traffic. Gage called ahead on the cell phone to alert the staff he was bringing in a very sick baby.

The automatic assumption for all infants running high fevers was meningitis. Gage and Jill were relegated to the waiting room. Jill turned vicious, blaming Gage for ignoring their baby, charging him with never wanting the child. Gage tried to reason with her, but she was beyond logic, beyond consolation, and a part of him believed she was right—not about not wanting his son, but about neglecting him.

The progress report they received wasn't encouraging. The doctor had done a spinal tap, which confirmed the initial diagnosis. He'd drained off some of the fluid to reduce the pressure and sent it to the lab. It turned out to be the bacterial variety. The physician administered massive doses of antibiotics.

They spent the night at the baby's bedside, staring at their beautiful creation, at the tubes and probes hooked up to him. Just as sunrise was tinting the eastern sky with the hope of a new day, the heart monitor let out a keening whistle. Ten minutes later the doctor pronounced Richard Allen Engler dead.

Gage and Jill clung to each other in that hospital room. Little did he know it would be the last time they'd connect. In spite of all the assurances from the doctors that getting to the hospital a half hour, an hour, even two hours sooner probably wouldn't have made any difference, Jill was convinced Gage was to blame for Rickie's death. He'd insisted on only calling the doctor when the baby had a fever instead of taking him in at once.

Then he'd failed to watch Rickie as he'd promised. Now their son was gone.

Gage hadn't needed Jill to tell him he had failed as a father and lost the most precious gift God could give him. What he did need was to hold her, but she wouldn't have anything to do with him. He sought professional counseling, something he would have considered weakness under any other circumstances, but he was desperate to try to make sense of a world gone insane. He begged Jill to go with him, but she refused.

"Give her time," a friend advised Gage. "My sister went through the same thing when she had a miscarriage. She got help and now has three beautiful kids."

That was another problem. There wouldn't be any more children. Rickie's birth had been complicated and the obstetrician had told them Jill wouldn't be able to conceive again. They hadn't told anyone, but he knew it weighed heavily on her mind. Before their marriage they'd talked of having a large family. Now they wouldn't have any.

A month later, Jill announced she wanted a divorce and moved out. She sought little from him through her lawyer. He gave her everything she requested and asked for nothing in return—except a baby picture.

"Do you still blame me for Rickie's death?" he asked now. "He was my son, Jill. I would have given my life for him. Don't you understand that?"

She remained silent. He watched her, waited. If, after all this time, she still blamed him, all hope for reconciliation was lost.

"It was a long time ago." Equivocating.

"Two years or twenty or fifty," he said, his throat tightening, "the pain of losing him will never go away."

"It will always come between us," she replied.

"What about the love we shared?"

She shook her head. He didn't know if she was denying what they'd felt for each other or disagreeing that it could ever bring them together again.

He cupped her chin and turned her face to his. Tears hung on her lashes.

He kissed her softly. She hesitated, and he could feel her desire to pull away, but this time, as his tongue nudged forward, she relented and admitted him.

Time stopped. Recriminations fled. He tasted her and felt her body react. She put her arms around him and melted into his embrace. For a few seconds the empty loneliness that had ravaged him since he'd heard the steady tone of that heart monitor fled.

"We need to start back," she said in a rush a moment after breaking off. Did she realize, he wondered, that she'd just acknowledged what she'd previously refused to admit, that beneath the heartache she still felt something for him?

Patience, he counseled himself. *Go slow. Give her time to accept what you already know.* That they loved each other. Still.

They arrived at the barn almost two hours after they'd left. The stable owner was waiting for them.

"How did it go, folks?" He reached up and held Jill's bridle while she dismounted.

"Nice horses," she said, dropping to the dusty ground. "We took it easy, but I suspect I'm going to feel it in the morning."

Earl's laugh was a low rumble. "Probably before then. Best thing is a hot bath."

"Sounds heavenly." She led her mount into the barn.

They helped remove the saddles, pads and tack. Gage paid the man and they left.

A few minutes later he pulled up in front of Jill's apartment building. Just as he'd done before, he got out, went around to open her door and escorted her up the stairs.

"How about dinner?" he asked.

"Maybe another time. I think what I need right now is that hot bath."

His eager mind conjured up an image of soap bubbles adorning her breasts, her nipples, like delicate lace. He felt himself harden. "I'll be glad to scrub your back, massage your feet."

He'd promised himself that he wouldn't crowd her, and here he was violating his own plan.

She tsked and rolled her eyes. "Don't push it, Gage." But there was a lightness behind the censure.

Any illusions he might once have had that she would run into his arms when she saw him had long been dispelled, but he'd learned something this evening. Protest as she might, she still felt something for him, something he was determined to build on.

"Good night, then," he said, and backed away.

"Gage," she called out.

He stopped.

"Thanks for the ride."

CHAPTER NINE

"WHY ISN'T MY HELICOPTER ready?" Gage was scheduled to fly this morning but had just been informed the Blackhawk wasn't available.

"It's due for a gearbox change," explained Paco Moreno, the chief flight mechanic. "But our supplier delivered the wrong transmission fluid."

"When did it come in?"

"Last week—"

"And you're just realizing now it's not what you ordered?"

"The invoice had it right, and that's what was used to post the inventory, but what was dropped off was wrong."

"Who signed for the shipment?"

Moreno lowered his head. "I did."

He was a short, chubby man in his early forties. Gage had gotten a background report on him from Sid. Moreno had been maintaining helicopters for twenty years, the last ten with the Customs Service. His record was spotless.

"It's my fault," he admitted. "I initialed all the items on the list, but I must have forgotten to physically verify the last one. When we went to get the oil from the warehouse this morning, we discovered the error. The supplier has never messed up on us like this before."

Or he could have received the right oil and someone later switched it in their storeroom?

Was that what happened with Doug's flight? The wrong lubricant? The wrong fuel? But the inspection team had double-checked everything and found no evidence of that kind of mistake.

"I've phoned in an emergency order. It should be delivered in a couple of hours. We'll have you flying this afternoon."

Gage wasn't pleased and considered reprimanding the chief mechanic, but nothing would be accomplished by doing so at this point. Not with so little evidence of who was to blame. Moreno's checks and balances had worked. No actual harm had been done.

Gage was also mindful of the other part of the report he'd received from Sid. It could explain Moreno's distraction, if that was the real culprit.

"How's Tina doing?" he asked. "She all right?"

Four years ago Moreno's then ten-year-old daughter had come down with a sore throat while camping with her Girl Scout pack in North Carolina. A local doctor had examined her, given her some lozenges and sent her back to camp without bothering to take a culture. At home, the sore throat worsened, so her mother took her to the emergency room where it was properly diagnosed as strep and she received antibiotics. The infection, however, turned out to be a virulent one and the medication—too little, too late—failed to cure the problem. More tests were performed. This time they'd discovered a congenital heart defect. The streptococcal infection, so long untreated, had caused serious heart valve inflammation and permanent damage that was now life threatening.

"She tires so easily," Moreno said. "Tina used to run everyone ragged. Now she hasn't got the energy to do more than sit and read. Even a short walk leaves her panting."

"Any word on the heart transplant?"

It was the teenager's only long-term hope. Government-sponsored medical insurance was picking up a major portion of the cost, but out-of-pocket and collateral expenses for this type of surgery could be daunting. Fortunately, people were very generous, especially when it came to children. Sid reported that the Morenos had a robust contingency account, thanks to donations.

"It may take months," he said. "We can only hope one becomes available in time."

"Hang in there." Gage laid an encouraging hand on the man's shoulder. "And let's make sure we don't have any more mix-ups like today."

"I'm real sorry, Gage. I promise it won't happen again."

The sound of activity on the hangar floor brought the conversation to a close. Jill's secretary was carrying a cardboard box toward a table that had been set up between two of the helicopters. Behind her trailed the other pilots, the flight mechanics and several staff members.

"What's going on?" Gage asked.

"Nita's birthday," Moreno explained. "Kim keeps track of dates and gets a cake to go with our morning coffee." He grinned and patted his round belly. "June is going to be a very fattening month. Six birthdays."

Nita played along at being astonished by all the attention, though she must have known it was coming.

The flight mechanics gave her a few gag gifts, all of them in good taste. She was well liked by the crews. The men treated her with the kind of affection they'd shower on a daughter or kid sister.

Lunchtime rolled around. Gage found Nita in the operations center studying charts, probably more out of curiosity than necessity. No one knew the local area better than she did. It occurred to him that she might be waiting for someone, Ruben, no doubt. But her expression told him her fiancé had forgotten what day it was.

"I'm sorry I didn't have a present for you, but nobody clued me in," Gage told her. Jill had arrived late and given Nita a small jadeite figurine of a horse. Nita was fond of the green mineral. "How about I treat you to lunch to make up for it?"

She hesitated. "That's okay. I'm not real hun—"

"I thought we might try the Spaghetti Western," he said before she could complete her refusal. The restaurant was an old-time saloon that had recently been restored and now featured Italian food.

She smiled. "I've been wanting to go there, but Ruben says lasagna gives him heartburn."

Gage chuckled. "I think there's more to Italian food than pizza, spaghetti and lasagna."

"That's what I keep trying to tell him, but he gets a notion into his head and it takes a bulldozer to remove it."

"Set in his ways, is he?"

She snorted, then her black eyes took on a shadowy sadness. "His father was very strict, and even though Ruben says he doesn't want to be like him, I think he takes after him more than he realizes."

"You said 'was,'" Gage observed.

"He died three years ago in a mining accident. Ruben had just had a big fight with him. Mr. Ortiz didn't like him becoming a policeman, said he was betraying his people. Ruben said his people were Americans. Told his father if he wanted to be a Mexican he could cross the border any time he wanted."

"I can see how that might put a strain on things," Gage said.

"Two days later his father was killed in a cave-in. Ruben has never forgiven himself for being so disrespectful."

"Does he think he was wrong?"

"Not about what he said. Our families have lived here for generations. It's not as if we're immigrants," Nita replied. "But Ruben has a temper and sometimes he says things he doesn't mean."

"We all do."

"In some ways he's very old-fashioned. He thinks children owe their parents absolute obedience and respect."

They arrived at the eatery. Lunch hour was already in full swing. Gage lucked out and snagged a parking space in the lot next to the restaurant just as someone was leaving. They mounted the three steps to the wooden sidewalk. The Spaghetti Western was decorated in the style of a nineteenth-century frontier dance hall with red-velvet wallpaper, dark wood and brass fixtures. The only table available was by the plate-glass window overlooking Allen Street.

"Hungry?" he asked when they were seated. Several men had turned to watch her. He couldn't blame them. Nita was a beautiful woman.

"Actually, I am," she said. "Mom called this morning to wish me happy birthday, then my aunt called, and my brothers. I was so busy answering the phone I didn't get a chance to eat." She opened the tall, laminated menu. "What do you suggest?"

While the waitress went off to fetch their iced tea, they discussed the various dishes. In the end, she left the ordering to him.

The waiter brought their antipasto salad. Only then did Gage realize he hadn't requested they hold the anchovies. To his relief, Nita liked them.

"When are you and Ruben getting married?" he asked. Except when she was flying, she wore her engagement ring, a modest, conventional diamond solitaire.

"The middle of September." Three months away. "He has a few credit cards he insists on paying off first. I offered to help with the bills, but he won't let me."

Gage's respect for the highway patrolman inched up.

Their main courses arrived. Manicotti for her, saltimbocca for him.

"This is delicious," she said after the first bite.

"Would you like to try a piece of this? It's veal with prosciutto ham and mozzarella cheese on a bed of spinach."

"Looks scrumptious. Can I?"

He cut off a piece. She reached across the table and skewered it with her fork.

"What the hell—"

Her fork clattered at the sound of the raised voice. They both looked up to see Ruben standing over their table.

"Ruben, what are you doing here?" she asked, her voice wobbly.

"I was just about to ask you the same thing. What are you doing here with him?"

"Whoa." Gage bunched the napkin in his right hand and rose to his feet. "You have no call to talk to her like that."

"Stay out of this, Engler. She's *my* fiancée. *My* woman. Not yours. Keep your hands off."

"Hold on, Ruben," Nita snapped. "Gage brought me here to celebrate my birthday."

"Your birth—"

"Which you obviously forgot."

"You were eating off his plate. What else have the two of you been sharing?"

Gage felt his temper rising. "You're out of line, Ortiz," he said through clenched teeth.

"Mind your own business."

"Ruben," Nita muttered. "For heaven's sake, keep your voice down. You're embarrassing me."

"You should be ashamed of yourself," he countered, his voice anything but lowered. "You're engaged to me and you humiliate me by eating in public with another man."

"I humiliate you?" She jumped to her feet and glared at him. "Look around, Ruben. You're the one making a spectacle of yourself, and me…of us. All I was doing was having lunch."

"This is your fault," he spat at Gage.

A waiter with a white apron tied around his substantial girth appeared at their table. "Is there a problem?"

"This *bastardo* is stealing *mi novia.*"

"Oh, for crying out loud," Nita moaned, and clasped her head between her hands.

"Gentlemen, I recommend you take this discussion

outside," the waiter said. "You're disturbing the other guests."

"Fine." Ruben glared at Gage.

"Ruben, please," Nita begged. "You've got this all wrong. There's nothing going on."

"Gentlemen, please," the server repeated. "I don't want any trouble. Take this outside or I'll have to call the police."

Gage tossed his napkin beside his plate on the table and led the way to the front door. Outside, he marched to the adjoining parking lot.

"You keep your hands off her," Ruben shouted to Gage's back.

Gage spun around to face him. "Take a deep breath, Ortiz. You don't want to do something you'll regret. I never—"

Before he could complete the sentence, Ruben had curled his right hand into a tight fist and swung.

Gage sidestepped. The trooper lunged past him. Regaining his balance, Ortiz renewed his assault. This time Gage ducked, put out his foot and tripped him. Unable to arrest his forward momentum, Ruben overbalanced and ended up on his hands and knees.

Gage shifted but stayed out of his immediate reach.

Ruben sprang to his feet, fists at the ready.

"Stop!" Nita stood at the edge of the parking lot. "Both of you, stop it this minute."

Like schoolyard brawlers in the presence of the principal, they lowered their guards.

"I don't belong to you, Ruben." Nita's hands shook as she tore the ring off her finger and tossed it to him.

Reflexively, he snatched it from the air with one hand, his eyes wide and confused.

"Our engagement is off. Over. I don't want to marry you. In fact, I don't ever want to see you again."

"Nita," he cried out, the ring in the open palm of his extended hand, but he was appealing to her retreating back.

"You're a damn fool, Ortiz," Gage said, adjusting his waistband. "Regardless of what you think of me, you should have had more faith in the woman you claim you love."

IF A DAY COULD GO completely to hell, this one had. Gage's helicopter didn't get fixed and what should have been a pleasant and innocent lunch had turned to horse dung.

After Ruben had barreled out of the parking lot, Gage had put Nita in the Jeep, gone back to the restaurant to leave money for the bill and returned to find her slumped in the seat, silent tears coursing down her face.

He'd wanted to console her, but what could he possibly say that would make up for the ugly twist her life had taken?

"It wasn't your fault," she assured him. "I don't want you to think it was. It's Ruben. He's so jealous."

"After you've both had time to calm down, you'll make up."

She shook her head. "I love Ruben, but I won't spend the rest of my life worrying about his jealousy…his violent temper. This isn't the first time he's acted this way."

BACK AT HIS OFFICE, Gage punched in his password on the desktop computer and brought up his e-mail.

Sid had come through. Bypassing the prefatory comments about the sources of his research and reliability of the information, Gage read the following:

Lester Keeling, 62. Attended Arizona State University; graduated from law school 36 years ago. Served as public defender for two years. Transferred to district attorney's office for four. Went into private practice as a criminal defense lawyer for the next decade. Handled several high-profile capital murder cases, winning acquittals or reversals of convictions on appeal. Was appointed to the bench twenty years ago. Wife died ten years ago from muscular dystrophy. Two kids.

Judicial record exemplary. Has reputation for being tough on crime. Metes out heavy sentences for violent criminals and drug offenders. Until a year ago he was rarely reversed on appeal. However, several recent narcotics cases have been vacated due to judicial error in refusing to admit exculpatory evidence, excluding defense witnesses from testifying or not following established guidelines in instructing juries.

In other words, Gage surmised, Keeling was becoming so hard on defendants that he wasn't giving them a fair shake. What had brought about this rigid stance, this willingness to stack the deck? Could his last ruling be an attempt to regain balance? If so, he'd gone too far the other way. Gage read on.

Clean bills of health on Keeling's kids. Older son is a professor of history in Sacramento, California. Younger son dropped out of college in his freshman year and enlisted in the army. Currently serving in Korea. Neither son has any criminal complaints or history of being in trouble.

Gage hit Reply to thank Sid for the information, then on an impulse switched to instant messaging and asked if he had anything on Keeling's social or medical history. The man appeared healthy enough, but his red-faced intemperance on the bench seemed out of character, based on his earlier record.

Sid replied:

No alcoholism or drinking problems. Member of the country club but not very active. Plays violin and belongs to a chamber music group that meets every Tuesday night. Spends most of his free time alone. Nothing to suggest physical or mental disorders. Review of Internet access files suggests no aberrant interests.

Of course if his mind was slipping—if he was in the early stages of Alzheimer's, for example—it might not be apparent for some time. Small inconsistencies in behavior were usually ignored until they became blatant.

Could he have felt unnerved by the presence of the esteemed J. Clanston Parks? Not likely. A young, inexperienced prosecuting attorney like Debbie might have been, but Keeling had been around too long to be impressed by a high-paid lawyer. Parks was a formidable presence whom opposing counsel no doubt dreaded seeing on the other side of the aisle, but the judge had clearly been in control of his courtroom.

That left only one other explanation.

Gage typed, "Any influxes of large sums of money in the past year?"

"Nothing," Sid responded. "He's clean."

But something was definitely wrong.

Sid added a footnote.

Re: Jill Manning. Clean financial bill of health. No loans outstanding. Car is lien-free. Pays credit cards on time without incurring interest or service charges. Has a modest cushion of savings and makes periodic deposits to a mutual fund that is doing fairly well in current market.

Gage typed, "What about Parks? Who paid him?"

"Latino Liberation League."

The LLL was an international nonprofit organization dedicated to representing Hispanics and other minorities in civil rights and criminal cases. Since no individual could be tagged for hiring the expensive attorney, this was another dead end.

CHAPTER TEN

NITA WASN'T SURPRISED by the knock on the door, and she didn't have to look through the peephole to know who it was. She checked nevertheless, took a small breath and opened up. She didn't step aside, however, to admit her visitor.

"What do you want, Ruben?"

"I brought you back your ring."

"I don't want it."

"Come on, Nita, be reasonable."

"That's what I wanted you to be today, but you weren't."

"Okay, things got a little out of hand—"

"You got out of hand, Ruben. Not things. You."

"I came to talk to you about that—"

"There's nothing to discuss."

"Nita…please. Can I at least come in?"

It was always the same, she thought. *He flies off the handle, then comes back and expects me to accept an anemic apology.* This time would be different. He gazed at her, waiting for her to invite him in, probably expecting her to fall into his arms. She'd done it too many times in the past.

Taking a deeper breath, she stepped aside and admitted him, then closed the door and leaned against it, facing him.

"I'm sorry. I screwed up today. I was out of line."

"Yes, you were." She wasn't going to let him off the hook. There would be no appeal to extenuating circumstances this time.

He held out the ring she'd tossed to him. "Please tell me you forgive me."

Her heart ached. God help her, she loved him, but this roller-coaster ride had to stop. "I can forgive you, Ruben, but I'm not going to marry you."

He gaped at her, and it occurred to her that he'd never really thought she would refuse him. Suddenly he looked scared, but she'd made up her mind.

She moved to the center of the room between the couch and TV. "I don't intend to spend the rest of my life worrying about your jealousy and your temper. You embarrassed me in front of a roomful of people today, practically called me a whore, then you started a fistfight with my boss. How do I know the next time you get some crazy notion in your head you won't take a swing at me?"

His eyes bulged. "Nita—" his tone was a soft plea for understanding "—I would never hurt you." He took a step forward, his arms extended. "*Querida,* I love you."

She backed away. "The way your dad loved your mom?"

Ruben froze. His father had struck his mother more than once and had transferred his rage to his son a couple of times when Ruben had tried to defend her. The last time Ruben had stepped between them, he had warned his father he'd kill him if he ever touched his mother again. The old man had raged at his son's disrespect and ingratitude, but he was smart enough to know the boy was stronger and faster than he was. No one, Nita included, had taken the threat literally, but no one doubted, either, that Ruben was capable of violence.

"I would never do that," Ruben said now, his voice shaky. He seemed outraged at the suggestion and appalled that she could think it. "I'm not like him, Nita. I could never hit a woman."

She believed he meant it, but that was no guarantee that he wouldn't abuse her. His father had probably said the same thing once, too, and he was contrite after each incident. Ruben's mother always took him back. Nita had no intention of living like that, waiting for the next blow.

"You need help," she said, her voice gentle. "Professional counseling."

He was insulted now; it showed on his face, along with the building anger. "You think I'm crazy?"

"I think you have a serious problem controlling your temper, a problem you can't overcome by yourself, and that I can't help you with. I've tried, Ruben. It hasn't worked."

"I love you," he repeated, and she knew the words, the entreaty in them, didn't come easily. He was acknowledging a need, which in his mind constituted a weakness, and it went against his every male instinct.

"I know you do," she replied, unable to hold back the tears that stung her eyes. "And I love you, too. But we can't go on this way. I won't live my life constantly on guard about your jealousy and anger, always wondering when you're going to turn on me—"

"You're afraid of me?"

Lips compressed, tears rolling down her cheeks, she nodded. "Yes."

He staggered to the couch and collapsed onto it. "You're afraid of me," he repeated in a shocked whisper. "I—"

She stood, facing him, agonized by the pain she knew she was inflicting. But if they were ever to have a chance together, it had to be based on honesty and trust. She was convinced he didn't want to hurt her, that he would never intentionally inflict physical pain. He was the sweetest, gentlest man until he flew into a rage over some real or imagined offense. His father had been charming, often considerate, too, and loved his family, but when things hadn't gone his way he'd become vicious.

Ruben sat there, rocking forward, his big hands bunched at his chin. His eyes glistened. Finally he rose to his feet and crossed the room to the door. Grasping the knob, he turned to face her.

"I love you, Nita. I would die rather than hurt you," he said, his voice hoarse.

He opened the door and walked out, letting the lock click behind him.

Nita collapsed on the coach and wept.

THE FOLLOWING MORNING, Chet Thomburg returned from leave.

"I think I'm suffering from mother-in-law syndrome," he said. "Thank God we live a thousand miles from her. Still, I'm not sure that's far enough. That woman can talk long distance without using a telephone."

Gage chuckled. He'd lost his own mother when he was eight, and Jill had never known hers. He wondered what it would have been like to have an older woman to talk to about the crises that had marked their lives, if it might have made a difference.

"One must honor one's elders," another pilot said.

Chet harrumphed. "Who said that?"

His colleague gave him a pitying look. "*My* mother-in-law."

Everybody laughed.

After being away a month, Chet was itching to get back into the cockpit, and Gage was eager to evaluate his flying skills. He'd flown routine surveillance patrols with the other pilots and could have postponed doing so with Chet for a few days. However, he'd just found out that Chet was due his annual check ride. The other instructor pilot qualified to give it to him was home with a stomach flu, probably for several days. If Gage didn't perform the eval this morning, Chet would be grounded, which wouldn't be fair to him or to the people who had to take up the slack.

The complicating factor for Gage was that he was scheduled to fly Jill to Benson this morning so she could look into a report of Mayan artifacts being smuggled into the country as souvenirs. He'd been looking forward to spending time alone with her, including a quiet lunch. He sighed in disappointment.

"We'll switch things around." He turned to Nita. "You and Hal take care of the chief. Chet and I will make your run along the border."

"Fine with me," Nita said. "I can do some shopping while I'm up there."

Chet completed the external inspection of the aircraft and the preflight checklist, then started the engines. Gage listened to the whine of the turbos and watched the blades begin to rotate and pick up speed.

The feel of the craft vibrating under him evoked a sense of power, of strength, of being in control. The only thing better, he thought, was sex. He hadn't had any of that in a long time.

Fuel flow, normal. Oil pressure, normal. Other gauges registered proper readings. All systems go. Chet gave the flight mechanic on the ground the thumbs-up and received the countersign. The pitch of the blades sliced into the still-cool morning air and the aircraft tilted forward. Gage felt that momentary tingling between his legs as the helicopter lifted off.

He kept one eye out the window for aircraft, the other on the instrument panel. Even through his headphones, he was tuned in to the sound of the engines. Flying was a multisense activity: sight, sound, smell, touch, sometimes even taste, if things weren't going right. Total concentration. Complete absorption. Pure existentialism.

They circled the field, then headed toward the border at a thousand feet. They were parallel with the northern edge of Fort Huachuca when something indefinable didn't feel right. He scanned the bank of dials and switches. Nothing appeared to be amiss, yet instinct born of years of flying had him on guard. He double-checked the bank of instruments. No warning lights flashed, but this time the seat of his pants presaged danger.

"Drop down to five hundred feet," he directed Chet. The younger man didn't question the order.

The land below them was rough and rolling. There

were no significant obstructions, not even a tall saguaro cactus, but there weren't any flat places of sufficient dimensions to set down, either.

"Make that three hundred."

Even as Chet complied, he asked, "Something wrong?"

"I don't know. Something just doesn't feel right." Gage called to the flight mechanic over the intercom, "Buckle up." He clicked on his radio. "Ground Control, this is Alpha-Zero-One."

"Go ahead, Zero-One."

"We're fifteen miles due south of the station and experiencing engine trouble."

"What's the nature of the problem?"

"Unknown at this time."

"Are you returning to base?"

"Roger that. ETA—" expected time of arrival "—two minutes."

The chopper shuddered, smoothed out, shuddered again. Gage's muscles contracted. "Correction," he said quickly into the mike, "we're setting it down here."

The fuel warning light flashed, yet the gauge said the tank was full.

"Switch tanks," Gage ordered.

Chet obeyed. The transition was smooth.

"I've got it," Gage said, assuming control.

Chet yielded without hesitation.

Another shudder. A pop. Torque dropped. They began to lose altitude. "Brace yourselves."

The engine quit.

The rotor above them continued to spin, propelled by the laws of dynamics. What is in motion tends to stay in motion. They were now in the phase called "autorotation." Gage could still control the pitch of the free-wheeling blades, which allowed him marginal maneuverability, but that wouldn't last long.

The ground rose up to meet them.

"GAGE'S CHOPPER IS DOWN!" Nita charged toward Jill, who was just stepping into the hangar for her flight to Benson.

Jill's heart lurched and a chill curled down her spine. "When? Where? Is he all right?"

"Called in a minute ago. Engine trouble. Was turning back. Then said he was setting it down." She veered sharply toward her chopper. "I'm going out to search for him."

"No," Jill shouted.

Nita stopped short and spun around, her black eyes wide, uncomprehending. "What?"

"I don't want you going after him." The last branch chief had been killed in a helicopter crash, the pilot seriously injured. Now this *accident*. She wasn't going to chance any more losses.

Her friend's mouth fell open and Jill realized she sounded as if she were refusing to rescue Gage and the others. She darted to the control tower, pulled open the door and bolted up the metal stairs, Nita right behind her. Their feet rang out and echoed in the square tin shaft.

"The other choppers are grounded until we figure out what's going on," Jill called out behind her.

"But Gage and—"

"We'll call D-M." Davis-Monthan Air Force Base was on the southeast side of Tucson. "They're better equipped to handle this type of emergency." She shot into the control room. "What do you have?" she asked the duty officer.

"Engler's last transmission was five minutes ago," the air-traffic controller told her. "He said he was going down, then nothing."

"No radio contact? Why not?"

"They should have battery power for guard frequency, but the equipment may have sustained damage."

"How about a location?"

"We had him on radar." The ATC directed her to a computer screen on which he'd already highlighted the area.

"Request D-M initiate an immediate search-and-rescue effort," she instructed, then picked up an admin phone to call over to the hangar.

Moreno, the chief mechanic, soon charged into the control center, breathless. "I don't know...what could have...gone wrong."

"When did you last perform maintenance on it?"

"We changed the transmission fluid three days ago. I did the final inspection myself. The gearbox was in perfect condition."

"Didn't you have a problem with the oil?" Nita prompted.

Worry ridged Moreno's forehead. "Our supplier delivered the wrong lubricant, but I discovered it before we put it in. I swear we used the right kind."

"What else could have happened?" Jill asked.

Moreno shook his head and bit his lip. "We've never had any problems with that bird. Nita will tell you."

So many things could go wrong on an aircraft. Engine parts broke. Bearings seized. Electrical connections shorted out. Fuel and lubricant seals leaked. Dust clogged filters. Foreign objects damaged rotor blades. The combinations of possibilities were endless.

Fifteen minutes crawled by, then the radio squawked. "This is Rescue Three. We have a sighting."

The air-traffic controller fingered the mike. "Go ahead, Rescue Three."

The Air Force commander recited coordinates. "Aircraft appears to be intact but is on its side. One of the blades is crumpled. No sign of life. I'm dropping in a team."

Until now, Jill had been able to concentrate on the things that needed doing, but that short message brought it all home. *No sign of life.* Gage was in trouble. Maybe he—they—were only injured. He couldn't be dead. Not him, too.

Her knees felt made of jelly. She slipped onto the wooden stool at the radio console. Seconds built into minutes, minutes into dread. Gage was an experienced, skilled pilot. He knew how to handle emergencies. He'd had some warning.

The radio speaker over the bench clicked. "This is Rescue Three. We have three survivors. Two ambulatory. The pilot was trapped, but we got him out. No indications of life-threatening injuries."

"Ask if he's conscious," Jill directed the controller.

"Affirmative," came the reply. "We're taking him to Tucson Memorial. ETA twenty minutes."

Jill slumped forward on the seat for several seconds before she realized everyone was looking at her. Taking a fortifying breath, she sat upright, then creaked to her feet.

"I'm grounding the fleet pending a complete investigation of this crash," she announced.

"Two crashes in two months," Nita muttered. "Something is wrong. It's too much to be a coincidence."

Nita's voicing what Jill was thinking, instead of being reassuring, heightened Jill's apprehension.

"I'll notify headquarters and request an inspection team ASAP," Jill said. "After the state police secure the crash site, I'm driving to Tucson. I want to get a first-hand report about what happened." And to assure herself Gage was all right.

"I'll go with you," Nita said.

GAGE'S HEAD HURT like hell. After freeing him from the cockpit, where he'd been trapped and dazed at the bottom of the tilted aircraft, the medics had put a foam collar on his neck and insisted he lie down on a litter, though he assured them he was perfectly capable of walking. He knew it was standard procedure and a sensible precaution, just in case something was seriously wrong, but he hated the helpless feeling of being carried to the rescue bird.

He'd asked about the other crew members and had been assured they were all right, but he wasn't satisfied until they came over to tell him in person. They had a few cuts and bruises, but they were mobile. He was the one flat on his back.

Suppose he really had injured his spinal column? He might end up like Doug, a paraplegic—or worse, a quadriplegic. He could feel all his extremities, he reminded himself. He could move his arms and his legs. But one wrong twist and the cord could be snapped, irreparably severed. As they loaded him onto the military aircraft, he experienced gut-wrenching panic. For the first time in his life, he knew what it felt like to be terrified for himself.

What if they told him he'd never walk again, never be able to hold his own cup, or…make love?

"Relax." The young guy at his side placed a comforting hand on Gage's shoulder. "We'll be there in just a few minutes. Chances are they won't even let you stay for a decent night's rest. They'll throw you out on your ear."

Gage struggled to smile. "Thanks."

Before he realized it, they were landing and strong hands were hefting his pallet onto a gurney. The young man raced beside him, rattling off blood pressure and pulse readings and other incomprehensible information to the waiting staff.

Under other circumstances Gage would have been less than cooperative, but the image of Doug lying helpless in his bed—and the memory of the man in the wheelchair missing an arm and a leg—rendered him compliant. He didn't even get dismayed when they cut off his flight suit, though he was sure he could have slithered out of it, if they'd given him a chance.

"Your crew said you lost consciousness," said a woman standing over him. From the name embroidered onto the breast pocket of her white coat, he knew she was a doctor, though she seemed awfully young. Intern, he decided. Still, she spoke with enough authority to inspire confidence.

"If I was, it couldn't have been for more than a few seconds."

"How do you know that?"

He smiled. "Okay, you got me. I don't."

"An honest man. I may have to keep you here for observation. I don't think we've ever seen this condition before." She said it with such a straight face, he almost believed she was serious—till he saw the twinkle in her keen brown eyes.

She made notes, ordered tests, then began a personal examination. He wanted to take exception to all the poking and prodding, but life was delicate, he realized—even his. He felt gratitude for these people who cared for others.

Then something unexpected happened.

The doctor placed her hand on the inside of his thigh to examine a bruise and he suddenly became erect. His face grew so hot he wondered if there was enough blood left to share with other body parts. He was about to apologize when she rearranged the thin sheet covering his abdomen and, without showing the slightest interest, returned to flipping pages on his chart.

He wanted to laugh, to cry, to sing. Maybe she wasn't impressed, but by golly, he was ecstatic.

"All your tests are coming back normal," she told him a little while later. "You have a laceration to your side from the seat belt harness, but you don't appear to have suffered any serious injuries. We need to keep you here overnight, though, to make sure you haven't suffered a concussion. We'll know by morning, and if everything is okay, you'll be able to leave then."

Gage nodded. If he had someone to go home to, he might object, but he didn't. And from what Doug had told him, hospital food wasn't all that bad these days.

They moved him to a separate room. A few minutes later a man with a badge poked his head in, introduced himself and asked Gage if he could answer a few questions about the accident. Gage had no reason not to cooperate, but he also had a feeling that, while the official investigation might find the mechanical reason for the crash, it wouldn't get to the heart of the matter. Someone was sabotaging operations at the Tombstone Customs station. Someone had tried to kill him. Or had Jill been the target?

CHAPTER ELEVEN

"I JUST WANT YOU to know," Nita said, "there's nothing going on between Gage and me."

"I never for a moment thought there was." Jill was driving. Keeping occupied was better than sitting idly in the passenger seat.

"Ruben was completely wrong."

"I'm sorry you two have broken up." Jill knew how much her friend loved the handsome highway patrolman.

"It's for the best," Nita said with a forlorn sigh. "Better I see that now than wait until after we're married."

"I guess you're right." Jill had thought leaving Gage was the right thing to do—until he came back into her life. She hadn't welcomed him, yet now all she could think of was that he was all right.

"I want to have children," Nita continued. "I don't want to get divorced and see my kids grow up without a dad, the way I did."

From late-night sessions, Jill knew Nita's family was Catholic, so her parents hadn't divorced. Her father had simply walked out of the house one day and never come back. He'd had a history of leaving and getting into fights but always turned up to heal. When he didn't, Nita's mother became convinced he was dead, but they never found out for sure. Without a death certificate, she hadn't been able to collect on his small life insurance policy.

In contrast, Jill's father considered parenting a sacred duty—an honor. It appalled her that Nita's father could treat his family so callously. Gage would never have done that. He'd paid a terrible price for a few minutes distraction, but he would never desert his family or intentionally do anything that would hurt them. His sense of duty, or moral obligation, was too strong.

Left with five children, all under the age of ten, Mrs. Gomez had gone to work in a sweatshop as a seamstress and brought home piecework to do at night. Nevertheless, her kids always knew she was there for them.

How does a woman give her children a sense of security after being abandoned? Jill wondered. How does she maintain her sense of worth after being discarded?

"You do what you have to," Mrs. Gomez had once told Jill. "It would have been even harder seeing my children separated."

Nita's oldest brother now owned a landscaping company. Her sister was married to an auto salesman. Another brother owned a restaurant in Tucson, and her younger brother was in the army.

Jill also knew the kids all sent their mother money, so she wouldn't have to work, but she did anyway. Not sewing, but helping out at her church's day care.

Mrs. Gomez had also made all her children promise not to get married before they were twenty-five. She herself had married at sixteen and was the mother of three by the time she was twenty-one.

"I'm sure Gage is going to be fine. Chet said he probably saved their lives," Nita said now.

"He's a good pilot." He loves flying, she thought. But suppose he can't fly any more? What will he do? How will he cope?

Nita glanced over and smiled. "Yeah, and I've seen the way you look at him when you think no one is watching. He's a great-looking guy and sweet, too."

Sweet.

Jill pulled into the hospital parking lot.

GAGE FIGURED SOMEONE from the shop would be coming to see him, but he hadn't expected Jill or Nita to show up. There was no denying he was glad to see both of them. Nita inquired about his injuries, showed relief that they weren't serious and then proceeded to grill him about what had happened. He explained the series of events. As an experienced aviator, she didn't question his intuition that something had been wrong before the engine had even started sputtering.

"What caused it?" Jill asked.

"About the only thing I can think of," he replied, "is some sort of fuel contamination. Maybe water in the line."

Jill eyed him. "Could that happen by accident?"

He shook his head. "In the wintertime in a damp climate, condensation is a hazard we take precautions against. But here, in the desert, in the heat of summer? No way. If there was water in the line, someone put it there."

Nita bit her lip. "Who would—"

"That's the big question, isn't it? When I talked to Doug—"

"Vogel?" Nita asked in surprise. "You know him?"

"We flew together back in Virginia years ago."

"Funny, you never mentioned it." Nita's eyes were like ice. She'd answered all his questions about the previous senior pilot without his ever indicating they were acquainted. It seemed she wasn't pleased by the omission.

"I have a friend who works down in pediatrics I'd like to say hi to." She turned to Jill. "I know you and Gage probably need to talk. I'll meet you in the coffee shop when you're ready. Take your time. I'm glad you weren't seriously hurt," she said to Gage. "See you back at the unit."

"Thanks for coming." He frowned at the closing door.

"What tangled webs we weave when first we practice to deceive," Jill said.

"If you want to trade clichés, how about 'people who live in glass houses shouldn't throw stones'?" Petty bickering had never been one of their games. "Don't worry about Nita. I'll explain that I hadn't seen Doug in years and didn't know if he might have changed."

"What really happened, Gage?" Her tone betrayed worry, and perversely made him feel better.

"Exactly what I told you and Nita. I was on the phone with Doug just before you came in. He confirms he experienced the same phenomenon. Except he was at a much higher altitude. It's a credit to his flying skills that he survived at all."

"You're convinced both incidents were sabotage?"

He saw fear flash in her eyes. She had been scheduled to fly with him to Benson in that helicopter.

She slid into a chair at the side of the bed. "You scared the daylights out of me."

Her concern for his well-being was the best medicine he could have received. "I'm going to be fine." *I'm still a man.*

The silence lingered between them for a long, tense minute.

"Jill, I don't know what you heard about the incident at the Spaghetti Western. I hope you don't believe Ruben's accusation."

"About you playing around with Nita? Even if I thought you'd hit on her, I know her too well to think she'd tolerate it—" she grinned "—even from a guy she thinks is great-looking."

Wasn't there some law against beating up on patients? "Gee, thanks, I think."

"She loves Ruben."

"And I love you."

"Don't." She jumped up from her chair and raised both palms. It seemed to him there was more fear than conviction in her voice.

"After you left, I toyed with the idea of being with other women—" she turned her back on him as he spoke "—but I never was. They weren't you."

"It's not important," she murmured, but they both knew it was. He could see by the rigid posture that she wanted to bolt. She didn't, however, and that said what words couldn't.

"I tried booze for a while, too," he continued, "but that didn't work, either. All I got were miserable hangovers." He let the silence between them linger a moment. "You never really answered my question the other night."

"What question?" she asked, her voice muffled, her back still arched.

"About whether you blame me for Rickie's death. Just so you know I do, or at least a part of me does, and always will. He was my son, Jill, and…" He let the words trail off, unable to go on.

She spun around, her eyes glistening, searching his. A tear fell. She wiped it away with the back of her hand. "I've relived that day over and over," she said in a soft voice, "day after day, night after night. I failed to do what every mother instinctively does, protect her child."

"It wasn't your fault, Jill. You didn't do anything wrong. I—" But she didn't seem to hear him.

"If I had insisted on taking him to the hospital the moment I realized he was sick…instead of listening to you If I had stayed home like I should have instead of being selfish and going out with friends—"

"You weren't selfish. You've never been selfish. I was the one who insisted you needed to get away. Remember? If anyone's to blame, it's me. Maybe if I—"

"Maybe a lot of things," she said. "But all the maybes in the world won't change anything. I wish we could go back, Gage, I really do. But we can't. What's done is done."

"So why did you come here?" he asked. "You should be in Tombstone where you're needed."

He realized too late it was the wrong thing to say. He sounded ungrateful, as if he didn't want her.

"I had to make sure you were okay. Apparently I've made a mistake." She turned toward the door. "I should go."

"No," he said in panic. "I'm glad you're here, Jill. I need you."

She paused, her head lowered, her hands knotted,

then turned back to him. "I've realized something since you arrived," she muttered, avoiding his eyes. "You're right. I did blame you for Rickie's death, and that was unfair." She grabbed a tissue from the box on the bedside table. "I'd forgotten how much you loved him."

Something that might have been a sigh soughed through Gage, releasing pressure, giving him hope. He'd waited two years to hear her say those words, two years for her to assure him he wasn't a monster. He threw his legs over the side of the bed and placed his bare feet on the cool floor. She still had her head bowed. He closed the narrow distance between them and took her into his arms, cradling her head against his chest. The warm contours of her body, the smell of her hair, the soft texture of her skin conspired to make him aware that all that shielded him from her was a piece of flimsy cotton.

His body's natural reaction had her moving away. "I need to go," she murmured. Her eyes flitted to the tenting of his hospital gown before she turned once more to the door. "I—I'll see you tomorrow." She was gone.

Gage's pulse raced as he leaned against the side of the bed. He would give anything to take the sadness from Jill's eyes. But how could he? She was willing to forgive him for what had happened, but how could he forgive himself? And how could either of them ever get past what they had lost? A child. Nothing was more sacred or more precious.

Coming here had been a mistake. He was pursuing an impossible dream. There was no redemption for him. He loved Jill, but he couldn't change the past. She had been right to leave him. If only he could escape the memories of what they'd once shared and be absolved of the guilt he bore for having lost it.

He climbed back onto the bed and covered himself with the white sheet. He was a man, but what kind of man hurt the people he loved? What kind of man let an innocent baby die?

GAGE WAS RELEASED the following morning with instructions to report back if he experienced severe headaches, memory loss or degradation of motor skills. He was assured, however, that aside from the minor bruising on his rib cage from the seat belt, he was in perfect health. He was thanking the doctor when Jill appeared, carrying the duffel bag containing an emergency change of clothes he kept in his Jeep. He'd called the station early that morning and asked to have one of the flight mechanics bring it up with his vehicle.

"You didn't have to deliver my stuff personally." But he couldn't suppress his elation at seeing her. "Did you bring my Jeep, too?"

"It's outside." She waited in the hall while he dressed.

"I was planning to drop by the rehab center to see Doug before driving back to Tombstone. Do you mind?"

"Good idea." She turned and started for the elevator.

The door opened just as they reached it. Inside, they were alone. He clasped her hand, relieved when her fingers meshed with his. She looked up at him and he saw something different in her gaze this morning. Wariness still lurked there, but he also glimpsed affection, the kind that had warmed her eyes when they'd first met.

Maybe a little fatigue, too. He wondered if she had slept as restlessly as he had.

"Thank you for coming," he said, hoping she could hear in his voice that he meant more than simple gratitude for a favor. But then, nothing between them was simple anymore.

She appeared to be searching for words when the door opened. "You're welcome." She strode toward the hospital's front entrance. "I feel bad about not keeping in closer contact with Doug. What happened to him is so unfair."

"Life is unfair," he reminded her as they stepped outside. He unlocked the passenger door of the Jeep for her, threw his bag in the back, walked around the vehicle and climbed behind the wheel.

"Where is my mangled chopper?" he asked.

"The NTSB showed up yesterday afternoon, examined the site and gave permission to move the wreckage." The National Safety Transportation Board investigated all flying mishaps. "D-M sent their Skycrane to relocate it just before sundown."

Davis-Monthan housed the famous "boneyard," the repository for derelict and obsolete government aircraft of every size and variety. Their S-64 Skycrane, a huge helicopter with a seventy-two-foot main rotor wingspan, resembled a praying mantis in flight. It was used to relocate everything from buildings to old B-52 bombers.

"It's in one of our cantonment areas."

The Customs station had several fenced-in compounds used to store confiscated vehicles and large items of contraband.

"Under armed guard," she added. "By the way, Chet Thomburg says you did one hell of a job getting them down safely, that by anticipating the problem you probably saved their lives."

He snorted. "Actually, I was trying to save my own."

She shook her head. "Why can't men just accept a compliment without making excuses for their good deeds?"

He grinned. "It's our natural modesty."

This time she laughed. "Yeah, right."

"Do you know if they've found anything yet?"

"The guy in charge of the investigation said he'd give me a progress report late this afternoon or early tomorrow."

"I want to be there when he does."

They arrived at the rehab center, but their timing was off. Doug had just gone to therapy and wasn't expected to return to his room for another two hours. Had Jill not come to pick him up, Gage might have sent whoever dropped off his Jeep back to Tombstone on the bus and hung around to see his friend, but Jill had already been away from her office longer than she could afford to be.

For a moment he considered having her go on ahead and taking a later bus himself, but spending time with her now seemed more important. They still had a lot to talk about. The atmosphere between them had changed. The world they'd known would never be the same; he could only hope they might build a new one. In spite of everything, they still loved each other.

"How's Mr. Vogel doing?" Jill asked the nurse on duty while Gage wrote a note to Doug saying he and Jill had stopped by and that he would phone him later.

"He's a dream patient. Does what he's told. Always cheery."

"Is he going to be able to walk again?"

The nurse continued to arrange the metal-clad charts in their slots. "Too early to tell. But he's a survivor."

Gage worried about his friend as they drove away from the center. Doug had always been upbeat; it was his nature. But what would happen if his optimism wasn't rewarded and he had to spend the rest of his life in a wheelchair, dead from the waist down? Alone. Gage acknowledged to himself that the real question was how *he* would cope under those circumstances. The answer: not very well.

"Do you have any idea who's behind what's going on?" he asked Jill when they were on Interstate 10, heading east.

She shook her head. "I wish I did. Before I became branch chief I began to suspect there was a mole in the office."

Which was whom the executive director had sent him here to find. "A pretty strong accusation. What makes you think that?"

"Our success rate was declining. The bad guys always seemed to know when we were coming."

"You changed that record with your last mission."

"And then the culprits got away."

"That wasn't your fault. Besides, they were small fry. We still have the narcotics." Something in her demeanor had him glancing over at her. "We do, don't we?"

"I got a call from forensics early this morning," she said. "What we thought was five hundred keys of cocaine turns out to be more like five."

He turned his head to take in her profile. "How can that be?"

She sighed. "Turns out only the top layer in each box

was pure cocaine. The rest was worthless powder with just enough coke to set the dogs off."

"We were set up." Gage slammed the palm of his hand on the steering wheel.

"Fritz Bradley's gut told him something was wrong," he added after a slow burn. "That it was all too easy."

"Smart gut."

"Who have you discussed your hunch about a spy in the outfit with?"

"Only Mack Robbins. The day before he was killed."

"What was his reaction?"

"I had a feeling I was confirming what he already knew…or at least suspected."

Gage remembered Doug saying Robbins had been preoccupied that morning. "Any chance he talked to someone else about it?"

"No idea. He was rather close-lipped. All I know is that he's dead and Doug's badly injured." There was a pause. "You might have been killed yesterday."

He exited the interstate onto Highway 80 at Benson, heading south toward Tombstone. "You realize I was originally supposed to take you here to Benson yesterday. Nita and I changed assignments at the last minute, which means that unless this was a random act of sabotage, you were likely the real target, rather than me."

"I'm well aware of that." She inhaled and let the air out slowly. "You'd probably like me to quit, wouldn't you?"

If he had his way he'd lock her in a tower away from all strife, except for the fact that she'd never be happy there, and her happiness was all that mattered. "I want you to be safe," he said.

She stared straight ahead, then squared her shoulders, as if she'd made a decision. "I understand that, Gage, and I respect you for it. But I'm not some weak female—"

He extended his arm across the back of the seat and stroked the side of her neck with his index finger. "I've never thought you were weak, Jill." She was painting him like some Neanderthal. "You're smart, tough and—"

Before he could add determined, she reached over and placed her hand on his thigh. A dangerous move in a speeding car, he wanted to tell her, but then she'd take her hand away and he didn't want that, either.

"I had a reason for leaving Customs when I got pregnant with Rickie. I don't now. This isn't a battle of brawn. It's a war of intelligence and will, and I'm going to prove I'm as smart—no, I'm smarter—than the son of a bitch who killed Mack. Who hurt Doug—and you."

"God, I love it when you get all hot and assertive."

She frowned and withdrew her hand, but before she could retreat into her corner of the cab, he clasped her hand in his. "I worry about you, Jill. I can't help it, and I'm not going to apologize for it. But I also want you to know I'm on your side. You have a job to do, and I want to help you do it."

"So you can protect me?"

He raised an eyebrow. "Is that so terrible?" He brought her fingers up to his mouth and kissed them.

She started to pull away but then relented. "No, it's not," she admitted, but slipped her fingers out from between his nevertheless.

They lapsed into silence. In about half an hour, they reached the outskirts of Tombstone.

"If you don't mind," he said, "I'd like to change into

something more suitable than jeans and a T-shirt before going to the station. I'll just be a few minutes."

"Fine."

He invited her to wait for him upstairs rather than in the Jeep. After a moment of uncertainty, she nodded and followed him up the metal steps.

His apartment, on the other side of town from hers, could have been its clone. Impersonally comfortable, it was more spartan, neater. He'd never been one for clutter. She left things out. He put them away, a habit she sometimes found aggravating.

"I need to shower and shave." He told her what she could find in the refrigerator and disappeared into the bedroom.

CHAPTER TWELVE

JILL WANDERED TO the kitchen, found a container of fresh orange juice and poured herself a glass, all the time trying to ignore the sound of the shower and the mental image of Gage standing naked under the steamy spray, rivulets of soapy water coursing down his chest, his belly.

In the living room she ran her finger along the row of books in the tall, narrow bookcase near the window. A few paperbacks, mostly mysteries and suspense thrillers. A small collection of nonfiction hardbacks, history, true crime, psychology. Tucked in one corner she found an old, leather-bound volume, the book of love poems he'd given her their first Christmas together. She'd left it behind when she'd packed her bags. Out of spite, she recalled. Out of bitterness. As a way of telling him she didn't believe in love anymore, that she didn't love *him*.

She saw nothing else around that had belonged to her. But he'd kept this. Her hand reached out and removed it from the shelf. Small, finely tooled. She opened it and read:

How do I love thee? Let me count the ways…
I love thee to the breadth…
Smiles, tears, of all my life;—and, if God choose,
I shall but love thee better after death.

The hairs on the back of her neck rose. She spun around, nearly dropping the precious volume. He was standing in the far doorway, buttoning the cuffs of a uniform shirt. She could see the double bed in the room behind him. Heat rose to her face. With a clap, the book closed, as if by its own volition.

"The nice thing about poetry," Gage said, "is that it doesn't change, yet it never remains the same." He stepped toward her, kissed her on the cheek, removed the book from her hand and slipped it into its assigned place on the shelf. "Ready?"

Her mouth was dry. Her insides quivered. She nodded.

They descended the stairs in silence. The drive to the Customs station passed without a word being spoken. Where three weeks earlier the tension between them would have been hostile, it was now intimate.

The mood in the main office when they walked in was somber. The usual workplace sounds—police radios, computer printers, news channel on TV—droned in the background, but the positive spirit that had begun to infect the place since she'd taken over was missing. Then, seeing Gage, everyone came alive and started talking at once, welcoming him with high-fives and slaps on the back. He returned their banter with the expected male posturing about his number not being up yet.

Jill poured herself a cup of coffee. "I'll see if the NTSB inspector is ready to brief us."

Once behind her desk, she phoned the safety board rep's cell phone number and asked if he could come to her office. While waiting for him, she browsed the stack in her In-box, her mind preoccupied with the man outside her door.

How do I love thee?

He was driving her crazy.

Scott Vargas rapped on her door. Fiftyish, with close-cropped brown hair and brown eyes, he smiled faintly and stepped into the room.

Jill introduced Gage, who'd trailed in behind him.

"Any idea yet what happened?" she asked after they were seated.

"Water in the fuel line."

Gage huffed. "That's what I suspected."

"Any idea how it got there?" Jill asked.

"Only two possible ways," Vargas said. "The source was contaminated or the water was added to the tank on the chopper."

"Have you checked the other aircraft?" Gage asked. "How about the fuel delivery truck?"

"We're running tests on every link in the chain."

"My chief of maintenance needs to be in on this discussion." Jill picked up her phone.

Moreno must have been waiting for her call because he appeared in less than a minute. He showed no surprise when the inspector explained the problem, admitting he'd already heard rumors on the flight line.

"When did you fuel up Zero-One?" Gage asked.

"Topped her off just before your flight," he answered.

"Did you see anything suspicious?"

"I would have done something about it, if I had."

"Have you had any problems of this nature before?" Vargas asked.

"Never."

"What about Vogel's crash?" Gage asked.

Moreno looked jittery, uncomfortable. "They said that was pilot error."

"He claims it was fuel contamination."

The chief mechanic had previously insisted Doug was one of the best pilots he'd ever met. Now he grew defensive. "He would, wouldn't he? No one ever found anything to prove it."

"We're reviewing the records of your supplier," Vargas said. "It's remotely possible you received a bad batch of fuel."

"Who was here yesterday morning?" Jill asked.

"The regular morning shift. Dave, Bobby—" He stopped. "Ruben was here when I arrived." His eyes widened. "Early for him. He doesn't usually come sniffing around until late afternoon, when Nita gets off shift."

"Ruben? What was he doing?" Jill glanced at Gage.

"Just standing around. Seemed fidgety. I heard about what happened in town the other day with Nita. Reckoned he'd come to grovel and beg her to take him back. Except he left before she showed up. I figured it was either time for his shift or he got cold feet."

Jill released Moreno to return to work a few minutes later.

The phone rang. It was for Vargas. He grunted into the receiver a few times and hung up. "Everything else is clean. The other aircraft, the main fuel supply tank and the truck."

"Which means the water was added directly into **Zero-One's** tank," Gage concluded.

"It appears to be the only option available."

"The question now is, who did this and why?" Jill said after Vargas had left.

"Someone familiar with helicopters," Gage reasoned. "The hangar isn't open to the public. This had to be an inside job. Maintenance people would be at the top of the list, since they have direct and unquestioned access to all the aircraft at any time."

"The pilots do, too." Jill rubbed her forehead.

"And Ruben."

Jill rolled a pencil between her fingers. "I really don't think he'd do a thing like that." But after her conversation with Nita, she couldn't be sure. "He's confused and angry, but—"

"He has a violent temper," Gage reminded her.

"But if he was going to lash out at someone, it would have been at you."

"Maybe he did."

She shivered at the idea. "His flight line pass is a courtesy. Mack Robbins pulled it once when Ruben got loud and obnoxious. I can rescind it, too."

"It's your call, but there are no operations going on now. You might consider giving him continued access so we can observe him."

She noted he was making a suggestion, not pushing his idea, which she had to admit had merit. "Good point."

"In the meantime, I'll snoop around to see what I can find." Halfway to the door, he turned. "Can I talk you into having dinner with me this evening? We need to put our heads together and see what we can figure out. Beside, I owe you for picking me up today."

She hesitated, knowing the invitation was about more than sharing a meal or returning a favor. She didn't know what to make of him, how to respond to his entreaties, his subtle pressures. His flight emergency had scared the hell out of her, and she didn't like being scared. She despaired of their ever having what they had once shared, what they'd been to each other, yet she wanted with all her heart to experience again the feeling of hope and security he alone seemed able to bring her. Playing with fire wasn't a good idea, but that didn't keep her from seeking its warmth—or enjoying the excitement.

"I won't be ready to leave here until at least six." She fanned the paperwork on her desk. "I have a mountain of catching up to do."

"I'll pick you up at seven."

DINNER WAS LESS THAN a gustatory success. Gage took her to a seafood restaurant in Bisbee. They were both fond of shellfish and the advertisement promised Alaska king crab and Maine lobster. Unfortunately those items were not available that evening, so they settled for overcooked swordfish. At least the salad was passable.

"Let's do a quick rundown of the people in the outfit," Gage suggested. "Maybe we can find someone with a motive."

They reviewed names, starting with the people in the administration building. Gage didn't tell her he'd already received reports on her secretary, Kim Oliver, and Victor Reyes, the intelligence officer. For the moment he tried to dismiss thoughts of her reaction when she learned his official reason for being in Tombstone. They discussed Pratt Dixon, the immigration officer. He certainly wanted Jill's job, and his reputation wasn't sterling. They put him at the top of the list.

"What about Fritz Bradley?" Gage asked. The border patrol chief was in an excellent position to mess things up and reap incredible profits from the drug trade. Gage knew his record was clean, but then, so was Dixon's.

"He reminds me of my dad, so maybe I'm prejudiced," Jill said. "I've never heard a hint of scandal about him. He lives simply, frugally. Everybody likes him."

"How long has he been on the wagon?" Gage had noted he was comfortable around alcohol but never touched it.

"About ten years. I understand he hit the bottle pretty hard after his wife died. I'm not sure he's a recovering alcoholic in the true sense of the word. I think he just chooses not to drink anymore."

Gage liked him, too, and would be very disappointed if he turned out to be the bad guy.

"Have you had your building electronically swept for listening devices? Maybe you're being spied on."

"A security team came in and checked out the entire place for bugs right after I took over—every office, every room, every phone and computer. The place is clean."

By the time the waiter presented the check, they'd exhausted the subject of a spy in their midst and accomplished very little.

Spies and customs houses weren't the real reasons for their dinner, however, and they both knew it. They didn't touch each other across the table, didn't hold hands, but their eyes met as if by compulsion, each occasion conveying undercurrents that went back to before Rickie was born, before their lives had been irrevocably traumatized.

Maybe the meal being a minor disaster was a good thing, Gage thought. If nothing else, it gave them something to grouse about and chuckle over. He'd wanted her when they separated and divorced, but being together in this casual, unpretentious place—hearing her voice, her laughter, seeing her eyes fixed on his, feeling the current flowing between them—want became need, and need hammered through him with the force of a pile driver.

Sitting across from him, witnessing the flash and sparks in his eyes, Jill felt herself slipping, falling, tumbling down a long chute of desire. She really had no choice but to allow herself to enjoy the moment. Nothing would ever be what it had been between them, but recriminations were useless and exhausting. For a few hours she wanted to put the past aside and experience the present for itself, to wrap herself in the care and warmth emanating from the man who'd once been the center of her universe. If she let herself forget, he could be again, at least for a while.

They left the restaurant. This time when Gage extended his hand for her to take hers, she let him, and they strolled like young lovers to his vehicle. It was only pretend, but sometimes make-believe was all anyone had.

"We can still salvage this evening." Gage turned onto the road to his apartment.

"Where are we going?"

"Dessert," he said. "I have some ice cream and crème

de menthe." One of her favorite after-dinner treats. It pleased her that he remembered. Stocking up had been a calculated move on his part, she realized, but she chose to feel flattered rather than manipulated.

"I don't know, Gage." She wanted to say yes. She wanted to be with him, but beneath the primal urges and a rare sense of well-being, fear still loitered. Of him? Or of herself?

"We can sit out on my balcony and watch the sunset," he said.

The western sky was already radiant. At best they had three-quarters of an hour of light left.

"I really ought to get home." To do what? Watch TV? Read a book? Wash her hair?

"If that restaurant had been any good, we'd still be there." A few minutes later, he pulled into his parking lot.

Her ambivalence seemed to encourage him. He opened her door and held out his hand. She took it and stepped down, only slowly withdrawing her fingers from his grasp. He let her precede him as they climbed the stairs.

He switched on lights and invited her to relax on the couch while he dished out dessert. Instead, she followed him to the kitchen and watched as he drizzled the green liqueur over vanilla ice cream. He motioned to a drawer and she grabbed a couple of spoons.

"Come on," he said, leading her into the living room.

"Where are we going?" she asked as he continued toward his bedroom door.

"To the balcony."

The bedroom was burnished bronze in the reflected light of the setting sun. She barely had time to glimpse his bed, the dresser and something low beside it. The brilliant sky beyond the sliding-glass door drew her as much as the man silhouetted against it. She stepped onto the small iron-railed balcony.

He handed her one of the bowls, his fingers brushing hers as she accepted the cold dish. The evening air was still, dry and pleasant. The land beyond the building dropped off steeply to an arid streambed. The effect was a sensation of being suspended in the golden glow of nature.

Gage rearranged the two deck chairs so they could sit side by side.

"Nothing compares with sunrise and sunset in the desert," he said.

"Hmm" was her only comment as she lifted a spoonful of minted ice cream to her lips.

The sounds of nature surrounded them. Birds fluttering to their nests for the night. Crickets chirping. In the distance a coyote cried out for a mate.

She understood the animal's plea. The longing for companionship, the craving to touch and be touched, to give and receive, to share life in a way that encompassed the physical yet went beyond it.

Suddenly they were wrapped in darkness, and the cocoon of color was replaced by an electric charge of tension. Gage was a few feet from her, but she imagined she could feel him above her, feel the hard texture of his warm flesh against her. The thought alone had her skin heating.

Without his saying a word or twitching a muscle, she realized he was aware of her. Did he know her body was rebelling against her determination not to be affected by the force field flowing between them?

If offer card is missing write to: Harlequin Reader Service, 3010 Walden Ave., P.O. Box 1867, Buffalo NY 14240-1867

NO POSTAGE
NECESSARY
IF MAILED
IN THE
UNITED STATES

BUSINESS REPLY MAIL
FIRST-CLASS MAIL   PERMIT NO. 717-003   BUFFALO, NY

POSTAGE WILL BE PAID BY ADDRESSEE

HARLEQUIN READER SERVICE
3010 WALDEN AVE
PO BOX 1867
BUFFALO NY 14240-9952

Get FREE BOOKS and a FREE GIFT when you play the...

LAS VEGAS GAME

Just scratch off the gold box with a coin. Then check below to see the gifts you get!

YES! I have scratched off the gold Box. Please send me my **2 FREE BOOKS** and **gift for which I qualify.** I understand that I am under no obligation to purchase any books as explained on the back of this card.

336 HDL DZ9W   135 HDL D2AD

FIRST NAME	LAST NAME

ADDRESS

APT.#	CITY

STATE/PROV.	ZIP/POSTAL CODE

(H-SR-07/04)

7	**7**	**7**	Worth TWO FREE BOOKS plus a BONUS Mystery Gift!
🍒	🍒	🍒	Worth TWO FREE BOOKS!
🔔	🔔	♣	TRY AGAIN!

▼ DETACH AND MAIL CARD TODAY! ▼

She snatched up the dish she'd earlier placed on the deck beside her chair. "Thanks for the dessert and the show. It more than made up for the entrée." Her smile was brittle, self-conscious.

"Please—" he didn't often beg "—you don't have to run off."

She stepped into the bedroom and halted, disoriented by the darkness, by the rough sound of his voice, by the tingling sensation of his closeness.

He came up behind her and flipped the switch by the door frame, lighting the lamp on his nightstand.

She had started to circle the foot of the double bed when she saw something and froze. On his dresser was the framed picture of Rickie. That was shocking enough, but in a way expected. It was the one thing he'd asked for when they split up, but that wasn't what made her heart stop. Beside the dresser was...the toy box.

She brought her hands to her mouth as she studied it, the fine craftsmanship, his labor of love. Unfinished. It represented all that had gone wrong with her life. The baby she still mourned, would always mourn, the children she would never have. The man who... She should hate it.

The toy box.

Without thinking, she crouched in front of it and ran her fingers across the top. The wood was still raw but satin-smooth. She remembered how carefully he'd researched the kind of varnish he would apply, one that was nontoxic, in case the little rascal ever decided to use it as a teething ring.

She didn't see Gage move up behind her, but she felt his presence.

"You kept it," she murmured. She hadn't expected him to. Surely it brought only sad, remorse-filled memories. Tears welled. She pressed her lips together.

He cupped his hand under her elbow and lifted her up. "I kept it." He turned her around and wrapped her in his arms.

She should resist. She ought to reject him, flee this room and never come back. But she didn't. She curled herself into his embrace.

"It's part of me," he whispered in her ear. "Part of us, Rickie and me. Just as you are a part of me."

Hot tears spilled down her face. She'd cried so many times over the past two years, but somehow these tears were different. Till now, she'd always shed them alone.

She rested her head against his chest. She could hear his heartbeat. Brisk. Steady. Relentless.

Was this his penance? Did he keep this object and Rickie's picture as constant reminders of what he had lost? She couldn't imagine seeing them every day without reliving the day their son had died. Her throat was raw with the pain those memories evoked.

"I love you, Jill," he said, words she hadn't heard in so long and feared she'd never hear again. "I want us to be together, but I'm willing to wait for as long as it takes."

He lifted her chin with the side of his finger and gazed into her eyes. "Take all the time you need, because there will never be anyone else for me."

When he brought his mouth down to hers, she was helpless to resist. His assault was sweet, gentle yet inescapable. The warmth of his hands on her skin, the heat he generated when he touched her breasts, the

taste of his lips on hers left her light-headed and rav-
enous. Something deep within her stirred. Her bones
turned liquid. All she was aware of was need, a throbbing pit of desire that only this man could satisfy.

She scraped her fingers along his back, fought to get
him closer, to make him a part of her. She fumbled with
his shirt, sent a button flying in her quest to make contact with the broad expanse of his chest, to rub and claw
at the ridges of taut muscle.

She closed her eyes when his fingers began to fumble with her blouse. He was trembling. She bit her lip
and savored the ecstasy of his hands touching her. It
took much too long for them to get naked. He yanked
back the bedspread. She lay on the dark blue sheet and
stretched out her arms. He settled beside her and proceeded to explore, to caress. She arched against his
probing. A soft moan escaped as he licked her breasts,
flicked his tongue across her nipples, suckled.

Torture. He was tormenting her, and she marveled
at his ability to inflict such exquisite pain.

"Please," she begged, her voice raspy, breathless.
"Please, Gage. I want you inside me."

She could feel his muscles go rigid as he entered her.
He was straining to be gentle. What he'd miscalculated
was her reaction. After two years of abstinence, she
wasn't about to be passive. Her mind, her body wanted
to give and then demand more. She cried out when she
convulsed the first time. Breathless, she gazed up at him
as he fought to hold himself back. Laughing, she said,
"Now it's your turn," and rolled him over onto his back.
Placing the palms of her hands on the slick muscles of
his chest, she leaned forward and brought her mouth

down to meet his at the same time she raised and lowered her hips.

This time she made sure they lost all control together.

THE KINGPIN HANDED OVER a six-pack of imported beer. A quality brew, not that his lackey cared. Bud would do him just fine. Beer wasn't what really mattered, anyway. The guy was in it for the money, nothing more. That, at least, he could appreciate.

He kept his manner mild, but he had no doubt the other man caught the menace behind it. "You screwed up."

"I did the same thing I did last time." The response was defensive, as it should be. "It worked with Vogel. Engler changed plans at the last minute. There was nothing I could do."

That was true enough, but it wouldn't get him off. "Why wasn't he killed?"

"He was at a lower altitude than Vogel when his engine conked. The guys with him said he sensed something was wrong before it happened."

The boss sipped from a hip flask. "It leaves us with a problem. Engler is still alive. So is Manning."

"Messing with the fuel won't work a third time."

"You'll have to come up with something else."

The other man remained silent. The kingpin washed down his expensive cognac with a mouthful of beer. Maybe it was time to get rid of this underling. He had a handgun with him. He could probably shoot him in the head and make it look like suicide or a gangland slaying. Like Cisco.

"What do you want me to do?" the guy asked nervously, as if he understood what was going through his benefactor's mind.

"Nothing for the time being." He was working on another plan to get the branch chief and her senior pilot out of the way. "Just keep your eyes and ears open and your mouth shut."

The harshness of the command had the other man retreating against the door of the vehicle, though he couldn't go far. The master control for the locks was on the driver's side.

"I have no reason to say anything to anyone," he reminded his boss.

"That's right, you don't. And don't ever forget it. You caused the death of Mack Robbins, a federal official, so don't entertain any notions of going to the police."

Dimwit wasn't likely to do that. He knew the kingpin's identity, but the only reward the authorities were likely to give him if he squealed was life in prison instead of the death penalty. Not much of a bargain. Still, desperate people were known to do desperate things. Putting the fear of God into him would ensure his silence for a bit longer, which was all that was needed.

"I told you last time, I'm cool."

Then why are you sweating? his superior was tempted to jeer. But why rub it in? They both knew he was scared. The key was to make sure he was more scared of him than of the law.

CHAPTER THIRTEEN

SUNLIGHT WAS DANCING on the ceiling when she awoke for the second time that morning. Gage had left just before dawn. Jill told herself she should be out of bed and dressed by now, as well, but for just another minute she wanted to stay where she was. Cocooned if not content.

Making love to Gage had been the most natural thing in the world last night. She'd savored the experience and wanted more, but as she curled up naked under the sheet and inhaled the scent of him lingering on the pillow, she had to ask herself if what she was doing was right. Having sex with Gage was wonderful, incredible, every bit as fulfilling as she remembered. They fit together as well as she could imagine any man and woman meshing. But lovemaking wasn't the same as love.

They'd loved each other once, but was love what they felt for each other now? She cared for Gage in a way she cared for no other human being, yet...

More confused than ever, she threw back the sheet and made her way to the bathroom. Gage had wanted them back together again. A part of her did, too, but how could they overcome the painful memories wedged between them?

He'd failed her once, failed himself and Rickie. He

was asking her to trust him again, give him another chance. She'd like to, but she wouldn't do it blindly. Not this time. He offered her his patience. Perhaps that was the secret. There was no hurry, no ticking clock. She'd make him prove she could trust him.

Don't let me down, this time, she muttered to herself, as she slipped into the shower.

THE SAFETY INSPECTOR was waiting for her when she arrived at the office at seven-thirty. He'd come to give her his final report and drop off the paperwork officially releasing the helicopters to her control. His team had performed a thorough examination of the two remaining choppers to ensure they were safe to fly. Jill thanked him and called over to the hangar, granting permission to resume normal operations.

A week passed. Patrols flew without mishap or incident. Small-scale confiscations of marijuana, hard drugs and other prohibited items continued to rise. Jill was signing a stack of forms pertaining to recent confiscations of proscribed horticultural plants when Pratt Dixon appeared in her doorway.

"We have another convoy coming through." He plopped into the chair across from her. "Two more eighteen-wheelers. Headed for Douglas again, carrying another five hundred kilos of cocaine."

She shoved the papers aside. "But it wasn't five hundred keys last time."

"That was a test."

"Did we pass or fail?" she asked.

Dixon studied his hands, then looked up. "My sources tell me the Black Hand didn't want to risk a big shipment the first time they used this ploy. They figure no one will be expecting them to pull the same stunt twice. Besides, the heat's off after Keeling's ruling, so this time they can go with a full consignment."

Reyes strode into the office. "Sorry to interrupt, Chief, but I have information of a shipment coming through—"

Dixon beamed up at him. "I already told her."

"About the terrorist weapons? How did you find out?"

"Cocaine," Dixon corrected him. "The Black Hand."

"The Green Turtle." Reyes held out a sheaf of papers. "I have it here."

Jill raised a hand to halt the debate. "One at a time." She nodded to Dixon. "Start again."

"Two eighteen-wheelers will be coming through Customs at Douglas—" he glanced at his watch "—in about twenty minutes. We'll have to act fast."

"It's a caravan of motor homes coming through Nogales," Reyes countered, "carrying five hundred kilos of plastique."

"You two agree on one thing," she concluded. "Somebody's coming through with eleven hundred pounds of something, either narcotics or explosives, through Nogales or Douglas. Now how do we figure out which?" She picked up the phone. "I'll check with Nogales. Victor, you call Douglas. If they're at Customs now, give orders to delay them. I'll do the same."

Reyes used the telephone on the small table at the other end of the room. Dixon rose and paced. Two minutes later both callers hung up. The news was obvious without either of them saying a word. They'd been too late. The two groups had already passed through Customs.

"What now?" Dixon asked. "We're short two helicopters and don't have the resources to track both groups at the same time."

Jill refused to give up. Another phone call confirmed Gage had just dropped off several members of the inspection team at Fort Huachuca and was coming back alone. The second chopper had just returned from a routine patrol and was being refueled. She hurried to the operations center and got on the secure radio link.

"Engler, this is Manning. Where are you?"

"About twenty miles out. ETA—"

She cut him off. "I need you to check out two groups immediately. One just transited the Nogales station, the other through Douglas." She described them.

He reported back a few minute later. "I see the caravan of motor homes that went through Nogales. I count sixteen, going west on Highway 289, probably headed for the Pena Blanca Recreation Area."

"Check out the trucks."

"Roger."

"Where's the other chopper?" she asked Moreno in maintenance over the phone.

"Ran into a problem, Chief. Getting a red light on hydraulics. It'll take at least an hour to troubleshoot the system."

She swallowed an expletive. "Safety first. I don't want any more accidents."

Time elapsed. Finally, Gage called in. "Are you sure there were two eighteen-wheelers? I see only one."

Damn. Was the other off-loading its stash somewhere?

"Pratt, call Douglas again and confirm two rigs went through," Jill directed Dixon.

He picked up a phone and hit a speed-dial button. After a brief conversation, he hung up.

"Two pharmaceutical company tractor-trailers passed Customs, all right, but one apparently experienced mechanical problems. It pulled off into the parking area on this side of the border and has its hood up. The other continued on."

Jill relayed the information to Gage and asked him for the current status of the advance truck.

"I have it in sight. He's out of the Mule Pass tunnel, traveling north at a normal rate of speed."

"Looks like a false alarm," Reyes said.

"He hasn't reached the Ellis ranch road yet," Dixon countered. "That was the drop-off point last time."

Reyes frowned. "What's happened to the other group, the motor homes?"

Jill asked Gage to check on them again.

"I was right," he reported twenty minutes later. "They've pulled into the camp area at Pena Blanca."

The mountainous area was classic high desert and exceptionally green after a recent rainstorm.

"Wait," Gage said. "They've joined up with a group that was already there." Another minute elapsed. "The two groups appear to know each other. They're exchanging items. I can't tell what. Totes of some sort."

"They're making their delivery," Reyes crowed and jammed a fist into the air. "We've got them."

The next move was Jill's. If this was connected to the terrorist threat against Fort Huachuca and she did nothing, a national catastrophe could result with far greater repercussions than more illegal drugs on the street. She asked Reyes how good his sources were.

"Multiple communications links. References to vanilla, a common code word for plastique, as well as an agent report referring to the same activity."

"The location is wrong," Dixon argued. "The caravans are boxed in. Smugglers pick spots that afford them quick getaways."

"Maybe they're counting on the unlikelihood of the setting to fool us," Reyes said. "Terrorists are getting more bold and imaginative every day."

Jill's mind was a jumble of frustration, fear and rage. After the screwup last time she couldn't afford another mistake. She was furious at the arrogance of these smugglers for putting her in this untenable position and at her superiors for not giving her adequate resources to respond the way she should. She had to pick now between two evils, the possibility of fifty million dollars' worth of hard drugs getting through or terrorist weapons destroying innocent lives. She had no choice.

"We're moving on Pena Blanca."

Dixon shook his head in despair but held his tongue.

She relayed the information to Gage. "I also need you to monitor the two eighteen-wheelers," she added. "They might be in the clear, but I want to make sure." She was stretching him thin and she knew it.

"Roger," he said. "Will do."

She checked back with Moreno in maintenance.

"Sorry, Chief. I was hoping it was only a switch that we could trade out quick, but it looks like we have a hydraulics leak. It's going to be a while before we can trace it and replace the line."

She didn't waste time lamenting the situation.

Gage announced he was en route back to Highway 80. "The rig has passed the Ellis ranch turnoff and is continuing north at moderate speed."

"Well, that tip was false," Reyes said. "There doesn't seem to be any resemblance between this shipment and the last."

Dixon scowled but still said nothing.

Gage's voice came across on the squawk box. "The target is pulling into the rest stop between Sierra Vista and Tombstone."

"What's he doing there?" Reyes asked over the radio. Jill was busy directing the forces moving into the Pena Blanca area.

"Nothing. Just sitting. Probably got a call from the other truck, saying the problem was fixed, and is waiting for him to catch up."

Jill took the microphone. "Engler, the highway patrol is blocking off the Pena Blanca group and we're proceeding with inspection. I need you to stay where you are and monitor the situation there."

She was worried about running into the same legal problems she'd encountered with Keeling last time—except this truck was on public property, not private. The caravan at Pena Blanca, too. That gave her some cover but not much consolation. If the judge was on the take, there wasn't much she could do to protect herself besides follow the rules.

Fritz Bradley had had a bad feeling about the first raid. She had a bad feeling about this one.

GAGE WAS CIRCLING the rest stop at high altitude, hoping his distance wouldn't draw attention to his presence until forces on the ground arrived, when he received another call on a different secure frequency.

"This is Zero-Seven, go ahead," he responded.

"Engler, this is Williams. Give me your exact location."

Being personally contacted while airborne by the executive director was more than unusual, it was unprecedented. He read off his coordinates.

"Aerostat in Sector Five is out of commission," said Williams. Aerostat was a series of tethered balloons positioned along the border. Its overlapping coverage was managed by a control center in San Diego, California, and provided real-time surveillance of the entire two-thousand-mile border between the United States and Mexico. "I need you to fill the gap for about half an hour until I can get other resources into position."

"I'm flying surveillance on a possible narcotics delivery," Gage explained.

"This takes priority. We were tracking a plane believed to be carrying senior Al Qaeda members to a meeting in the desert south of Ajo, when our balloon in that sector shut down, leaving us blind. We're diverting a P-3—" an electronics surveillance aircraft "—but we want you to verify that the plane landed—"

"Is the Aerostat malfunction related?"

"We can't be sure, but we think it is."

If that was true, these people were heavyweights.

Williams gave a description of the aircraft and the location of the suspected meeting site. Ajo was nearly a hundred miles away. If Williams wanted him to do no more than confirm the presence of the plane, this recon should take less than an hour. But a lot could happen in sixty minutes.

"Roger. I'll inform the branch chief—"

"This mission is top secret. No one is to know until we determine otherwise."

"What do I tell her when she finds out I'm not—"

"As far as she's concerned, you're on the mission she assigned you. Make something up if you have to."

Gage didn't like it. Deception was part of the cat-and-mouse game the good guys played with the bad guys, if you considered matching wits with drug runners and terrorists a game. But lying to his own people—especially his boss, particularly Jill—rubbed him the wrong way. Not letting her in on his clandestine mission when he'd first arrived was bad enough, but he'd consoled himself that that was deception by omission. This was by commission, and he dreaded her reaction when—not if—she found out.

"Understood," he said and tried to ignore the dirty taste it left in his mouth.

Jill called him twice over the ensuing period, requesting the status of the tractor-trailer.

"No change," he reported, counting on her being too tied up with the other group to demand elaboration.

He located the plane Williams had identified at the end of a short dirt runway. Not far away was a small cabin where two pickups and a van were parked. He communicated the information to Williams.

"Maintain surveillance," his boss ordered. "We have forces on the way. If they attempt to take off, you are authorized to employ whatever measures you deem necessary to prevent their escape."

"Roger." This was the kind of mission Gage thrived on. Too bad he couldn't enjoy it.

A quarter of an hour elapsed before he saw ground forces converge on the lone building and a SWAT team barge in. A few minutes later, six men were led out of the cabin in handcuffs.

"Who are they?" Gage asked over the secure radio.

"Thanks for your assistance, Engler," Williams responded without answering the question. "You are relieved to return to your previous assignment."

He headed directly to the Tombstone highway. The director's unwillingness to answer his questions didn't surprise him. Gage might never know what went down at that remote site. He just hoped the diversion hadn't been in vain.

To his amazement and relief, the pharmaceutical truck was still at the rest stop when he arrived there, the second one nowhere in sight. Then he saw something that disturbed him. As the rig started pulling out of the lay-by, so did six pickups that hadn't been there previously. Half of them drove to the turn-around and headed south, the others continued north. In their beds they carried what appeared to be identical cargoes, square containers shrouded under tarps.

Had they off-loaded boxes from the trailer?

He attempted to read their license plates with binoculars, but they were obscured by hitches or were bent in ways that made deciphering more than one or two characters impossible. It was hopeless. They were all so ordinary that even his descriptions wouldn't help find them later. He followed the ones headed north, then realized he'd soon lose them in Tucson's traffic. He should have gone after the southbound trucks, but it was too late. They'd already dispersed or found cover. Besides, he was running low on fuel.

Had he just missed a major drug transfer while he had been deployed on what might have been a wild-goose chase? Had fifty million dollars' worth of high-grade cocaine just slipped through on his watch?

JILL PACED THE NARROW aisle between the wall and a bank of computer consoles in the operations center.

The search of the motor homes was turning into a fiasco even bigger than the one with the motorcycles a month and a half earlier. At her behest, the highway patrol had detained the caravan at the recreation area, along with the group of tourists already there. Customs showed up and a meticulous search of both groups of vehicles—which included using sniffer dogs and portable radars to search for secret compartments—and yielded absolutely no contraband, not even a reefer or an unstamped bottle of whiskey.

For good reason. Both groups were devout Muslims. They had been trading spices, including vanilla, legitimately bought and declared at the Mexican border.

When finally released after six hours of searching, both caravans had returned to Interstate 19 and driven north to Tucson. There, a spokesman for the now-consolidated group had called a press conference to complain vociferously of religious harassment and racial profiling. He even showed camcorder footage no one had been aware was being shot of government personnel removing personal items from motor homes and appearing to interrogate women and children. The situation had turned from an unfortunate mix-up to a nationally televised political outrage, and Jill Manning was being ridiculed by name as an incompetent, racist bureaucrat.

"Okay, so you had a little setback today," Gage said, as he lay beside Jill on his bed.

"Little?" She looked over at him, her mouth twisted in derision. "It's been the most humiliating day of my life."

"You'll get over it." He tried to sound upbeat, positive.

"I've embarrassed the service, been mocked in the media and called all sorts of names." She steamed. "I've made an absolute fool of myself, and all you can say is get over it?"

"Hold it." He rolled onto his side and lowered his voice while he stroked her cheek. "I didn't say get over it, Jill. I said you *can* get over it. And you will." He kissed her on the lips. "You know every mission isn't going to work out. The important thing is that you made the right decision today. You have nothing to blame yourself for." He shifted so he could run his open mouth along her naked breast. "Let the politicians worry about the politics."

She squirmed under the distraction of his tongue circling her left nipple. "If only it were that easy," she tried to object, but the words were coming out in whispered pants without much conviction.

The heat of her silky skin was almost enough to dispel thoughts of his role in the day's activities. He'd dreamed for two long years of the places he wanted to touch her, and the fantasy was coming true. Last night their lovemaking had been untamed, reckless, madcap. They'd collapsed, exhausted, dazed and grinning. She'd remembered what pleased him and accommodated him with a generosity that surpassed pleasure and bordered on hallucination. Escape was exactly what he needed. Escape from memories of his old failures. Escape from the secrets he was keeping from her now.

This morning had been slower, as if she were trying

to find in physical pleasure a different kind of satisfaction. Wild and thoughtless, measured and intense. He didn't care. All he wanted was to please her.

He slid his hand down her belly. "We fit together," he said.

"Sex was never the problem." She ran her hand along his chest, the sensation tickling, arousing.

He peered down at her. "I think what we've been experiencing was more than sex."

She held his gaze, her eyes twinkling. "It has been spectacular." She moved her fingers lower on his abdomen. "Do you think more-than-good can get better?"

His breath caught. "I always strive to improve myself."

She chuckled and cuddled more intimately against him.

"Marry me, Jill," he whispered.

Her kneading slowed but didn't stop. "You said you wouldn't rush me."

The message he heard was that she wasn't saying no.

"I won't. Today, tomorrow, next week, next month." He smiled at her and subtly tightened his hold. "Drive me crazy for as long as it takes for me to prove you're the only woman I'll ever love." He ran a finger between her naked breasts, down to her belly button, lower still.

She burrowed closer, her leg coming up to cover his. As she cradled her head against his shoulder, he sensed sadness, disappointment. He kissed the top of her head and closed his eyes. He knew what she was thinking.

They'd dreamed of a big family, of a house filled with toys and laughter. They'd cried when they learned Rickie would be their one and only contribution to posterity. It had made him all the more special, all the more treasured. Their son was supposed to be the part of them that would live on.

"Let's adopt," he said. "A girl to start with, then a boy, then maybe another girl, perhaps twins—"

"Whoa!" She chuckled. "Where will this end?"

"Where indeed." He brushed his lips against her temple. "We have so much to offer, you and I. The sky's the limit."

"It's not in our future," she said, a little sadly. "At least not right now."

"Because of your job." When they'd been married, she'd been willing to put her career on hold to have a family. Now having a family was taking second place to her career. He was disappointed, but he'd promised her time. At least they were talking about marriage now. He was making some progress.

"I've worked my way to a leadership position," she said, drawing her index finger across his navel. "I'm certainly not going to quit now, when so much is at stake."

"Your predecessor was murdered," he reminded her, "and there's every likelihood you were the target of this latest crash. It was only by chance that you weren't in the chopper with me." He positioned himself more intimately against her. "Is the job worth your life?"

She turned her head to stare at him. "That's a strange question coming from you. When you got here, you said you were proud of what I've accomplished."

"I am," he insisted.

"But—" she said, adding the word he hadn't voiced. When he didn't take the bait, she went on. "If and when I decide to turn in my badge, it's going to be when I'm at the top of my form, not out of fear. I can sacrifice a lot of things, Gage, but my pride isn't one of them."

"I would never ask you to." He nuzzled her neck. "You must know that. It's just that—" he stroked his knuckles along her cheek "—I worry. I don't know what I'd do if I lost you."

"Does this mean if I agree to marry you you'll give up flying helicopters?"

He lifted his head to gape at her. "Why would I do that?"

"Because it's dangerous," she said. "Because I don't want to lose you, either. Seeing you in the hospital after the accident made me understand that you're still very important to me."

He moved up and kissed her on the forehead. "Flying is actually safer than driving a car."

"Tell that to Doug Vogel."

The image of his friend lying helpless in bed jolted him.

"So you'll at least give up flying for the Customs Service?" Jill asked.

A minute elapsed in silence.

She swung her legs over the other side of the bed. "I guess I've got my answer," she said, as she padded back to the bathroom.

CHAPTER FOURTEEN

TWO MORNINGS LATER Pratt Dixon stood in the middle of the doorway, his arms outstretched to the frame. "Just thought you'd like to know, Chief—" sarcasm and disdain were etched in his words "—the cocaine shipment got through just fine."

Jill lowered her pen and glared up at him. "What are you talking about?"

"The rig that pulled into that rest stop south of here, the one I told you about—"

A sick feeling churned in her stomach.

"Half a dozen pickups pulled up behind it, unloaded the consignment and left, and the eighteen-wheeler went on its merry way to Tucson."

"That's not possible." How could Gage have missed goods being unloaded from the tractor-trailer? She'd never known him to miss a beat. What the hell was going on? "We had the rig under surveillance the entire time."

She picked up the phone, called over to the hangar. "Is Engler there? I want to see him as soon as he gets back."

"Five hundred kilos of first-quality uncut coke," Dixon crowed as she hung up the phone. "The price of powder on the street has dropped, at least temporarily.

It'll go up again as soon as they get a few more suckers hooked."

"I don't believe it."

His chuckle was bitter. "I didn't think you would. My sources don't seem to count for much around here. Check it out yourself." He disappeared.

She was tempted to call him back to demand more information, but he'd already told her enough to make her stomach ache. She got up and walked down the hall to Reyes's office. The expression on the intelligence officer's face answered her question before she asked it.

"I was just coming to see you," he said. "It appears we were bamboozled."

"How is it possible? You had multiple sources."

"The ploy was well orchestrated," he agreed.

Her hunch was right. The two organizations were in cahoots. "That means the tourist caravan was part of the plan."

Reyes shook his head. "They were members of the Rolling Sheiks, a recognized travel club. Anybody can go online and with a click of a mouse find out where they plan to go and what routes they'll be taking. I suspect the Black Hand simply used their established movements to mask their own."

"Except for one thing." Jill peered at him and saw that he understood where she was going. "You received the information on the caravan from Green Turtle sources. Which means the two are working together."

Reyes closed his eyes and nodded.

Further discussion was sidetracked when Jill's secretary interrupted to announce Brent Williams would be arriving via government airplane in twenty minutes.

Jill had a sinking feeling her boss's surprise appearance wouldn't brighten her day.

Gage still wasn't back. Dammit. She needed answers. Now.

She waited on the tarmac as the Cessna Citation jet rolled to a stop in front of the hangar. Was Williams coming to relieve her of duty? His personal appearance suggested as much.

The clam door of the airplane opened, its steps unfolding onto the broiling pavement. An armed guard descended the stairs and looked around, then nodded up to the open doorway. The executive director, dressed in a gray pin-striped suit, white shirt and blue tie, stepped out onto the tiny platform, took in the surroundings with a glance and descended the stairs. He made brief eye contact with Jill in the process but showed no reaction and offered no greeting.

Jill waited in the sun with dread, then moved forward to meet him halfway. "Welcome to Tombstone," she said in a vain attempt at convivial hospitality. She wished to hell he wasn't here, and she was sure he knew it.

"Is it always this hot?" He didn't extend his hand.

"Only in the summer," she assured him. "And during the day. This is high desert, so it cools down at night. Gets downright chilly sometimes."

"I'm not planning to be here long enough to find out. Where can we talk?"

"My office." Jill pointed in the direction of the administration building. "This way."

She wanted to ask questions, but his demeanor didn't encourage them. They crossed the blacktop between the hangar and the main building in silence. Inside, she signed him in at the reception desk and gave him a visitor's badge that identified him as having the highest level of clearance. He could go unescorted wherever he wanted. She trusted her people to support her, but she hoped he chose not to exercise the prerogative. She didn't need any more surprises.

Jill's secretary stood behind her desk when they entered the outer office and greeted their visitor by name, showing the deference appropriate to his high status. Williams barely acknowledged her greeting.

Jill motioned him into her office. She half expected him to appropriate her place at the desk, but he didn't. Was that a good sign?

"Close the door," he instructed.

Maybe not. She followed orders. He waited for her to take her accustomed seat, then he sat.

Lacing his fingers over his belly, he began. "I'm concerned about the job you're doing here, Jill, and I feel obligated to discuss it with you face-to-face."

She clamped her jaw and vowed to keep her responses minimal. The adage "never volunteer information" came to mind, and she intended to follow it.

"Three cases have been seriously mishandled at this station in the short period you've been in charge," he said. "Two of them will cost the department valuable funds that could have been spent more productively. That bothers me, but it isn't my main problem. I recognize things don't always go as planned. Mistakes and miscalculations occur, and sometimes we have to settle valid and occasionally spurious claims against us. What disturbs me is the pattern of poor judgment that has led to them."

She was tempted to slouch, to wilt under his intense

glare. But long ago she'd made up her mind not to crumple under pressure, whether it was from the bad guys or, in this case, her boss. Folding her hands to keep from wringing them, her pulse throbbing, she waited for him to go on.

"The first pharmaceutical convoy was unfortunate. You caught a judge on a bad day."

"Or one on the take," she couldn't help mentioning.

"We have no evidence of that."

She wanted to laugh. "A judge dismisses a fifty-million-dollar drug bust, and you don't suspect him of sleeping with the enemy?" So much for her other resolve not to be argumentative.

"We're looking into it," he conceded. "In fact, the heist turned out to be only paltry."

"The judge didn't know that, but the bad guys undoubtedly did," she observed. "So why did they bring out a big gun like J. Clanston Parks?"

Williams huffed an impatient breath. "I said we're looking into it. Let's take a closer look at the other two situations."

He settled back in his chair, clearly prepared to go on for some time. Jill had no choice but to listen.

"Hiding plastique in assembled motorcycles rather than the transport vehicle carrying them is a novel approach, I grant you, and certainly worth pursuing. Careful analysis of the proposition, however, would have disclosed that the probability of significant amounts of explosive being hidden in them was slim. When the tear-down of the first bike yielded nothing, that should have been a clue the others didn't contain any illegal substances, either. Why didn't you stop there?"

She started to remind him that this represented a terrorist threat, that only a few pounds of the high-grade material could wreak political and physical havoc, but he held up his hand to indicate he didn't expect an answer and wasn't interested in what she had to say anyway.

"You wasted more than a hundred man-hours in a consistently unproductive effort to disassemble machinery. Even if the very last bike had come up positive, the amount of contraband you found would have been negligible. Poor judgment, Jill. You weren't using your head."

She swallowed. Maybe he was right, but she'd been determined to prove she was thorough.

He got up from his chair and began pacing. "This last incident, however, is far more serious. You failed to evaluate the situation objectively." He placed his hands on the back of his chair and leaned forward. "What the hell were you thinking?"

She remained silent, partly because she refused to be taunted into making excuses but also because she knew he was right.

He shook his head and started walking again. "You had a group of tourist motor homes in an isolated area with no escape route, meeting another group of motor homes—in a recreational park. While campgrounds have been known as settings for exchanging a few joints of pot, they're hardly the place for major terrorist weapons transfers. Strike one."

He made a cursory examination of a commendation on the wall by the door. She'd received it several years ago in Florida, before she and Gage had split up.

"You ordered state troopers to move in and detain over a hundred people, then searched them because you had an intelligence report that they might be carrying vanilla, which you interpreted as code for plastic explosives. When our people got there, they found they did indeed have large but legally declared quantities of vanilla extract, a very popular export from Mexico. Strike two."

He sat down again and folded his hands in his lap. "Then, having discovered these people were devout Muslims, a group of people who are at present politically very high profile, you proceeded to spend hours subjecting them to an unreasonable search. I'm not even going to mention the videotaping your people failed to notice or stop. Strike three."

"My intelligence was from reliable sources," she pointed out. He was making her look and sound like the head of the Keystone Kops and she resented it. "We had a threat advisory about terrorists targeting Fort Huachuca."

"Your job is to distinguish between good intelligence and bad." He threw the words in her face. "If you believe every cockamamie story you receive you'll find yourself spinning your wheels, which is exactly what you did this time. While you were causing an international incident and a political uproar, a real drug deal, the biggest ever in this sector, was going down. You didn't know it, because you were focused on this unlikely scenario."

Her heart was pounding. Why had he given her this job if he thought she was so incompetent?

"Jill," he said, his tone softening, "I know you want to prove yourself, but for God's sake, use the brain power I know you have. Trust your instincts, not just words printed on paper. One of the reasons I appointed you branch chief is that you have an excellent confiscation rate, which you achieved by going after the little guys. Maybe that's where you should continue to concentrate your efforts, instead of grandstanding big busts that have a much higher and more visible potential to backfire. It doesn't matter where your statistics come from, low-level mules and pushers or higher-level intermediaries. It's the numbers that count." He pursed his lips. "Believe me, if I didn't think you could handle this job, I would never have assigned you to it. Now I'm beginning to wonder. There are plenty of other candidates out there who would love to take your place, one of them right here in your own organization."

He made hard eye contact to ensure she got the message. She did.

"I don't want to come across as selfish here, but your bad judgment reflects on me, too. Keep it up and I'll have no choice but to relieve you of duty to protect my reputation. As it is, I'm placing a written reprimand in your file for failure to exercise sound judgment in dealing with this political hot potato."

Her heart sank. A letter of reprimand would kill her chances of getting permanently assigned to the branch chief position now or in the future. Her career might not be over, but it definitely wasn't going anywhere.

"We need more choppers," she said, standing, as well.

"I'm working on it. Lousy timing, I'm afraid. We lost a Blackhawk in Alaska last week, another one in the northeast the week before, and there's talk of grounding the fleet because of hydraulics problems. For the time being, you'll have to make the best of what you've got."

He moved toward the door. "I don't want you or any of your people making any statements to the press. Nothing. Refer all questions from whatever source to our public affairs office. We'll handle the firestorm you've stirred up from there. Is that clear?"

"Yes, sir."

She reached around and opened the door for him. Ten minutes later, he was gone without a trace, as if he had never been there—except for the reprimand that would soon appear in her personnel folder.

AFTER WILLIAMS LEFT, Jill picked up the phone and called over to the hangar. Told Gage was inbound, she repeated her request that he report to her office as soon as he landed.

She accomplished little during the ensuing twenty minutes. Her mind was too busy trying to sort things out. She'd followed the wrong lead. Her mistake. No excuses. But how could she have missed the pharmaceutical connection? In spite of Keeling's ruling against the small-fry who had delivered the cargo and the fact that the cargo itself was a fraud, the episode proved the shipping line and the route were conduits for drug trafficking.

Was the Latino Liberation League a front for smuggling commodities and people across the border? Or had the head of the Black Hand suckered them into doing his bidding? Either explanation could explain why J. Cranston Parks had been hired for the defense. Law enforcement was as much a match of wits as it was a matter of witnesses and hard evidence, especially when it came to apprehending the brains behind multimillion-dollar schemes. The gang leader wasn't concerned about the welfare of replaceable pawns; he was interested in intimidating his enemies. It was all a mind game.

Then there was Pratt Dixon. He was playing with her mind, too, running hot and cold, hostile and supportive. Giving her good information, then watching her fumble with it. He wanted her job, and what better way to get it than to help her fail? Or had he handed her the tools to succeed and she'd dropped them?

Was he a bad guy, an opportunist or someone genuinely interested in mission success, but frustrated by leadership that dismissed him as peripheral? As far as she could tell, he hadn't given her any false information or recommended inappropriate action. In the purest sense, he couldn't be blamed for her mishandling of the intelligence he'd presented.

"You wanted to see me." Tall, lean, powerful, he filled her doorway in his blue flight suit. He was breathless, his broad chest expanding and contracting.

"Close the door and sit down."

He complied, his attention riveted on her. "What's the matter? Are you—"

"When you were keeping the pharmaceutical truck under surveillance, did you see any other vehicles in the rest area?"

His eyes shifted for a second before he got them under control. "Several." He peered at her. "A couple of sedans, a horse trailer, a few pickups."

She studied him. His body language was wrong. Defensive. "Were any of them parked near the rig?"

He was normally so sure of himself, so decisive, observant. Now he seemed uncertain, searching for answers. Searching for the right answers. "Some of them. So what?"

"Did more show up?"

"Of course they did." His hesitation had turned to annoyance. "There was a constant stream of traffic in and out of the place, Jill. It's a rest stop, for heaven's sake."

She let out a breath. "Did you see them get anything out of the trailer?"

This time he froze and studied her. There was a long pause. Too long. "No, I didn't. If I had—"

"Were you there the whole time?"

"What's this about, Jill? What—"

"Just answer my question, dammit. Were you there the entire time?"

He paused again, as if collecting his thoughts. "If you recall, you told me to monitor both trucks, the one at the rest stop and the one at the border."

She'd forgotten about the second rig. Had she told him to keep it under surveillance, too?

"I flew over to Douglas to verify it was still there."

"You what?" Her temples felt as if someone had just tightened a clamp on them. "Why?"

"I—I had misgivings about your tourist caravan scenario," he said. "I thought it might be a decoy to divert attention from another coke shipment, a real one this time."

So he'd figured it out but never said a word to her.

"I watched the rig at the rest stop for a while, but nothing was happening. Then I realized it could be a decoy, a diversion. Maybe the truck near the border was the one we should be watching. So I flew down there."

"You could have checked on it via secure radio," she argued.

"I did, but all they could tell me was that the rig had passed Customs and moved on. They didn't have the resources to monitor it beyond there."

"How long were you gone?"

He shrugged. "I don't know, maybe thirty, thirty-five minutes. I was following your instructions, keeping an eye on both—"

Her heart sank, overcome with a sense of futility. "My last instructions to you were to maintain surveillance on the eighteen-wheeler at the rest stop, not go flying off to Douglas." He started to object, but she shook her head. "While you were away, five hundred kilos of cocaine made it through."

"I don't believe it." But he didn't sound all that convinced. More in shock than denial.

A wave of depression washed over her, leaving behind a riptide of anger. She bolted to her feet and began pacing, feeling trapped. "Dammit, Gage—" her voice was raised, but she didn't care "—you disobeyed my orders. As a result, fifty million dollars' worth of coke is on the street." She was as angry as she'd ever been. "So much for your pledge of support." She forced air into her lungs and let it slowly out. Her heart was pounding. "I trusted you."

He stiffened at the rebuke and gazed at his hands before looking up. "All right," he said, his voice sharp, "I used poor judgment, but I was only trying to help."

"Then why didn't you tell me what you were doing?"

"You were busy with—"

She pounced. "It wouldn't have taken thirty seconds to tell me then what you just told me now. I would have agreed with you—"

"Then what's the problem?" he argued.

The blood racing through her head and heart left her legs weak. "The problem—" she clawed her fingers through already tousled hair "—is that you left me in the dark. Brent Williams, the executive director, was here a little while ago. He's putting a letter of reprimand in my folder—"

Gage exploded with an expletive and jumped to his feet. He reached for her, but she shied away from his grasp.

"You screwed up, Gage. You screwed up big-time, and as a result I'll probably lose my job." Thank heavens she was too incensed to cry. There would be plenty of time for that later. "I should fire you on the spot, bring charges of insubordination and dereliction of duty."

He worked his jaw. "You're the boss. It's your call."

If she reported him now, after being reprimanded herself, it would look like retaliation against one of her subordinates for her own incompetence. She'd also have a difficult time defending herself if he countered that he was following her specific orders, which he'd be forced to do to protect his own reputation. She couldn't be sure how she'd phrased her last instructions to him, and in the excitement of the moment she doubted anyone had been listening to her end of their exchange closely enough to validate her version. The deck was stacked against her—an acting branch chief with a record of failures versus one of the most highly decorated members of the Customs Service.

If she pushed too hard, their previous relationship was also bound to come out. Her deception in not disclosing it wouldn't weigh in her favor—or his. She was the superior. He could testify she'd ordered him to keep it secret. Not a high recommendation for an aspiring branch chief.

Did she seriously think he had undermined her position on purpose? Of course not. He hated the drug trade as much as she did, and he had a record of fighting it that rivaled anyone's in the bureau. Still, he had acted independently. Even with the best intentions in the world, it was the wrong thing to do, an attitude that couldn't be tolerated.

What was the right thing to do? If she relieved him of duty, she would further diminish her already marginal operational capability. Given Gage's popularity, she'd also have a serious morale problem on her hands. On the plus side, she would be sending a message that she didn't tolerate incompetence or insubordination.

"What are you going to do?" he asked.

None of the alternatives was very attractive. She sat down. "Get out of here. I need to think."

"Jill—"

"Get out, Gage."

He nodded meekly—a stance she wasn't used to seeing from him—and left the office, closing the door behind him.

Jill picked up a ballpoint, rolled it between shaky fingers and threw it across the room. A minute later the tears began and she was afraid they wouldn't stop. Why had he come to Tombstone? Why had she let him back in her life? Why was she such a fool to want him, to love him? And where would she go from here?

CHAPTER FIFTEEN

GAGE MADE A FEW PHONE calls and learned the executive director was spending the night in Tucson before flying back to headquarters in the morning. He was outraged at the way Williams had treated Jill. Even more, Gage was furious that he had been forced to lie to her. He'd never done that before, and he vowed he never would again.

He found Williams ensconced at the Hilton, although he could have been billeted more economically in government quarters at Davis-Monthan. Perks. But Gage wasn't interested in that now. The corpulent bureaucrat was in the lounge enjoying a post-prandial libation and chatting with a sexy barmaid.

The set of the older man's mouth indicated he wasn't pleased to see Gage, but the way he sucked in his cheeks also suggested the visit wasn't a complete surprise, either.

"Let's move to that booth," he said, motioning toward one in the far corner. "Would you like something from the bar?"

The cocktail waitress, who'd backed off, approached.

"Club soda with lime."

Williams held up his glass to indicate another of the same and rose to move to the designated booth.

"What you're doing to Jill Manning is grossly unfair," Gage said after they were settled and their drinks served. "She's a damn good branch chief. You shouldn't be laying this mess on her back."

"And who should I lay it on?" Williams asked. "She's in charge. She's responsible. I might also point out that you were given this assignment to ferret out a mole. You've produced squat."

Williams was right in that regard, but this wasn't about him. "You were supposed to uncover the Al Qaeda connection," Gage countered, "which you obviously failed to do, otherwise this caper wouldn't have gone down. There's also the matter of clearing Vogel's record, which you haven't followed through on."

His subordinate's boldness in pointing out Williams's failings had the man on the brink of sputtering.

"Manning is supposed to catch the bad guys, not harass honest law-abiding citizens and cause international incidents," Williams said.

"Cut the crap. You haven't been honest with her or given her the resources she needs to do the job properly."

"Everybody's shorthanded. You do the best with what you've got."

"Right," Gage said, failing to keep the sarcasm from his voice. "We're authorized four choppers. We should have six, but we're down to two. Of course we have to learn to work smarter, not harder. Why, after a while, we'll be so good at doing better with less, we'll be able to do everything with nothing. That's bull, Williams, and you know it."

The executive director grew still; his jaw tightened. "Watch your tone, Engler. You take orders from me. Remember that."

"And don't play games with the people who work for you. That's a hell of a way to earn loyalty and respect."

Williams's jowly face grew red. "Be careful, Engler. You're skating on very thin ice," he said in a menacing voice. "I'm warning you. You're on the edge of insubordination."

Gage took a huge breath and released it, all the time staring at his boss. "You're right. I am," he admitted. "If you want my resignation, say so. I'll give it to you verbally now and follow up with it in writing in the morning. You can have the paperwork on your desk by noon."

The big man gaped at him, appearing shocked by the explicit challenge and the hostility behind it. A long minute of eye contact told him the threat wasn't hollow.

Gage knew he was taking a chance, but it was a calculated one. His resignation over this incident would reflect poorly on the executive director. Losing control was far worse than outright failure in this business.

At last, Williams blinked. "Oh, shove it," he said in disgust and gulped down his Scotch.

"Why was I diverted?" Gage demanded.

"I can't give you details. I will tell you this. Your time wasn't wasted."

Gage wasn't sure he believed him. It was an easy statement to make and an impossible one to verify.

"You owe Jill Manning an apology," he said, taking advantage of the upper hand he'd gained.

"She's not going to get one, not from me or anyone else." Williams motioned to the waitress for another drink. "Look, Engler, Manning has her orders, you have yours, I have mine. Is it always pretty? No. Is it always fair? No, again. But that's the way it is. You've been around long enough to know how the system works. Now suck it up and get back to catching the bad guys."

Gage studied the man sitting across from him. "I don't know what your game is, Williams," he said, "but I can tell you this. You're not giving Manning a reprimand." The portly man started to object. Gage cut him off with the sharp slice of his hand through the air. "Because if you do, I'll blow the whistle on your diverting my helicopter. I won't compromise security because I won't say where I was sent, but I will make it plain that I was taken off station by your direct order behind the back of the branch chief, and as a result, fifty million dollars' worth of illegal narcotics found its way into circulation."

Williams was seething when Gage got up and left him.

JILL NEEDED SOMEONE to talk to, someone who could help her sort through the emotional quagmire she found herself in and a new, more personal worry that was beginning to plague her.

She left work early, drove to a Sierra Vista supermarket that had a delicatessen section and bought a large Greek salad, corned beef, Swiss cheese, a jar of sauerkraut, a bottle of Russian dressing, a loaf of pumpernickel bread, two kosher dill pickles, and a small cheesecake. Backtracking, she went to Nita's house on the southern edge of Tombstone.

Her friend looked startled when she opened the door and saw Jill. "What's wrong? Has something happened to Ruben?"

That she regarded Jill's presence as a harbinger of bad news indicated how little they'd seen each other in the last few months. Before Jill could answer, Nita realized her visitor's arms were loaded with groceries. "What's this?" she asked, her worried expression evaporating.

"I need a Reuben, and I thought you might, too."

Nita laughed. "I suppose you're talking about the sandwich."

Jill grinned. "What else would I possibly have in mind? May I come in?"

Nita opened the door wide and grabbed one of the brown paper bags. "I've missed you," she said as they unloaded things in her small kitchen.

"I've missed you, too." Jill felt guilty for not keeping in closer touch. Her new job had eaten up her working hours and, lately, Gage…had preoccupied the others.

They set about the task of building sandwiches bigger than either of them would eat.

"I've got some wine," Nita offered. "A fine generic in a pretty green jug."

"Not for me, thanks," Jill responded. "I'm going to stick with mineral water for now, but you go ahead."

Nita eyed her for a brief moment, then shrugged and selected a soft drink from the refrigerator for herself.

They sampled their spinach salads while the sandwiches toasted on the griddle.

"Now, what is it that has you so strung out?" Nita asked when they sat down to their impromptu Reubens.

"That obvious, huh?"

"In two years I've never seen you as uptight as you have been this past month. I've been hoping you'd come by so we could chat. Then I thought maybe with you being the branch chief—"

"Oh, Nita." Jill lowered the thick sandwich she was about to bite into. "It's not like that. I've just been so busy. Actually, I was hoping you'd stalk in and rescue me."

Nita chuckled. "I should have." She crunched on a pickle. "It's about Gage, isn't it?"

"What are—" No use playing word games with her friend. "How did you know?"

"I told you I've noticed the way you look at him and he at you." She smiled. "Don't worry. No one else seems to have a clue. Men are too obtuse to pick up on things like that. But it is about him, isn't it?"

Jill pinched a clump of sauerkraut that had slipped from the side of her sandwich and brought it to her mouth. "Yeah."

"Well, don't just sit there." Elbows on the table, Nita held her bulging sandwich with both hands. "Tell me what he's done—or hasn't done."

Jill nodded. "There's something's going on I don't understand." She toyed with a piece of Feta cheese in her salad. "The fiasco with the tourist caravan the other day… He was supposed to be monitoring the pharmaceutical truck from Mexico that had pulled into a rest stop but he left his post. While he was away, they off-loaded five hundred keys of cocaine."

The news didn't shock her friend. Obviously word had gotten out. Who blew the whistle? Dixon?

"Did he explain why?" Nita asked. "I've only worked with him for a couple of months, but I can't imagine him doing anything that would compromise the mission."

"His explanation made sense," Jill admitted, "but he's hiding something. I can feel it."

"Like what? Surely you don't think he's involved—"

Jill shook her head. "He's not a traitor. Besides, things were going wrong around here long before he showed up."

"About this five-hundred-kilo transfer," Nita mused a minute later. "Are you sure it happened? I mean… you're certain? Last time it turned out to be a hoax."

"Reyes's reports confirm it. Dixon says the price on the street has dropped, though it won't stay down for long. Just long enough to hook more victims."

"Pratt Dixon isn't one of my favorite people," Nita mumbled around another bite of her sandwich, "but his information is usually accurate. The guy's got snitches in every stink hole for six counties around."

Jill made a dismissive gesture. "I'm probably being paranoid. It's just that there was something funny about the way Gage reacted when I confronted him. I accused him of dereliction of duty, but instead of getting angry, he became quiet. Attacking his devotion to duty is like attacking his manhood."

"Don't tell me about the male ego." Nita scowled and washed the words down with her soft drink. "But I see what you're getting at. He should have gone ballistic."

"Why didn't he?" Jill asked, even more confused now that her friend agreed with her.

"Men. They're only good for one thing, and some of them aren't very good at that."

Heat rose to Jill's face. She chuckled. "He's good," she said, then concentrated on her food.

"So's Rube," Nita replied with a sly, conspiratorial grin. "Dammit, I miss him."

"Are the two of you really washed up for good?" Jill asked, concerned.

Placing the remnants of her sandwich on her plate and forking up more salad, Nita sighed. "I don't know. Maybe with counseling he can get his head straight and his temper under control."

"Has…has he ever hit you?"

She shook her head. "If he had, I would have washed my hands of him long ago, without a second thought, even if he is the sexiest male I've ever met." For a moment she had a faraway look in her eyes. "He can be the sweetest guy…."

Jill folded a hand over Nita's. "You'll work it out. He loves you. Anybody can see that. Give him time. He'll do whatever he has to to win you back."

"God, I hope so." Her dark eyes grew glassy. "I can't imagine life without him." She chomped her salad with a vengeance. "We were talking about Gage," she said after swallowing. "The mission the other day isn't all that's bothering you about him. What else is going on?"

Jill chugged her mineral water. "We used to be married."

Her friend's jaw dropped. "Oh, wow. I thought maybe you two had a history. But married? I hadn't expected that. You never mentioned ever being married. Why did you split up?"

Jill regretted not telling her friend more about herself earlier, but she'd wanted to put it all behind her. Now she was afraid Nita would get upset about her holding back. No, she decided, Nita might be a little miffed, but when she heard the whole story and understood how painful it was to talk about, she'd understand.

"We had a baby," she said.

"You're a mother. You never said a word."

"He died."

"Oh, Jill. I'm so sorry." She reached across the table and stroked the back of her friend's hand. "Truly."

Jill told her the story of how Rickie had contracted meningitis and died within hours. "One day he was perfectly fine."

She recalled feeding him the night before, the way his soft, warm, little body felt tucked under her breast, the sensation of him suckling on her nipple, the little smile he produced when she burped him afterward. "The next day he was dead."

Neither woman said anything for another minute.

"You blame Gage for his death," Nita concluded.

"Yes and no. I mean, I never thought he willfully neglected our baby. He was just inattentive, careless—" Jill sipped her water, hoping it would douse the fire in her throat.

"The doctor said it wouldn't have made any difference if we'd brought Rickie to the hospital a couple of hours sooner, but…I needed to blame someone."

"No parent should ever have to bury a child," Nita said. "I can't imagine what it must have been like for you."

Jill bit her lower lip. "I was furious when he showed up here two months ago. I thought I'd put him out of my life." She looked away. "He's asked me to marry him again."

This time when her friend's eyes went wide, it was with delight. It quickly faded, however. "You've forgiven him, but you can't love him anymore. Is that it?"

Jill didn't respond right away, perhaps because she didn't understand the answer herself.

Nita stared at the half-empty bottle of mineral water. When they'd shared late-night meals at home like this, they'd invariably had wine or beer. "You're pregnant, aren't you?"

Jill lowered her head and breathed through her mouth. At last looking up, she mumbled, "I…think…I might be."

"Does Gage know? Is that why he's asked you to marry him?"

"I haven't told him. For one thing, I'm not sure. I'm usually so regular, but this time—"

"You're afraid of how he'll react."

Jill shook her head. "I know how he'll react."

"But you don't want to have children now, after Rickie, is that it?"

"I want kids."

"You're afraid Gage won't make a good father?"

Jill pushed aside her plate. "He'll be a good dad. If anything, I'll have to watch that he isn't overprotective."

Nita couldn't hide her confusion. "You're pregnant. You love him. He loves you. He wants to marry you. You both want to have more kids. I guess I'm missing something. What's the problem, Jill?"

"When Rickie was born the doctors said I wouldn't be able to conceive again."

"Well, obviously they were wrong."

"But suppose I can't carry this baby to term. Suppose—"

"Whoa. Slow down." Nita got up, knelt beside Jill's chair and held her hands. "You can drive yourself crazy with what-ifs." She smiled. "The first thing we're going to do is dig into that cheesecake. If you are pregnant, the baby needs the nourishment. If you're not, you owe it to yourself." Her eyes twinkled. "Then you're staying here so we can talk half the night away. I won't let you come this far and not give me all the…wonderful details. Tomorrow, you buy a pregnancy kit and make an appointment with my GYN. You'll like her. She's great." Nita kissed Jill on the cheek and stood up. "Now, do you want more sauerkraut or can we get right to the cheesecake? If you want kraut on the cake, you probably don't need to bother with the pregnancy kit."

Jill exploded with laughter, grateful for her friend's good sense and unconditional support. "Not yet. How about some tea?"

"Herbal tea coming up."

As soon as he returned to his apartment that evening, Gage phoned Sid Regis.

"I was getting ready to call you," the researcher said. "I have the final report on Jill Manning."

Gage had all but forgotten he'd asked for it. He didn't need outsiders telling him she was clean. "Good. What have you found?"

"Nothing much. No police record, not even for speeding. She seems to be something of a workaholic, routinely puts in sixty-hour-plus weeks, but you probably know that already. Not very active socially. Doesn't belong to any organized clubs or associations, though she is a regular speaker at groups for at-risk teenagers, advocating abstinence from drugs and premarital sex. Only close friend appears to be a pilot at the station, Nita Gomez. Haven't been any men in her life since the divorce, as far as I can determine."

Gage received the report with mixed feelings. His male pride was pleased to hear she hadn't been romantically involved with anyone else, but the life Sid described also sounded lonely. She deserved better, whether it was with him or someone else.

"Thanks, Sid. Now I need something else from you. Aerostat in Sector Five went down last Wednesday. I'd like to know why. Also, there was a raid on a cabin near a dirt strip south of Ajo during that period. See if you can find out what it was all about. Who was taken into custody? What agencies were involved in the lead-up and follow-on to the arrests? And, Sid, be discreet. You may ruffle feathers otherwise."

"Gotcha."

"One other thing. I'd like you to find out all you can about Brent Williams."

"The executive director?" After a moment of silence, the researcher said, "Will do."

CHAPTER SIXTEEN

THE FOLLOWING MORNING Gage was signing the coming week's duty roster when his phone rang.

"Reyes just called me from the hacienda," Jill began. "He took leave today to be with Selinda." Her voice softened. "It's the first anniversary of Cisco's death."

Gage shook his head. He and Jill both understood the pain of losing a son.

"Anyway," Jill continued, "Dixon contacted him to report information he'd received about a meeting between leaders of the Black Hand and Green Turtle gangs."

So there was a link between the two. "When is this meeting scheduled to happen, and where?"

"It's supposedly taking place right now. Dixon had a veiled reference to a location, but he couldn't decipher it. He thought Reyes might be able to, but Victor can't get his car started. He thinks it's the alternator. He asked if you could fly down to the hacienda and pick him up. He needs to research the archives here ASAP."

"No problem, but why did Dixon call him? Why not you?"

"I wasn't in yet. I tried calling Dixon when I arrived, but he wasn't in his office and isn't answering his cell phone. I left a message for him to call me back as soon as he gets a chance. Going to Reyes is a positive sign. Maybe he's finally becoming a team player."

Gage didn't argue the point. He ordered his mechanic to get Zero-Nine prepped for immediate take-off.

With only two helicopters operational, pilots and navigators were sitting around, not doing much of anything besides grumbling. Gage would have been disappointed if they didn't. He was grouchy, too. Among other things, his repeated calls to headquarters for replacement aircraft had so far yielded nothing.

One crew was out flying surveillance in the other chopper. Gage was slated for a routine mission that afternoon.

"Let me go," Nita begged. "Doing nothing is driving me crazy. Besides, I need to make myself scarce for a while."

Gage raised an eyebrow.

"Ruben's coming out to beg me to take his ring back, and I don't want to face him right now."

"You're not going to accept it?"

"I am, but on my terms, like counseling, and he's probably not going to like them. I really don't want to discuss it with him here, in front of everyone."

Gage chuckled. "Good for you. Go ahead and pick up Reyes. Have you landed there before?"

"Last year, when he got word about his son being found, I flew him home rather than let him drive. He was a mess, kept blaming himself. I thought he was going to have a nervous breakdown."

"I can imagine." Vividly. Gage still woke up at night sometimes in a cold sweat, his chest pounding, his mind racked with guilt over Rickie's death.

Nita was about to dash out to the waiting chopper when Ruben's patrol car pulled into the parking lot.

Gage looked at Nita. "I'll send him packing if you want me to."

"It's all right," she said, her eyes on the police vehicle.

Gage took a step back but remained visible, ready to come to her rescue if things got out of hand.

Her heart thudded as she watched Ruben lope toward her. "Nita, honey, I'm sorry. I want you to know that. You're right, I do need help. I've already contacted a counselor about taking an anger management course. She says I can start next week."

Nita grinned in delight. "You're really going to see a counselor?"

"It's what you want, isn't it?" He sounded unsure of himself.

"Yes, oh, yes." She threw her arms around his neck. She'd been afraid he would refuse to seek help, and here he was swallowing that macho pride of his for her. If she didn't watch out, she'd start crying.

"I love you, Nita." He kissed her on the forehead, his hands bracketing her narrow waist. "I'll do anything to make sure you're not afraid of me. I would never hurt you. I want you to be certain of that. I can't live without you, Nita. Tell me you'll take my ring back."

She bit her lip. "I will, Ruben, when you finish your counseling."

He looked disappointed by her reply, but he didn't argue with her. "If that's the way it's got to be. I want you to be happy, Nita. I want us to be happy."

"I'm happy already, Ruben." She pulled his head down and kissed him hard on the mouth. "We'll talk more when I get back." She separated herself from him.

"I love you, Nita."

Joy bubbled inside her as she walked to the waiting copter. She was so proud of Ruben. Knowing how much it had cost him to admit he needed help made her love him all the more. No, he wasn't like his father. Not now. She would have to assure him that facing his problems made him stronger in her eyes, not weaker.

If all went well, they could get married in the spring. Nita imagined his hand holding hers as he slipped the wedding ring on her finger and the tingle on her lips when he gave her that first kiss as her husband.

Time to shift gears, refocus. She went though her preflight checklist, perused the readings on the gauges, noted whether appropriate lights were on or off, flicked switches to confirm settings and informed the tower she was ready for takeoff. Receiving confirmation, she pulled back on the stick.

Flying had become as natural to her as driving a car was to a professional chauffeur. Training and experience had honed her skills and given her the confidence that made the difference between a competent pilot and a darned good one. To fly had been her dream since she had been a little girl. Even after a thousand hours of cockpit time, slipping the surly bonds still hadn't lost its thrill. She smiled to herself as she veered south toward the Reyes's hacienda.

She scanned her instrument panel. Everything was in order. It took only a few minutes to reach the ranch. She looked down. In the distance Reyes was waving her in. She adjusted the throttle to begin her descent.

Suddenly there was an earsplitting bang.

The entire craft bucked.

Nita's belly went hollow. Her skin tingled as terror swept through her. Her fingers fisted on the control yoke. The instrument panel was completely dark. The engine silent, powerless.

Nita pulled back on the stick to begin autorotation. It was slack in her hands. She looked up. The main rotor blades were gone. Her stomach rose as the aircraft plummeted in free fall. In that split second of eerie stillness, she knew she was going to die.

Only one thought possessed her. *I love you, Ruben.*

THE PHONE ON JILL'S DESK rang.

"What?" Her face froze. "Are you sure?" The receiver shook in her hand, her eyes went blank, her jaw slack. She seemed to have trouble catching her breath. "Call rescue immediately." Her voice warbled. "Keep me posted. Do you hear? I want to know everything the moment you do." Her expression turned to granite. Her eyes welled up. She sat motionless.

"What is it?" Gage stared at her across the desk. He'd come to her office to own up to the reason for his assignment here, to tell her about the diversion, to beg her forgiveness for his deception.

"It can't be," Jill said.

"What?" The horror on her face scared him. "Tell me."

"The noise we heard a minute ago—" She mumbled, her hands trembling. "That was the tower on the phone. They lost radar contact with Nita the moment it happened. They think—"

Gage went cold, then hot as rage consumed him. Not Nita, not that beautiful, vivacious young woman who had everything to live for.

The phone rang again. Gage lifted the receiver, listened to the short message with growing nausea, then hung up.

"Reyes. He saw it happen. The chopper exploded as it was making its approach to the field next to his house."

Gage ran out to the emergency exit in the corridor and peered to the south, Jill on his heels. Twenty miles to the south, a gray cloud rose from the ground. His stomach clenched, then with pounding heart, he bolted out the door.

"Wait," Jill called out. "I'm going with you."

He spun around on the concrete landing, placed his hands on her shoulders. "Stay here."

Her face grew red and her eyes blazed. "That wasn't a request, Engler. It was an order." She pushed past him, ran down the metal stairs on rubbery legs and dashed toward her official vehicle.

"We'll take my Jeep," he called out. "It's four-wheel drive, better suited to rough terrain."

With barely a second's consideration, she altered her course and jumped into his passenger seat. "Let's go."

The sport utility vehicle roared to life and Gage backed out of the parking space. Jill gripped the handle over the door as the Jeep careened in a semicircle and shot through the main gate.

The police radio squawked with news of the crash. Gage turned the volume down, slipped his cell phone off his belt, flipped it open and hit a button.

"They've struck again," he said, raising his voice enough to be heard above the scream of the engine. "Blew up a helicopter in flight this time. I don't know yet. Send a forensics team at once I'm on my way now… Yes, I'll take charge… No, not yet. She's sitting next to me. As soon as I hang up, I'll fill her in… I'll get back to you."

He wasn't surprised to see Jill gaping at him. She was confused; in a minute she'd be furious.

"Who was that?" she demanded. "Fill me in about what?"

"This isn't the way I'd planned to tell you, but there's no choice now. That was Brent Williams."

"The executive director? Why would you call… How is it you have instant access to him?"

"I'll explain later." He turned left onto the secondary road that would take them to the hacienda.

Tugging on the shoulder harness of her seat belt, she shifted around to look at him more squarely. "Not later. Now. What the hell's going on, Gage?"

He imagined he could hear her heart pounding. "I'm working for Internal Affairs," he said. "I was sent here to investigate Mack Robbins's death and a possible leak in the outfit."

She gaped at him. Her next words were slow in coming. "You came here to spy on me?" She drilled him with her eyes while her jaw flexed. "You've outdone yourself." The words were barely audible, but he got the message.

"I'm sorry."

She said nothing. He glanced over. No tears, just a stone mask.

"I know this comes as a shock. I wish none of it had happened, but we're going to have to work together if we hope to solve this problem. Do you think you can do that?"

"Solve this problem?" Her words were razor sharp.

"You make it sound like we have to decide what brand of laundry detergent to buy."

"I'm not trying to minimize the situation, Jill. Nita is probably dead. Things don't get much worse than that." *I'm losing you. Again.* "If you can't work with me, say so."

"And what?" she snarled. "You'll call Williams and have me replaced?"

After a brief pause he said, "Yes."

The answer obviously jolted her. Her breathing stopped. He waited for her to erupt and call him every name in the book.

"Does he know we were married to each other?" she demanded.

He glanced over. "No."

"So you lied to him, too. Seems to be a habit of yours. I wonder how he'll react when he finds out."

He started to say something, but she cut him off. "Give me your cell phone."

"Jill—"

"I said give me your cell phone. Now."

He hesitated, for once unsure what to do, what to expect. He removed it from his belt and handed it over.

She opened it. "Which speed dial?"

"Jill—"

"You're wasting time, Gage. Now or later, I'm going to talk to Williams. It's your turn to make a decision. Either you cooperate or you don't. I'll ask you only one more time. Which speed-dial button?"

He was tempted to ask, "Or what?" as if they were playing a game of dare. He'd threatened to get her fired. What would she threaten him with? Maybe it was better not to ask, not to provoke her.

"Six," he said.

She hit it. "Mr. Williams, this is Jill Manning… We're on our way now." Her tone was level, almost conversational. "I'm sorry you didn't trust me enough to keep me informed. Yes, I understand all that… I would like to clarify one point, however. I have no objection to Special Agent Engler heading the investigation of this accident. I'm sure he's qualified for the job and will be thorough. But I must ask about my status. Am I still the branch chief?" A single word on the other end. "That's all I needed to know. I'll tell him… Yes, of course. I'll be sure to keep you informed. Good day, sir."

Jill closed the device and tossed it to her ex-husband. It landed between his legs. "We're independent. You're in charge of the accident investigation. I'm still the branch chief. Neither of us answers to the other. I don't take orders from you, is that clear?"

A vein in his neck stood out. She could see the blood pulsing through it. "Yes."

"Nita was my friend, Gage, my *best* friend." She fisted her hands to keep them from shaking. "I'm giving you fair warning. Keep me fully apprised of what's going on. Say or do anything that undermines my authority, and I'll blow the whistle on you. It may cost me my job, but I guarantee it'll cost you a lot more. I don't think your friends and colleagues will have much respect for you when they find out you came here to spy on your ex-wife and, as a result, an innocent young woman got blown to bits in your place."

"Dammit, Jill…"

"Have I made myself plain enough?"

"Don't threaten me," he said through clenched teeth.

"I am threatening you," she snapped back. She was frightened of her own ruthlessness. "What are you going to do about it?"

He smoldered but said nothing.

"Good. Now that we have that settled, how do you want to proceed at the crash site?" Realization that they were again talking about Nita being dead hit like a punch to her gut, and for a moment her stomach heaved. *My baby. Oh, God. My baby.*

"I think it would be best—" his voice was gravelly with emotion, as well "—for you to announce that you have talked to headquarters and they've agreed to put me in charge of the investigation."

Her insides quaked. She had to struggle to concentrate. "I'll instruct everyone to cooperate with you and answer all your questions. If you run into any resistance, let me know."

The road was already crowded with emergency vehicles, their lights flashing. Ahead, a tall black plume marked the site of the disaster. The cortege snaked through the gate of the hacienda and sped over the caliche road, kicking up a dense plume of fine white powder.

People—there was no immediate way to determine who they all were—were busy putting out the small brush fires that dotted the desert floor. All that remained of the once powerful flying machine were mangled, blackened scraps of metal. One overhead rotor blade, still attached to the distorted fuselage, hung limp and twisted. The tail assembly was gone, no doubt among the pieces strewn over the treeless landscape.

Gage dashed to the fire chief, Jill only a few steps behind him. They identified themselves and she explained that Gage Engler would be in charge of the accident investigation.

"Did the pilot survive?" Jill asked.

"We can see a body still inside. Do you know how many people were on board?"

"Just one," Gage answered.

"Her name was Nita Gomez," Jill supplied in an undertone. *She was my friend.*

"Too hot to get to her right now," the fireman explained.

"Any idea what happened?" Gage asked.

The chief shook his head. "Not at this point. That guy over there says he saw it."

Reyes stood alone, his hands in his pockets, his head bowed.

"I'll go talk to him," Jill told Gage. "I'm sure you have other things to do here."

As she approached the intelligence officer, she saw that his eyes were bloodshot. Tears ran down his cheeks.

He shrugged when she came up beside him. "I waved to her. Then—" his voice was dull, flat "—the explosion knocked me off my feet."

Jill placed a hand on his back. "There was no warning? No indication of engine trouble?"

He kept shaking his head. "For a second I didn't understand what had happened." He bit his lip. "How could this…"

"We'll find out. Engler is taking over as investigating officer."

"Engler?" He looked first confused, then resigned. "Investigating won't bring her back. She was so young. So beautiful. This isn't fair." He turned away and began walking toward the house, where Selinda was probably waiting for him.

Gage came up beside Jill. "I'm going to call Davis-Monthan and request military assistance."

Under normal circumstances Customs would use their own resources to secure the area, as they'd done when Mack Robbins was killed, but now everyone was a suspect.

"I know the security squadron commander there," she said. "Do you want me to call her, or will you?"

"I'd appreciate it if you would. I need to make sure the crime scene doesn't get contaminated."

CHAPTER SEVENTEEN

FRITZ BRADLEY APPEARED a few minutes later. Until the air force arrived to guard the site, his border patrol people were to establish a security perimeter. Gage was coordinating details with him when a highway patrol vehicle sped toward them under a rolling cloud of dust.

Ruben jumped out and ran toward the still-burning chopper. Gage bounded after him and had to all but tackle the man before he was able to stop him. Fritz caught up a few seconds later.

"Let me go," Ruben shouted, and threw a punch that nearly connected and would have done serious damage if it had. Ruben's adrenaline was pumping and his strength was as massive as his rage and grief.

With Fritz's help, Gage strong-armed the flailing trooper into immobility.

"Calm down," Gage said in the man's ear. "There's nothing you can do. She's gone."

Ruben struggled. "Let me go."

"Not until you get hold of yourself. You can't help her and you're not helping yourself by losing control."

"If I have to, I'll cuff you," Bradley added. "I don't want to do that, Ruben, but I will. Now what's it going to be?"

Ruben's dark face grew darker, then his features

crumbled and his whole body went limp with a heart-wrenching moan. For a moment the other men had to hold him up.

"I'm sorry." Fritz relaxed his grip as the younger man regained stability, but he didn't completely let go.

When Ruben started to struggle again, Fritz dug his fingers into the policeman's forearms. Ruben stared at the burned-out shell of Nita's chopper. Tears filled his eyes. This time Fritz released him.

"What happened?" Ruben asked, his voice raw.

"We won't know until we investigate," Gage said.

"Why was she flying?" Ruben stabbed Gage with bloodshot eyes. "You were supposed to be on duty today."

A myriad of ideas ricocheted through Gage's brain, each more disturbing than the last. Ruben knew their flight schedules. Who else outside the organization did? If this was sabotage—and he fully believed it was—was Nita's death the result of miscalculation? Was a terrorist intent on killing someone, anyone, as a means of demoralizing the unit, or was the Gage the sole target? "We switched at the last minute."

"If you had anything to do with this," Ruben muttered, "I swear to God I'll kill you."

"That's enough," Fritz interceded. "Come with me." Ruben hesitated.

"Or I'll place you under arrest for threatening a federal official."

Ruben glared at him. "He's a damn helicopter pilot."

"He's in charge of this investigation."

"I want you to leave this crime scene," Gage said with quiet authority. "We can talk about this later, but right now I have things to do and can't afford to put up with your interference."

"You son of a b—"

Bradley grabbed him by the neck and pulled him away before he could finish the epithet. Just then, Gage heard the unmistakable whop-whop-whop of a helicopter approaching. He looked up to see the familiar star and chevron of the air force on the fuselage.

While Bradley escorted Ruben back to his vehicle, Gage met the security detail. Within minutes the area was under the protection of military personnel in camouflage uniforms wielding loaded M-16 rifles. Another chopper landed, this time carrying a forensics team.

They had just removed the body from the burned-out fuselage when Dixon showed up at the crash site. Gage made the preliminary identification, but Nita's body was so badly burned they would have to use dental records to confirm it. Watching from the sidelines, Dixon turned an ugly shade of green just before the remains were covered. He still looked on the cusp of being sick when Gage began his interrogation.

"You called Chief Manning this morning. What time was that?"

"I tried to," Dixon corrected him. "About eight-thirty. I was surprised she wasn't in. She's usually there by then."

Gage had let her statement that she hadn't yet arrived when Dixon called slip by without questioning it. "She tried to call you back. Where were you?"

"Meeting with my contact, trying to get more information. He's very cautious. Checks me out for bugs and won't let me carry a cell phone."

"Who is this guy?"

Dixon mulled the question before answering. He'd resisted revealing his sources in the past, but the sight of Nita's charred body seemed to have altered his disposition. "He's a *federale* in Aqua Prieta, just across from Douglas."

"And his tip was?"

"That the heads of the Black Hand and Green Turtle were meeting today to discuss an alliance."

Weren't they already working together? Was this related to the gathering Gage had been sidetracked to monitor south of Ajo? A formal alliance? Why would a group of zealots who abhorred the use of narcotics join forces with a cartel that dealt in them?

"How did he know about it?"

"He had his hand in a lot of jars."

"Does he know who the heads of the two organizations are?"

"Claims not to."

"He knew they were meeting but not where?"

"He didn't have a specific location, only that it was in a house on this side of the border, because one of them lives here."

"Did you believe him?"

Dixon shrugged. "He's always given me good information in the past."

"Is he a double agent?"

"Probably." Dixon shook his head in apparent frustration. "This is the game we play, Engler. Short of militarizing the border, only a fool would believe we'll ever make real progress in halting the traffic in people and goods between the two countries. So what we do is demonstrate to the mindless public that we're doing something. From time to time we make a few high-profile arrests of low-level operatives, confiscate a few weapons, burn a few stacks of marijuana and puff out our chests. The smuggling goes on, and it'll continue because it's profitable for both sides."

"Reyes was unable to find anything in his intelligence sources to substantiate your information." Jill had had a trooper drive Reyes into the office. He had reported back that he could find nothing to confirm the tip, and headquarters had come up blank, as well. "How do you explain that?"

"He wasn't able to substantiate my report of a second shipment of cocaine coming through on eighteen-wheelers, either, but it did. Maybe you should be asking him to explain his lack of good intelligence instead of questioning the validity of mine." The brief eruption of temper ended when Dixon saw the ambulance roll away from the scene. "God, she was so beautiful. How could anyone do that to her?"

"We don't know it was intentional yet."

"Engler, if you believe that, you're an idiot." He strode to his car, climbed in behind the wheel and drove away without a backward glance.

By midnight Gage was ready to quit for the day. There was one more thing he had to do, however. He approached the head of the forensics team.

"Any theories you're willing to share with me yet?"

They were standing on the edge of the intensely bright lights that had been installed around the wreckage, both for security and so investigators could continue their gruesome work.

"Not much question what happened. There was a bomb on board," the team chief answered.

"What kind of bomb?"

"Our best guess at this point is that C-4 plastique was crammed into the engine compartment. The blast instantly blew the engine apart and ignited the fuel."

"How was it detonated?"

Gage knew the options: a timing device set for a prescribed number of minutes after takeoff; the device was altitude-sensitive, so that when the plane descended to a preordained level it went off; or the timer was triggered by someone on the ground.

"Remote control," the bomb expert said. "Whoever pushed the button was probably within a three-mile radius, either on the ground or in another aircraft."

A check with all the radars in the area, including Aerostat balloon coverage, had found no other flight activity in the vicinity of the Blackhawk at the time of the explosion, so it had to be someone on the ground, probably in a car or truck.

Gage drove back to town. He'd seen Jill leave an hour or so earlier with one of the crew members. She hadn't stopped by to inform him she was going, which was disappointing but not surprising under the circumstances. His dashboard clock said it was almost one in the morning. He doubted she'd still be up, but he decided to drive by her place anyway.

He experienced a combination of relief and depression when he saw her apartment lights on. The need to be with her was as strong as ever, but awareness that their meeting was not likely to be pleasant soured his anticipation. His stomach growled. He hadn't eaten all day. He ought to find an all-night convenience store, pick up a stale sandwich and go home to his empty bed for a few hours' sleep.

He should, but he didn't. Instead, he parked in the visitor's slot at the end of a row of cars, got out and mounted the stairs.

RUBEN ORTIZ FED another bill into the jukebox in the corner of the bar, made his selection and returned to the table he'd been occupying all evening.

"I'm getting damn tired of listening to that stupid song," groused an unshaven hulk of a man wearing a dirty baseball cap.

The small group of hangers-on in the place didn't pay any attention.

"You hear me?" the guy yelled to Ruben.

Ruben shot him the finger.

The guy sprang from his bar stool and stormed toward Ruben's table, his meaty fists clenched, ready for a fight.

The bartender, a strapping young man, bolted out from behind the bar. Before he got to the aggressor, however, a tall, big-boned waitress blocked the way to Ruben's table.

"Calm down, Larry," she said. "He needs to hear that song real bad right now. His girl got killed in a helicopter crash today."

The guy looked at her, trying to determine if she was telling the truth.

She put her hand on his wrist. "Let him be," she ordered him. Her sincerity seemed to convince him.

He muttered an uncouth word, went back to the bar, polished off his drink, threw down a couple of bills beside the empty glass and stomped out the door.

Ruben watched it all as if it were a movie scene.

His head felt hollow. *His girl just got killed in a he-*

licopter crash. The words rolled around inside, bouncing, echoing, causing unbearable pain, yet he felt numb.

He'd been drunk only once before in his entire life. When he was fifteen, two of his buddies had swiped a bottle of tequila from somewhere and shared it with him. He hadn't cared for the taste of the liquor, and he'd liked the hangover the next day even less. He nursed a beer once in a while now to be sociable, but that was all. And Nita liked a glass of wine sometimes when they went to a nice place for dinner. He really didn't understand what made wine so special. Still, he sipped it. He'd do anything for her. She'd wanted him to see a counselor. He'd hated the idea, but he'd signed up. For Nita. Now she was gone.

He heaved a forlorn sigh. He'd never be able to tell her how sorry he was for upsetting her or how much he loved her. They'd never make babies together or laugh or kiss or smile at each other across a room. He wouldn't be able to touch her soft skin, feel her curled against him.

He brushed away the tears running down his face, picked up the fat little glass in front of him and tossed down the cactus juice, then doused the fire with the beer next to it. Raising his right hand, he signaled to the waitress to bring him another round.

The room was nearly empty now, except for a cowboy and his girlfriend necking in the corner booth. The waitress—what was her name? Crystal?—came over and sat across from him.

"You've had enough, Ruben." She rubbed the back of his hand. "It's time for you to go home."

"She's dead," he moaned.

"I know, honey. I'm sorry."

"Somebody killed her."

"Go home, Ruben, and get some rest."

"He killed her, and I'm going to kill him."

"You've had a lot to drink," Crystal reminded him.

"I don't care what happens to me. I'm going to kill him."

She shook her head. "That won't bring Nita back. Go home, Ruben. Sleep it off."

He stood, tipping over his chair in the process. The waitress looked up, watched him. The bartender meandered toward them.

"We can't let him drive home," he said.

"I'll get him there." Crystal went to the end of the bar and snatched her purse from under the counter.

Ruben staggered to the door. "I'll kill him."

"Sure you will." She put her arm around his waist and steered him toward her car in the parking lot. "Sure you will."

CHAPTER EIGHTEEN

JILL ANSWERED THE DOOR wearing a bathrobe, her hair damp from the shower, her eyes puffy.

"What do you want?" she demanded, standing in the open doorway.

"I thought you might like an update."

"There was a bomb. I already know, unless you've come to tell me who did it."

He shook his head. "The forensics people have determined it was remotely detonated." She looked exhausted. For a moment he wondered if she'd been drinking. "May I come in?"

"Why?" She was peering through him rather than at him. "You've already given me the report. That's all I need." She started to close the door.

He blocked it with his hand. "Jill, we have to talk about this."

He expected her to ask what *this* was. Nita's death? His betrayal? But apparently she realized there was no point in continuing the duel of words. Rather than inviting him in, she simply walked away from the door, leaving it open. He entered and closed it behind him.

"Gage, whatever you have to say—" she kept her back to him, her shoulders stiff "—please get it over with and leave. I'm tired. I need to get some rest."

He doubted sleep would come easily for either of them. Today had been a tragedy that would never go away. Whether or not they found the person who had blown up the helicopter, he was certain he would spend the rest of his life blaming himself for letting Nita take that flight. But self-recrimination wouldn't bring her back, just as it hadn't brought back Rickie. What he had to do now was deal with the living, this woman he loved, the woman he had broken faith with—again.

She sat in an easy chair across from the couch and tightened the upper and lower parts of her bathrobe with clenched fists. Not out of modesty, he realized, but in a ritual for finding some sort of inner warmth and security. He'd robbed her of that. He'd failed her over and over.

He perched on a corner of the couch, his elbows on his knees, facing her. "I'm sorry I wasn't able to be up-front with you about my reason for coming here. The secrecy wasn't my idea. In fact, I fought it. But I was under orders. You understand that."

"Of course." She wasn't conceding. She was placating, condescending, patronizing. Calling him a liar.

"I wrangled this assignment because I wanted to see you, to be with you, to protect you."

"Too bad you couldn't protect Nita, too."

He closed his eyes and tried to block out the pain of her indictment. "I guess I deserve that."

She sprang from her chair and gazed out the dark windows on the far side of the room, her head bowed, her shoulders rigid. Turning slowly, she said, "No, you don't. That was a horrible thing to say."

She plopped down in the chair again, her arms folded across her waist, as if in pain. "I'm so angry with you,

Gage, I don't know what to say or how else to feel, other than betrayed, used. Deep inside I suspect what you've done has been with the best intentions. The road to hell…" She closed her eyes, shook her head and waved the comment away. "I want to hate you for not confiding in me, while at the same time I understand the position you were in. Williams was simply being a good bureaucrat, covering all the bases by considering me a suspect. After all, I profited by Mack's death. Success, achievement is always suspect, isn't it?" She bowed her head and took a shuddering breath.

Gage wanted more than anything to gather her in his arms, to soothe and console her, and maybe find some solace for himself. "I never believed for a moment you were responsible—"

She snorted. "I guess I should take comfort in that." She inhaled and let it out. "Regardless of whatever honorable motives you might have had, the fact remains that I can't trust you. You've kept important secrets from me, not for my good, but for someone else's."

"It was for your good."

"Really? How was I better off not knowing I was suspected of treason or that you were spying on my people?"

When he failed to answer, she shook her head. "No, Gage, you did it for the good of the service, for your career. I don't doubt that you wanted to protect me, too, and for that, I suppose, I ought to thank you. My gallant defender, rescuing a beleaguered damsel in distress." She sneered. "Is that how you think of me, Gage—weak, vulnerable, needing deliverance from the clutches of fire-breathing dragons?"

"Of course not. I respect you—"

"If you ever thought there was a chance for us to get back together, Gage, I'm afraid it's out of the question now."

"Jill—" He'd planned to tell her about Williams's diverting his flight, but under the circumstances he doubted she'd believe him. He couldn't blame her.

She rose almost regally to her feet. "Thanks for dropping by. I appreciate the personal report. I'm sure we'll be called upon to work together in the days and weeks ahead. You can count on me to be open and candid with you, because I know you're a very good agent and will do everything in your power to catch whoever did this."

She moved to the front door and put her hand on the knob.

He huffed out a sigh of frustration and climbed to his feet. "Sorry to keep you up," he said when he was beside her at the door. "The forensics people will be at it all night. I'll let you know as soon as I get any information of value."

She opened the door wide.

He stepped out into the shadowy darkness. "Good night, Jill."

"Good night." The door closed behind him with a click. A moment later he heard the dead bolt slide into place.

JILL WAITED UNTIL the sound of Gage's Jeep faded into the night before she allowed herself to break down. All the things she'd said to him had been true. She did respect his skills as an investigator, his integrity in following orders. She believed him when he'd said he wanted to tell her his true objective in coming to Tombstone was to be with her. But also inescapable was the fact that she would never be able to completely trust him. If he could hold back something as important as his being assigned here to spy on her, how could she be certain he wasn't keeping other secrets?

She turned off the lights in the living room and wandered to her bedroom, hoping for but not expecting to get any sleep. In the bathroom she caught sight of the pregnancy kit on the shelf under the medicine cabinet. She sobbed, spun around and ran to the bed, where she collapsed, facedown.

The tears came in quantities she'd never imagined possible. Time passed. She leaned against the headboard, drew up her legs and wrapped her arms around them. She was a hypocrite and a liar. Worse even than Gage.

She'd been late to work this morning because of a side trip she'd never expected to take.

In spite of the gynecologist's assurances that she would not be able to conceive again, her cycle had always been like clockwork. Except now. She was a full week late. But there could be all sorts of explanations besides pregnancy. The turmoil in her life these past months had been horrendous. Taking over as branch chief following the violent death of her predecessor and Doug Vogel's injuries. Gage's unexpected appearance in itself produced enough tension to throw her hormones into panic. Making love to him again after more than two years—two years of celibacy—was bound to affect her regularity. Wasn't it?

This morning, after oversleeping, she'd left Nita's house and purchased a pregnancy kit at the pharmacy in town. Nita had said she hoped Jill was pregnant, that she deserved another chance at motherhood, that she thought Gage would make a great father.

Jill was sure of only one thing: she desperately wanted

this child. She wanted to be a mother, and the realization that a new life might be growing inside her brought a sensation like no other in the world. Sure, there were problems, obstacles she—they—would have to overcome, but…

She'd asked Nita to be the baby's godmother—if she was pregnant. Her best friend's face had lit up and she'd hugged her. Less than twenty-four hours ago, and now Nita was gone.

Jill stared at the kit. It said on the box the test was only ninety-nine percent accurate. It would be just her luck to hit the one percent false positive. Maybe it would be better to wait. She was, after all, only a week late. She could start her cycle tomorrow.

If the test came out positive, would she be able to carry the baby to term? If she did, would it be healthy? The thought of losing another child frightened her even more than the fact that she might be pregnant.

And what about Gage? She'd played a cute word game with him tonight, but at some point she would have to tell him he might become a father—again. He had a right to know, to share in their child's life. Would it be another boy or a girl this time?

When should she tell him? Not right away. She'd wait awhile, until after she'd seen a doctor. If she lost this baby, he would never have to know. Everything would be easier that way. For him. For them.

She needed to give things a chance to return to normal, though how that could happen with Gage still around and Nita dead, she didn't know.

GAGE REMOVED an individual pepperoni pizza from the freezer compartment of his refrigerator, glanced at the instructions on the back and turned on the oven. He popped the top on a beer and riffled through the mail he'd picked up on his way in. Chucking the junk variety without opening it, he scanned the bills and set them aside. After dotting the pizza with a few slices of jalapeño, he shoved it into the oven, set the timer, then went to his bedroom, pulled off his boots and stripped off his clothes.

The shower refreshed him marginally. At least he felt clean. The oven timer dinged. Barefoot and wearing only skivvies, he returned to the kitchen.

The beer tasted flat, the pizza like cardboard. He ate only half of it but decided to give the brew a second chance.

Sitting on the couch with his feet on the coffee table, he tried to fit together all the pieces of today's disaster. Better that than dwell on Jill and the look he'd seen in her eyes when she said he'd destroyed any chance of them ever getting together again.

THE MEMORIAL SERVICE for Nita Gomez was held Saturday morning in the small Catholic mission church in Bisbee where she had been baptized and taken her first Holy Communion. Lots had been drawn at the station to see who would attend the funeral mass, since they couldn't all be there. Victor Reyes brought Selinda, who commiserated in Spanish with the grieving family. Pratt Dixon and Fritz Bradley showed up. With the one remaining helicopter grounded indefinitely, all the pilots and flight mechanics came together. Paco Moreno was red-eyed and devastated by the death of the young woman he'd treated like a daughter. Ruben Ortiz, his mother and sister sat behind the Gomez family.

In spite of her vow to stay away from Gage, Jill had

little choice when he came up to her at the church and took her hands in his. Making a scene by rejecting him would only complicate an already complicated situation. Besides, she couldn't expel him from her life, not if she was really pregnant. And she couldn't pretend she didn't find comfort in his familiar, gentle touch.

In their pew at the back of the church, he continued to hold her hand. An overflow crowd filled the side aisles and fanned outside into the bright July sunlight. Dozens of wreaths, baskets and potted plants jammed the sanctuary, their scents perfuming the air.

At ten o'clock the casket was borne in on the shoulders of Nita's brothers and cousins. A gray-haired priest in black vestments met them in the center aisle and sprinkled the casket with holy water. The church was soon filled with the added aromas of beeswax candles and burning incense. Nita's eldest brother gave the eulogy, celebrating—sometimes with a strangled voice— the cheerful, sparkling life of his precocious sister.

Through it all, Jill found herself squeezing Gage's hand, grateful for his closeness and strength and wishing she could find solace in the ancient rituals of grief.

From there, the cortege proceeded to the cemetery, where a benediction was recited. Nita's mother collapsed when the priest sprinkled holy water over the flower-strewn casket.

JILL LAY IN HER BED that night, staring at the ceiling. She still hadn't started her period, so she'd given in and used the kit. There could be no doubt now. She was pregnant.

This should be an exciting time for her, a redemption of herself as a woman, the bearer of life; yet she was miserable. She would have to tell Gage. It wasn't fair to keep it from him. He'd be thrilled. He'd want them to get married right away. The realization that he would find joy in what she should be celebrating, as well, only increased her depression and sense of shame. She was carrying a new life inside her and as much as she wanted it, it also terrified her.

He'd want her to resign, of course. For the baby's sake. How could she argue with him when her predecessor had been killed? When Gage's crash had probably been an attempt on her life? When her best friend had just been murdered?

Two more sleepless nights went by. She'd purchased a second kit. The result was the same, but she still hadn't made an appointment to see a doctor or told Gage.

She was beginning to experience morning sickness now. At least her office had a private bathroom, so no one saw her bolting to throw up. She'd always loved coffee, but now the smell of it nauseated her. Nobody noticed—or at least no one commented on it—her shunning coffee in favor of herbal tea. Eventually they'd figure it out, if she didn't announce it herself first.

She remembered Gage's comment about wanting to make an honest woman of her, and the sadness she had felt in dismissing the notion. They hadn't used protection in their lovemaking. After all, she wasn't supposed to be able to get pregnant, and she'd believed him when he'd said he wasn't sleeping around.

How would she manage to raise a child as a single parent? Marrying Gage was out of the question. Before she'd found out the extent of his lying, she might have accepted his proposal. For the baby, but also for herself. In spite of everything, she still loved him. Always had.

Maybe their marriage wouldn't have been ideal, but they could have made it work—if he hadn't deceived her.

She called him at the hangar late Monday afternoon, just before quitting time. "I need to see you. Privately. This evening, if possible."

"Your place or mine?" A note of anticipation buoyed his tone. Stringing him along was unkind. This wasn't a ploy, but she didn't want to discuss it over the phone. "Or do we need neutral ground?"

"I think my place would be best." The nearness of Rickie's toy chest in his apartment would only remind her of what had been. "Grab a bite first, then come over to my place around seven."

"How about I take you to dinner?"

"No," she said.

"I can pick up a pizza, pepperoni and mushroom. Your favorite."

Her stomach flipped. "Gage, please just do as I ask." She knew she sounded bitchy, but dammit, that was the way she felt. "Get yourself something to eat—or don't, I don't care—then come over."

She could picture the quizzical expression on his face. "Sure. Okay." A pause. "See you at seven."

She hung up the phone and after making sure the door was closed, she lowered her head and cried.

CHAPTER NINETEEN

"You're certain?"

Gage's heart did a somersault the moment she told him. He could barely contain himself. He wanted to jump up from the couch, sweep her off her feet and dance around the room. She was pregnant with his child. They were going to be parents—again. He would never forget Rickie, but they needed to focus on this new life, this second chance.

"I'm sure," she said with a dullness that took the wind out of him.

He cocked his head to one side and studied her, standing in front of the cold fireplace, her arms folded across her middle as if she were trying to hold herself in. In spite of her neat tan slacks and spotless green blouse, she looked somehow rumpled, worn out. He wondered how long it had been since she'd slept.

"This is wonderful news, Jill. Why aren't you happy? You've always said you wanted more children."

"This baby will never come to term, Gage."

His heart stopped. He gaped at her. "What are you saying, that you're going to have an abortion?" He knew his mouth hung open, but he couldn't close it, couldn't catch his breath. She couldn't do this. He wouldn't let her do it. There must be some way to stop her.

"Of course not," she said with as much anger as contempt.

He closed his eyes, exhaled and let his shoulders sag. "Then what? Has the doctor—"

"I haven't been to a doctor yet."

Why the hell not?

He climbed to his feet. "Jill, you have to," he pleaded with outstretched hands. "As soon as possible. Right away."

"It's only been four weeks." She sat in the easy chair by the window.

"But you're sure."

"I did the test twice," she explained. "Just in case the first one was a false positive."

He still couldn't understand why she wasn't happy. This was what they'd always wanted, hoped for. Getting married wasn't an option now but a necessity. It would be difficult for a while. He didn't delude himself into thinking they didn't have unresolved problems to work out. She didn't trust him and it would take her a long time to forgive him for not being open with her, but she was an intelligent woman. In spite of everything, she still cared for him. Hadn't the way they'd made love proved that?

"But…why do you say it won't come to term?" he asked, trying to comprehend.

She bit her lip. "You heard what the doctor said last time, that I couldn't—"

"That you couldn't get pregnant. But she was wrong. You are pregnant."

"That's what the kit says."

"Twice," he pointed out. "Jill, you have to see a doctor right away—"

"I intend to," she snapped, and jumped up again.

She always became annoyed when he tried to tell her the obvious, as if she didn't have a mind of her own. But he wasn't dictating. He was just confirming what she must already know. She was worried, afraid. He was, too. For her. For their baby. About whether he would be a good father. He'd tried to be the last time, but wanting, trying, wasn't enough. He'd failed then; he wouldn't fail again.

"I'm not right inside, Gage. We both know that. I'll miscarry."

The agony in her voice tore at him. "Oh, honey…" But when he approached her, she backed away, unwilling to let him touch her.

"We know only what one OB/GYN said, and she was obviously wrong." He was losing patience with this uncharacteristic defeatist attitude. "You don't want this baby, is that it?"

She glared at him. "Of course I do. But I have to be realistic."

"Then see a doctor." He softened his tone. "I'll go with you. We'll find out exactly what needs to be done for your health and for the baby's. If your obstetrician says you have to stay in bed for the next eight months, that's what you'll do, and I'll bring you all the pickles and ice cream you want."

She didn't even crack a smile.

"Jill, listen to me," he implored her. "I love you with all my heart, with all my being. I understand at this moment you don't feel the same way about me. I hope one day to change that, but right now you and I aren't important. Our baby is the only one that really matters."

She nodded. Tears filled her eyes.

He coaxed her cheek against his chest. "We'll go to a doctor. We'll get married and—"

Her head shot up. "I'm not quitting my job, if that's what you're about to say." She stepped out of his embrace. "Not until I find out who killed Nita. She was my friend, Gage. She was the sister I never had. I can't abandon her. I won't."

"I'm not asking you to," he assured her. "We'll find whoever did it."

"I'll find him," she shouted back, her voice raw.

"Jill, the situation is getting more dangerous every day. You're not safe."

"I'm able to take care of myself."

He felt helpless against this strong-willed woman who was letting emotion cloud logic. "Of course you are, but these aren't ordinary circumstances. Remember the saying about discretion being the better part of valor?"

"Don't patronize me."

He swept his hand down his face in frustration. "What I am trying to do is make you see reason. You're pregnant. That changes everything." He held her gaze and took a breath. "I was wrong to ask you to quit your job the last time. I admit it. Williams told me he picked you ahead of other qualified candidates because you were the best choice for branch chief."

"He discussed my selection with you?"

The wrong thing to say, he realized too late. "Only when I asked how you were doing. After the choice was made, not before. I agree with him, Jill. You're good, very good. You took over under terrible circumstances.

I don't know of anyone who could have done as well as you."

Her expression mellowed with his praise, but the underlying doubt and anger didn't subside.

"If it were just you and me… But this isn't about you and me anymore. Your…our first priority has to be our baby."

She squeezed her eyes shut. He knew she couldn't deny the truth of anything he'd said, yet—

"I'll make an appointment to see a doctor. And we'll go from there." She pinned him with her tear-stained eyes. "Getting married isn't a slam-dunk decision, Gage. And whether I continue to work isn't up to you, either. It's my choice."

"You're carrying my child, Jill. I sure as hell have a say, morally, if not legally."

She huffed out a breath and wilted onto the couch. After a moment she looked up at him. "Gage, I don't know what is right anymore. I want this baby more than you can imagine." She squeezed her eyes shut and shook her head. "No, I believe you can imagine. You want him or her as much as I do. This child deserves to grow up in a family with two parents who love each other. I'm just not sure marrying you is the right thing to do for the baby—or for us. There are too many issues between us."

"I love you, Jill. I want to protect you."

"I'm not looking for a protector. I need someone who respects me enough to be open and honest with me. Maybe you haven't actually lied to me so far, but you've held things back that I had a right to know. You won't trust me and I can't trust you."

"Are you refusing to marry me? You would rather let this child be brought up in a broken home?"

"I don't know what I'm saying," she acknowledged. "I have a lot to think about, and so do you. Let's wait until I find out what the doctor has to say. We still have time."

"Not much."

"Please don't put any more pressure on me than I already feel, Gage. Please."

He studied the sadness and worry in her eyes, the defeated posture. Why couldn't she see what seemed so clear to him? Reestablishing the commitment they'd once shared wouldn't be easy after all they'd been through, after all the pain and sorrow he'd brought her. Forming a new bond would require hard work and dedication on both their parts. But he was convinced they could succeed if she would just give them a chance, give *him* a chance.

He knelt at her feet and took her hands in his. "Make your doctor's appointment. I'd like to go with you, if you'll let me, but that's up to you. Tell me what you find out."

"I will."

"We'll go from there." He touched his lips to her cheek, tasted the salt of her tears. "I love you, Jill. Just remember that. Whatever you do, whatever you decide, never forget that I love you and I always will."

She nodded, even as fresh tears coursed down her cheeks.

"I'VE HAD ENOUGH. I want out. Killing Nita wasn't part of the bargain. If I had known—"

"She's dead," the kingpin said. "You killed her. You planted the bomb."

"You pressed the button," the tearful underling shouted. "You didn't have to. How could you do that when you knew— I told you it wasn't Engler aboard."

"I had no choice."

"But—"

"There are no buts and there is no out. Not now. Not ever."

"I HAVE SOME INFORMATION for you," Sid announced.

Gage used the hands-free feature on his cell phone as he drove to the Customs station. He felt drained. He hadn't slept all night. After his discussion with Jill, he'd gone home and gotten out his woodworking supplies. He had a reason now to finish the toy box. A child. His child.

First he'd given the entire chest a fresh sanding with the finest-grit sandpaper, then he'd carefully applied varnish to the raw wood and watched the rich grain come to life. While his hands had moved with measured precision, his mind raced.

He'd pictured Jill's swollen face, the uncertainty and fear he'd seen there. Maybe she was right. Maybe he wasn't a fit father. Maybe he didn't deserve to be a parent. But he—they—were being given another chance. The miracle of a new life was growing inside her. He would sacrifice anything to protect that precious gift.

She'd said their baby deserved to be brought up by two loving parents. Didn't that imply that they lived together? Suppose she did refuse to marry him? What then? Living apart from her had been torture. How much worse it would be if he was separated from his child, too?

"Gage, you there?"

"I'm listening, Sid," he told the intelligence specialist.

"I thought I'd lost you for a minute. Look, I got curious about this guy, Pratt Dixon. Checking his address and auto registration, I noticed he seems to have expensive tastes."

"He lives in a small house in town," Gage said. "I've driven by the place. Didn't strike me as luxurious, and his pickup is several years old. You sure we're talking about the same guy?"

A chuckle greeted him from the other end. "That's only one of his residences and one of his vehicles."

Gage slowed to take a sharp curve. "Go on."

"He also owns a town house in Tucson and a condo in Vail. As for transportation, in addition to the six-year-old truck, he has a new four-wheel-drive Land Rover he keeps in the mountains and a BMW-8Z in Tucson."

"The sports car alone costs about twice what he makes a year as an immigration officer."

"And the houses are paid for, free and clear."

"Family money?" Gage asked.

"Nope. Parents are farmers in Nebraska. They're scraping by, not exactly living high on the hog, pardon the pun."

"Drug money?"

"Maybe not. He likes to play the stock market, usually wins."

"Really?"

"He's got two brokerage accounts, one is full service with Krauthammer and Lapierre, the other with a discount house. Has assets in both that top the seven-figure mark."

Gage emitted a low whistle.

"He started investing in penny stocks about fifteen years ago and consistently lost. Not unusual. They're speculative. The miracle would have been if he'd profited. Then he switched to Dot-Coms just before the craze took off. Again mostly losers, but not all. Cashed in a few big winners six years ago, about the time they were peaking, and collected a bundle. Since then he's been more conservative. Hasn't made as much, but he hasn't lost, either. Grossed about a quarter of a million last year in his trading and dividends."

"Neat," Gage said. "I wonder if he'd be willing to handle my portfolio. So he doesn't have to work at all. Why does he, do you suppose?"

"Maybe he's just a dedicated civil servant."

The notion wasn't outrageous. Gage had met a number of wealthy agents and operatives. They thrived on dangerous work, the high it gave them. Some even did it for patriotic reasons, because they wanted to make the world a better place.

Gage wondered if he would stick with his job if he could afford to quit. Probably, but maybe not. It wasn't making him rich, but that wasn't important. He was living well enough. He could even afford a few indulgences, though he wasn't a slave to any of them. Gambling didn't interest him. Or drinking. As for women…

He loved only one woman, and she was carrying his child.

"There is one other tidbit," Sid said. "Dixon has a couple of offshore accounts. One in Switzerland, another in the Caymans. I haven't been able to determine how much is in either, though, or the source of the income."

CHAPTER TWENTY

THE DAY HAD BEEN hectic. At the Naco port of entry, they'd seized over five hundred pounds of marijuana, hidden in a tour bus, and a hundred and fifty pounds of heroin in a van an hour later. These seizures brought them above last year's total, and they were only seven months into the year. That aspect of Jill's job, at least, was going well.

Later in the day, she'd met with officials at Fort Huachuca, reviewed security issues and laid out provisions for a new detailed exchange of intelligence. Then she'd been interviewed by representatives of a joint task force of FBI, CIA and other federal agencies investigating the recent rise of drug and weapons transfers from Mexico. The treasury department was also putting an additional emphasis on U.S. currency being smuggled out of the country.

She was in bed, alone, beginning to doze off, when the telephone shattered any chance of sleep. She glanced at the alarm clock, which read eleven-fifteen, and lifted the receiver. "Manning."

"Jill—" Gage's voice. "Keeling's been shot."

She levered herself upright. "Judge Keeling? Where? How?"

"Don't have any details yet. Apparently a drive-by shooting at his home."

"Is he still alive?"

"He was when the medics took him away."

"How did you find out about this?" An unreasonable wave of jealousy washed through her that he had contacts she didn't. Had he preempted her authority and given orders that he was the point of contact for any new developments?

"I heard it on the police scanner."

Of course. He had one in his Jeep as well as at home. She had turned hers off over an hour ago when she'd crawled into bed. "Where are you now?"

"At his house."

"What's the address?" She jotted it down. "I'm on my way."

Fifteen minutes later she saw the red and blue lights of police and emergency vehicles flicking through the darkness as she approached the street in the quiet neighborhood where the judge lived. Cruisers blocked the thoroughfare and uniformed policemen were posted to stop pedestrians—there weren't any at this hour—from contaminating the crime scene. She parked her Taurus at the curb, got out and approached one of the sentries.

"I'm Jill Manning." She displayed her badge. "I'm looking for Special Agent Gage Engler."

"He's at the judge's house," the young man responded. "Said for you to meet him there." He lifted the yellow tape stretched across the roadway.

She ducked under it and strode toward the redbrick residence that was ablaze with floodlights. Through the open main entrance she could see men and women moving about inside.

Gage was standing near the half-raised garage door, talking to a middle-aged woman in uniform, who nodded and entered the house. He turned to Jill, having already acknowledged her presence with a wave of his hand.

"Sorry if I woke you." He must have recognized the sleep in her voice when he'd phoned. He'd always been perceptive about details, except the ones that really counted. She gave herself a mental slap. The thought was unfair and unkind, as well as unproductive. "But I knew you'd want to be called."

She didn't look at him but at the late-model silver Cadillac a few feet away. The rear and side windows were shattered. Bullet holes pockmarked the chassis. On the ground beside it, footprints radiated from a pool of dried blood.

She tried to ignore the coppery taste in her mouth and redirected her attention to the man standing only a few feet away. He was wearing faded jeans and a black T-shirt. The glare of artificial lights accentuated his sinewy muscles and rugged masculinity. She'd touched that hard flesh. At the moment, she was so tired and confused she wanted only for him to put those strong arms around her and hold her tight. Annoyed by her errant thoughts, she demanded, "What do we have so far?"

"Keeling came home about ten o'clock from his weekly chamber-music session, pulled into the driveway and got out to open the garage door."

"No automatic opener?"

They stepped aside when a pair of technicians began measuring various points of reference.

"According to the guy across the street, he'd been having trouble with it lately. Sometimes it works, sometimes it doesn't. He'd just gotten out and started to raise the door when a pickup roared by and opened fire."

They moved again when another member of the forensics team rushed inside carrying a boxy satchel.

"How do you know all this?" In spite of the warmth of the late-July night, she felt cold inside.

"The neighbor saw him when he was locking up his house for the night."

"Any description of the vehicle or occupants?"

"Sketchy. An old, faded-green pickup with a crumpled left front fender. Two males in the cab, possibly Hispanic. The guy in the passenger seat opened fire at Keeling, then they sped away. No plate number. The neighbor immediately called 9-1-1. He was doing CPR and trying to stop the bleeding when the paramedics arrived. Probably saved the old man's life." That explained the bloody footprints.

"A good Samaritan." Her words sounded cynical.

She noticed Fritz Bradley across the street talking with a couple of the guards on duty and suggested they join him, away from the flow of foot traffic and the glare of the bright lights. Gage agreed. As they approached the border patrol officer, the two uniforms wandered off.

"Any idea who did this?" Jill asked.

"He was a hanging judge. I'm sure he made his share of enemies. The cops are checking on parolees recently released, as well as any threats on file."

"Do you think this might be the work of the Black Hand or the Green Turtle?" she asked.

"Don't know why the Black Hand would go after him," Bradley said. "He let their people off. I suppose it could be the Green Turtle sending a message that they didn't appreciate his supporting their rival."

"Except the latest reports indicate they're not rivals

anymore," Gage pointed out. If the two gangs had met, as Dixon had reported, no one had found any evidence of it.

"The possibilities are endless," Jill observed.

A flatbed pulled up in the middle of the street and lowered its ramp. A man wearing a gold badge on the belt of his civilian clothes and sporting latex gloves and paper booties got into the Cadillac and started the engine. A minute later, he drove the car up onto the trailer. Two other guys put chocks under the wheels and the truck moved out of the circle of light and down the dark street.

"I suppose this could have been a random act of senseless violence, maybe part of a gang initiation. But given all the other things going on lately, the helicopter crashes—" her last picture of Nita's burned corpse shivered through her "—and Keeling's decision to let those drug smugglers go, I'm more inclined to believe this attack was personal. Any way we can find out?"

"Have you asked Dixon?" Bradley inquired. "He brags about having his ear close to the ground. Maybe he has information that will help."

"I tried calling him earlier," Gage said. "He's not answering his home, office or cell phones."

"Interesting," Bradley said.

Jill hung around for another hour to observe the forensics team collect evidence. Shell casings in the street established that the weapon was an AK-47 assault rifle. Slugs were also recovered from the judge's vehicle. Depending on their condition, ballistics might be able to match them to the specific weapon, if it was ever recovered. The chances of that happening were slim. More promising would be leads from the kinds of sources Dixon cultivated: snitches and paid informants.

"No need for you to be here," Gage told her. "There's really nothing you can do. Why don't you go home and get some sleep? Tomorrow is going to be another busy day."

He was trying to persuade her rather than insist she leave. Maybe that, plus the fact that she had already been dog-tired when he'd called her, convinced her to follow his advice.

"You'll call if you learn anything?"

"You have my word," he said.

"See you in the morning then." She retreated to her car and drove home.

It was after two by the time she got to bed. Sleep eluded her, however. She kept recounting the conversation she'd had with Gage and Fritz.

Having never tried to contact Dixon outside the normal workday, she didn't know if his non-availability tonight was common. It seemed unusual for someone whose job revolved around being accessible. The man was still a conundrum to her. Erratic, hostile, helpful, recriminatory. At times she wasn't sure whose side he was on. Plainly not hers, but in the bigger picture, where did his loyalties lie? Was he the mole? Was he the secret head of the Black Hand? Or…maybe something had happened to him, too.

His report about the truck convoy had been accurate, but she couldn't discount the idea that it was all part of a mind game he was playing with her, giving her valid information but subtly robbing it of credibility, knowing she wouldn't follow through on it. A cynical *gotcha*.

Why target the judge? Revenge? To keep him quiet?

If Keeling was on the take, part of a conspiracy, his co-horts would want to keep him around, unless he'd had a change of heart. He'd served honorably on the bench for twenty years. What would drive a man of integrity to violate his deepest values? There were no indications he needed money. How about a threat against something or someone he considered even more precious than his name and reputation? Only one answer came to mind: his children.

From Gage, she'd learned the judge had an unmarried son in Southern California, a major corridor for a variety of illegal activities. His younger son, Ronny, had dropped out of college last year and enlisted in the army. A smart move on the part of a kid who lacked focus, or was it a convenient getaway? What could Ronny have done to place him in jeopardy? One possible answer was drugs. Who would have knowledge of it? A slew of law enforcement agencies: the police, the sheriff's department, the border patrol, members of the Customs Service.

Which brought her right back to Dixon.

SHORTLY AFTER JILL LEFT the crime scene, Gage drove by Dixon's house in Sierra Vista. The place was dark. He rang the bell and knocked on the door. No answer. Using his flashlight, he peeked through the window of the garage. His truck was gone. Concluding the guy wasn't there, Gage went home. He needed sleep and a clear head; he had the nagging feeling he was missing something important.

At seven o'clock the following morning his alarm went off. He crawled out of bed and into the shower. Three hours' sleep wasn't too bad. A cup of strong coffee would bring him back to life.

His mind focused on Jill, and he wondered what she was doing, what she was thinking. He hadn't missed the distrust in her eyes when he'd told her he'd keep her apprised of developments. Why not prove his sincerity by inviting her to go with him to Dixon's office? Sharing his investigation with her ought to prove he didn't have anything to hide. He started to dial her number but then remembered her sheer exhaustion the night before. Not only was she grieving for her dead friend, her *best* friend, but she was pregnant and worried sick about being able to carry the baby. She needed her rest. Stamping down images of her curled up in bed and memories of their nights together, he clicked off the phone.

Dixon's truck was parked in front of the immigration office, a snug building on the southern edge of town. The man was perusing papers at his desk, a cup of coffee at hand. He looked up when Gage appeared in front of him.

"What can I do for you, Engler?"

"Judge Keeling was shot last night."

"I heard it on the radio this morning. Is he going to pull through?"

"He's still critical. We tried to get hold of you."

"I was in Tucson, visiting a friend. Forgot I had my cell phone turned off."

"Uh-huh. I'd like to ask you a few questions."

"Sit down." He offered coffee, which Gage declined.

"I'm conducting the investigation of Nita's crash—"

"Apparently, you've been undercover since you arrived," Dixon said with a smug sneer.

"I'm doing my job."

Dixon smiled. "That's what they all say. I have to

admit, I wasn't surprised when I found out you had ulterior motives for being here. Like your ex-wife."

There was a moment of silence. "How long have you known?"

"Since your second day."

"How did you find out?"

He chuckled. "I have friends in various places. I did some checking. You seemed too sharp to be just a helicopter pilot."

"You don't think it takes brains to fly a chopper?"

"No disrespect to pilots, fixed-wing or rotary. I've never met one I didn't think was intelligent. But your interests and expertise seemed to go beyond playing with your stick."

Gage couldn't help but laugh. "Thanks, I think."

Dixon grinned back and for a moment the two men shared a sense of camaraderie.

"Who have you told?" Gage asked.

"No one. I figure that's between you and Jill. Believe it or not, Engler, we're on the same side."

Gage found himself hoping it was true. "I've done some checking on you, too."

The smile didn't fade from the other man's face. If anything, humor intensified it. "And what have you discovered?"

"That you have offshore banking accounts."

Dixon poised the cup at his lips and spoke over the rim. "Am I being accused of something?"

"No."

He drank and set the coffee down. "But you think I owe you an explanation."

"Under the circumstances, it seems a reasonable request. Two people associated with the Customs and

Border Protection office where you work have been murdered, another crippled. A judge has been gunned down at his home and may not survive. Under the circumstances I should think you'd be eager to clarify the situation, assuming you have a legitimate explanation that will bear scrutiny."

Dixon toyed with the handle of his cup, then appeared to come to a decision. "I don't owe you a damn thing, Engler. Let's establish that from the get-go. I'm sorry about what happened to Robbins and Keeling. But senior officials and judges take their chances when they accept high-risk jobs. That includes you since you're more than you pretend to be. But Doug was just a pilot and Nita…she didn't deserve what happened to her. So I'll answer your questions to get you off my back and let you go about finding the real villain."

The playful tone was gone, superceded by anger. Dixon sat straight in his chair, folded his hands on the desktop and made unflinching eye contact with his visitor.

"I have investments in South America and the Far East," he said. "Offshore banking makes trading easier. I also pay federal and state income taxes on the income. I'm surprised your sources didn't discover that."

Sid had gotten what he could, except for the information from the IRS.

"According to my attorney and accountant," Dixon continued, "I haven't broken any laws, and I'm not on the take, if that's what you're hinting at. Do I shake down some of the sleazebags I have to deal with in my work? You betcha. I admit it. But not for money. For information."

"And favors?" Gage asked, man to man.

Dixon snorted and shook his head. "If you're referring to sex, you're barking up the wrong tree. I have too much respect for myself to blackmail some chick into doing me in the back seat of a car. I'm no saint, Engler, but I haven't sunk quite that low."

He rose from his chair and Gage realized the man was seething, though he controlled it very well. For that Gage held him in grudging respect. "Now, unless you're prepared to formally charge me with a crime, this meeting is over."

Gage climbed to his feet and started for the door, then spun around. "One other thing. What are your sources telling you about the attack on Keeling?"

"Nobody knows a damn thing," Dixon replied. "The guys who did it aren't local." He shifted to one hip. "And if your next question is who's behind the killings and everything else that's been going on—" his demeanor reverted from belligerent to professional "— I've been trying to get an answer to that since before Robbins was killed. All I can say is whoever it is has someone on the inside, someone who's privy to our plans. Someone close to the top."

The immigration officer's smile was wry. "I don't imagine I'm telling you anything headquarters hasn't already figured out, otherwise you wouldn't have been sent here to spy on us. A dirty job, but like mine, somebody has to do it." He scowled. "I'll tell you this. The very idea that one of *us* has sold out sickens me. If I had any information I thought would help you, I'd hand it over to you, and I'd help you bring the bastard down."

"Thanks." Gage held out his hand.

After a slight hesitation, Dixon accepted it. No crocodile grin, but Gage still had to wonder if he was dealing with a chameleon.

ANOTHER NONSTOP DAY. In the early morning hours they confiscated a cache of more than a hundred assault weapons being smuggled through Nogales. Whether they were associated with the terrorist threat to Fort Huachuca was not certain, but the hundred pounds of plastique they found with them suggested as much.

All that activity, however, didn't keep Jill's mind from pursuing other matters. She replayed her conversation with Nita about Gage, and Nita's complete confidence that Gage wouldn't do anything dishonorable regarding national security. Jill agreed, yet fifty million dollars' worth of cocaine had gotten by him. Why?

The more she thought about it, the more trouble she was having buying his story about flying to Douglas to check on the other eighteen-wheeler. Gage could be secretive; he could be deceptive; but he wasn't stupid. His explanation for missing the drug transfer was feasible on the surface, but it didn't hold up under close scrutiny. Why hadn't he radioed her that he wanted to check on the truck in Douglas? It was a logical move, one he must have known she would approve. Something else was going on, but what?

He worked for her in name only. She understood that now. His real boss was Brent Williams. Unfortunately, she was in the doghouse as far as the executive director was concerned. Asking Williams point-blank what was going on would earn her an admonition to mind her own business. She'd just have to approach this problem from another angle.

The following morning, a little past seven, she called Doug Vogel at the rehabilitation center in Tucson.

"Hope I didn't wake you," she said.

"Sleep I have plenty of time for. Conversations are in short supply."

His comment, whether intended to or not, made her feel guilty for not keeping in closer contact with him. "How are you doing?"

"Progress. They took the cast off my arm yesterday. At least I know two of my limbs still work." There was a note of impatience, even bitterness, in the flip reply.

"I bet that's a relief."

"It sure makes things easier. What can I do for you, Jill?"

So he knew this wasn't the casual call it should have been.

"You were spying on me when you were here, weren't you?" she said casually, as if it were an inside joke. She wanted to set the record straight, but she also knew she couldn't afford to alienate Gage's friend—her friend, she hoped—when she needed his help.

She was greeted with silence on the other end.

"For Gage," she elaborated in the same nonaccusatory tone. "That's how he knew I was here, why he was so eager to get the pilot's job."

"I didn't have you under surveillance, if that's what you mean." Doug's voice was defensive. "But yes, I was keeping him posted on how you were doing. He was concerned about you, Jill, especially after Mack's death. He was worried sick when he found out you'd been appointed the new branch chief."

"Was his assignment here your idea or his?"

"It was mine. Since he was so interested in you, I

suggested he put in for my position. A few days later I received a personal phone call from the deputy commissioner, asking how I was doing. We're not close, but we are friends. I put the bug in his ear that he ought to send someone to Tombstone because I was convinced my helicopter had been sabotaged. I specifically recommended Gage as the best man for the job. I figured a little politicking couldn't hurt. Gage didn't think his prospects of getting the assignment were very good. Tombstone isn't exactly in the same league with the high-profile cases he's been handling the past few years."

"Unless he could uncover inside corruption," she pointed out.

"He was as convinced as I was that there was something underhanded going on, but if you think he came here to spy on you, Jill, you're wrong. His primary objective was to protect you."

It made sense, Jill decided. In spite of the tension between them, Gage wouldn't have suspected her of responsibility for Mack Robbins's death. However, he *would* accept the Internal Affairs assignment as a way of keeping a close eye on her—for her safety.

"There's still the little matter of fifty million dollars' worth of narcotics getting through on his watch," she said.

"What are you talking about?"

"I guess Gage didn't tell you." She explained about the drug transfer Gage had missed.

"He wouldn't do that," Doug said. "That's not the way he operates."

"I agree, but I need—" What did she need? Verification? As if she still didn't trust Gage or her own instincts?

"I need some help with a theory I've developed, and I'm wondering if you could do something for me," she said.

"Name it."

She hung up a few minutes later, her spirits bolstered.

What drove them down again was a feeling that they were approaching the end-game, the most dangerous part of any operation.

CHAPTER TWENTY-ONE

RUBEN ORTIZ SAT in his highway patrol cruiser, radar gun at the ready, waiting for the next speeder to come flying over the peak. The grade on the other side of the rise wasn't steep enough to slow most vehicles, and the long open stretch of this rural highway was an irresistible temptation to lead-footed drivers. A small stand of salt cedars hid Ruben's position from view.

He heard the scream of an oncoming vehicle, a car rather than a truck from the sound of it, approaching at a good clip. He raised the speed gun and pointed. The readout was close to ninety for the old yellow Buick convertible—well over the posted limit. The open car careened off the main drag and shot past Ruben down the secondary road, kicking up a huge rooster tail of dust as it skidded along the inside shoulder.

Flipping on his siren and flashing lights, Ruben pulled out. His souped-up patrol car was capable of catching the offender, but safety on this narrow, poorly maintained byway was a consideration. He'd recognized the local car and the driver.

Most motorists cursed and slowed when they saw a cop in their rearview mirror. Ruben would have put this driver in that category. Not today, though. If anything, he'd accelerated. Was he drunk?

Ruben picked up his radio handset.

"This is One-Adam-One. Headed east on Twenty-two." He described the car, then added, "It's Paco Moreno."

The dispatcher, familiar with many residents in the small community, asked, "What's he doing out there?"

"Search me, but the way he's driving he's going to get himself killed."

Ruben was doing close to a hundred on the next clear stretch but slowed down when he came to a succession of winding curves that dipped and peaked through gullies and washes. Still, he was able to keep Moreno in sight without narrowing the distance between them.

At the next curve Moreno's convertible bounced high into the air and landed with a bottoming-out screech. Sparks flew from the undercarriage. The vehicle continued to hurtle forward. Reaching a tight curve to the left, Moreno yanked sharply right. The topless car catapulted over a high-banked shoulder, became airborne, landed crooked and began tumbling in a bone-crushing series of rolls.

Ruben clicked on his mike. "He's rolled. Five miles east of the junction with Highway 80. Request an ambulance, pronto."

"Any fire?"

"No. The vehicle is approximately a hundred yards off the road. Am going to assist the driver."

Ruben rocked to a halt, grabbed the first-aid kit attached under the dashboard and shoved open the car door. He raced toward the convertible, which had come to rest upside down, the frame of the windshield flattened.

Had Moreno been wearing his seat belt, he would have been crushed under the heavy vehicle, but Ruben had seen him tossed like a circus clown just before the car's last, fatal touchdown.

The man was a battered mess. Blood oozed from his ears, nose and mouth. He'd ended up on his back, his left arm pinned beneath him. A sharp, pinkish piece of bone stuck through the shoulder of his shirt.

Forcing down the bile that threatened to rise, Ruben touched the man's neck. A pulse. Then he saw the rivulet of blood seeping out of his belly.

Moreno moaned.

"Hang in there, Paco. Help is on the way."

Ruben knew better than to try to move the injured man. Doing so could easily snap whatever wasn't already broken. But he also knew he had to stanch the flow of blood from the man's gaping abdominal wound. His hands shook as he fumbled with the first-aid kit and tore open an envelope containing a large gauze pad. He applied it to the bleeding gash. It was instantly saturated. He removed the handkerchief from his hip pocket and placed it on top of the gauze.

Moreno's lashes fluttered. He looked up at Ruben.

"I'm sorry," he moaned. "I never intended…for Nita to get hurt."

Ruben's chest constricted. What had he said?

"Forgive me."

Ruben prayed he'd misunderstood. He must have. Paco could never… "You sabotaged the chopper?"

"I didn't mean it for Nita."

Ruben felt a level of rage he'd never before experienced. His muscles went rigid. His vision clouded. White-hot heat infused his bones. His respiration halted. He wanted to strike out as he'd never felt a need to pummel before.

This was the man who had killed Nita, murdered her, robbed her of life. Stolen from him the woman he loved, the woman he'd intended to make his wife, the mother of his children.

The hand that held the bandage to Moreno's belly shook.

"Don't let Tina know," the dying man begged, and a tear ran down his dirty, bruised and bleeding face. "I never wanted to hurt anybody. Tina…"

Ruben's chest rose and fell. His mind was filled with the image of his last moments with Nita before she climbed into her helicopter. The look of adoration and pride she showed in him, the soft way she put her hand to his face and said everything was going to be all right. The last sweet, impulsive kiss.

He wanted to kill this man. He could do it so easily. No one would know—except him.

"You're dying, Paco. I don't know if anyone can save you."

"Let me go. I can't live with what I've done. Please, let me die."

I wish I could, Ruben thought, *but then I'd never be able to wash your blood off my hands.*

Ruben applied as much pressure as he dared to the gushing wound. In the distance, he could hear the wail of an ambulance.

"You weren't in this alone." Ruben struggled to keep the man from bleeding out. "Tell me who is behind it all."

Moreno mumbled a name just before he fell unconscious.

GAGE WAS BACK IN HIS Jeep when his cell phone chirped. He clicked it on and held it to his ear. "Engler."

"I have something you might find interesting." Sid's tone held a note of satisfaction. "I did some discreet inquiring into Williams's background. Career bureaucrat. Nothing particularly impressive in his record. One of those guys who gets promoted because he avoids making controversial decisions and doesn't shy away from taking credit where it's due someone else. He likes to live well, too. Paid cash for a half-million-dollar home about eight years ago, buys a new Mercedes every two years, and takes pricey cruises to Alaska, the Caribbean and Europe annually."

Gage's interest was definitely piqued. "Where does he get the money?"

"Claims his wife came into an inheritance about ten years ago. Trouble is, I can't find any records to substantiate it."

"So he's dirty," Gage concluded.

"Maybe. I'm still digging. You're going to like this second piece of information even less, though."

Gage braced himself. "What do you have?"

"That raid south of Ajo on the twenty-seventh? The Feds and the locals combined forces to bust up a crack house."

"A crack house? That's it?"

"A small one at that. Customs wasn't even involved."

Gage had been set up. If he weren't driving a car, he'd kick himself. He should have smelled a rat sooner. Executive directors don't personally task pilots on the spur of the moment, even with top-secret missions. Gage slammed the heel of his hand against the steering wheel. He'd been an idiot, a stupid, blind idiot.

"Any idea who his contact is here in Tombstone?"

"Nothing obvious so far, but now that I know what I'm looking for, I should be able to come up with a name pretty soon."

"Thanks, Sid. You've been an eye-opener."

That took care of one piece of the puzzle, but there were still important pieces missing.

JILL DRESSED, fixed a cup of decaffeinated tea and toasted a bagel, which she slathered with cream cheese. She was actually hungry this morning. After cleaning up, she grabbed her handbag and headed for the door. Her cell phone chirped.

"You were right," Doug said. "I just got off the phone with Williams, bluffed him like you suggested, said I knew about his reprimanding you and asked why he hadn't told you he'd diverted Gage's flight." He snickered. "I caught him off guard. He started to demand how I knew, then realized he'd let the cat out of the bag and tried to cover up by saying he had no idea what I was talking about."

Jill blew out a pent-up breath. She'd been right. She marveled that it had taken her so long to figure out what was so obvious.

"Williams diverted Gage from the mission I gave him? Why would he do that without telling me, then hold me responsible for the disaster that resulted?"

"To cover his own ass," Doug replied. "He's a bureaucrat, Jill. At his level, secrecy and manipulation are the keys to power. Whatever mission he gave Gage, it must have been highly classified, and Gage was sworn to secrecy."

It made sense now. She pictured Gage at their meeting, his discomfort as he tried to explain not seeing a multimillion-dollar drug deal taking place under his nose. He'd been caught between two allegiances and was forced to choose the one he thought would do the least harm. Until his priorities got rearranged by her pregnancy.

"Thanks, Doug. You've been a lifesaver, more than you realize."

Gage hadn't been completely truthful, but the purpose of his deception hadn't been to protect himself. Ironically, he could have accomplished that by telling the truth. The key thing was that he hadn't been trying to undermine her. It was all backward, but somehow it made sense, too.

"Jill, I don't understand all the issues between you and Gage. They're none of my business." Doug's voice warmed. "But I do know he loves you."

She sighed. "I know that, too. Thanks again for your help. I promise to come visit you soon and fill you in on what's been going on."

"I'll hold you to that."

She clicked the off button, her mind in a whirl. A minute later morning sickness struck and she darted to the bathroom. Strange how she could be kneeling over a toilet bowl and still feel so good.

Five minutes later she shoved her cell phone into her purse and charged out the door. She was in her Taurus, heading for the office, approaching the street where the hospital was located, when she changed her plan. The one unexplained anomaly in the events of the past three months was Keeling's dismissal of the case against the drug traffickers.

She dug out her phone and called the office. Her secretary had asked for the day off, so Glenn picked up in the control center and confirmed that nothing significant had transpired overnight.

"I'm stopping by the hospital to see how Judge Keeling is doing," she told him. "I shouldn't be more than an hour."

The hospital on the outskirts of Tombstone was small and compact, little more than a clinic for emergency care and routine births. Most other medical procedures were referred to larger facilities in Tucson. The receptionist also handled private appointments for two local doctors, one of them the OB/GYN Nita had recommended.

"She has an opening next Wednesday at nine."

Jill would have preferred something sooner, but that was unrealistic. She'd tell Gage about it and see if he still wanted to come with her. Her lips twitched. He'd jump at the chance. Would he also want to know beforehand if it was going to be a boy or a girl?

"That'll be fine." She accepted an appointment card from the woman. "Now, can you tell me where I'd find Judge Keeling's room?"

He was in one of the few private rooms in the small hospital. When Jill arrived at the nurses' station, she identified herself and inquired about his condition.

"About the same," the nurse on duty told her, which didn't say much.

"Did they have to do surgery?"

She nodded. "Removed his spleen and one kidney. His liver was also nicked."

"What's the prognosis?" Jill asked, not really expecting a useful answer.

"He's in serious condition, but unless there are unforeseen complications, he should pull through. We'll be transferring him to Tucson this afternoon."

"Is he conscious?"

"He was talking this morning. Complaining." She smiled. "That's a good sign."

"Has his family been notified?"

"They called his son in California. He's due in late this afternoon. I understand he contacted the Red Cross so his brother in the army could come home on emergency leave."

"Would it be possible for me to visit the judge for a minute or two, just to let him see a familiar face?"

The nurse paged the doctor on duty. He agreed to allow her a brief visit.

An armed guard was posted outside the door. He insisted on examining her ID before allowing her to enter. The physician accompanied her, checked the monitors, pointed out the call button, paused a moment, then left when his pager emitted a low buzz.

Not a big man, Lester Keeling looked even more diminutive in the white bed, and much older than his sixty-two years.

His eyes fluttered open when she took his hand, then closed again, clearly disappointed. His reaction made her feel like a vulture standing over his body. In truth, she wasn't there to console as much as to cajole. He had information she needed, information that might lead to Nita's killer.

"Can you tell me who did this?" she asked.

He turned his head away. Did he realize by doing so he'd answered her question? The rhythm of her pulse accelerated.

"You know we'll find out," she said. "If you were in any way involved in what's been going on these past months, please tell me. I can help you set the record straight. What happened, Judge? Who did this to you? And why?"

His eyes glazed over, and for a moment she thought he might be dying. She was about to press the call button when he began to speak.

"I received a threat against Ronny a few days before the hearing."

His younger son. "What kind of threat?"

"The caller knew he was stationed in Korea, even named the unit and his job, said it would be easy for him to have an accident. He's always been good at mechanics. The army has him working on heavy machinery. A couple of months ago one of his buddies was severely injured in a work accident. The caller said Ronny's accident would be fatal if I didn't cooperate."

"Why didn't you notify the police or alert the military?"

Keeling shut his eyes, paused, then opened them again. "I wanted to, but the caller said involving the authorities would mean my son's death. He had resources in Korea ready to kill him. He also had spies in other places who would report any contact I made with the law."

"It could have been a bluff," Jill mused, more to herself than Keeling.

"I knew that," he snapped, "but I couldn't take the chance."

"Of course not," she assured him, not wanting to further agitate the sick man.

"So I talked to Victor."

"Reyes?" Jill hadn't expected that. "Why him?"

"He's a good friend. He came to me last year and alerted me that Ronny was involved…with bad companions."

"You mean, using drugs?"

Keeling grimaced. "Worse. Dealing. Victor found his name in an intelligence report and brought it to me. He recommended I get Ronny away from here. Said if he had done that with his son, Cisco might still be alive."

"Cisco was dealing?" Reyes had never mentioned that, but then why would he? And what about this intelligence report that mentioned Keeling's son? Divulging classified information to uncleared personnel, including judges, was a security violation that could have gotten Reyes fired, even charged with a federal crime. And what happened to the report? She'd never seen it. Had he destroyed it?

"Selinda doesn't know," Keeling added. "She thinks Cisco was an innocent victim."

Reyes loved Selinda. Wanting to protect his wife would be as instinctive for him as it was for Gage.

"Was Victor able to help you this time?" Jill asked.

Keeling's angular jaw flexed. "I'd hoped he'd be able to trace the call, uncover who was responsible, find out if the threat was real."

Reyes never said anything about this when they were discussing why Keeling had dismissed the charges against the drug runners at the preliminary hearing. Maybe he was trying to shield his friend. Or perhaps he was afraid disclosing the connection would lead to revealing his own little secret about Cisco. "Was he able to help you?"

Keeling shook his head. "He said the call was probably made from a disposable cell phone."

"So you decided to dismiss the charges."

"No," the judge retorted in a raised voice, then calmed. "At least, not right away. I was still trying to figure out what to do the day before the hearing when I received another phone call, reminding me what would happen if I didn't cooperate. I tried to explain that dismissing the case wouldn't work. The prosecutor would reframe the charges and present them to a grand jury. He told me not to worry about it, that he would furnish me cover—"

"In the person of the distinguished attorney, J. Clanston Parks," Jill concluded. She had been correct. The high-priced mouthpiece had been hired as a means of intimidation.

And the stratagem had worked. Debbie Sanchez had not gone to a grand jury. "You didn't recognize the voice?"

"He used some sort of distortion device. I can't even be sure it was a man."

"Why were you shot? Do you know?"

"I found out from my older son that Ronny has been transferred. He isn't in Korea anymore. I took a chance that he was safe and called the sheriff's office Tuesday afternoon. I wanted to confess, to expose this conspiracy, but he wasn't in, so I hung up. I didn't identify myself, but the deputy who answered could have recognized my voice."

A tap sounded on the door, then Victor Reyes entered the room.

"I heard you'd come here to visit my old friend," he said to Jill with a broad smile. "What have you two been talking about?"

That was when it hit her. She knew who the mole was.

CHAPTER TWENTY-TWO

GAGE CHECKED THE Jeep's dashboard clock. Nearly 9:00 a.m. He hit the speed dial on his cell phone. Jill would be in the office by now. He wanted to tell her about his conversation with Dixon and his report from Sid. Together they'd work out the last piece of the puzzle. Mostly, though, he wanted to hear her voice, weigh her mood, her attitude. She was worried about the baby. He'd promise to be there for her every step of the way. No matter what happened, he loved her.

Glenn in the control center answered the phone.

"This is Gage Engler. Let me speak to Chief Manning."

"She's not here, Mr. Engler. Called a little while ago to say she was going to the hospital to visit Judge Keeling. You can probably reach her there."

"How about Reyes?" Maybe he would have some ideas.

"Left right after she called to join her at the hospital. Said he needed to talk to her about something."

"Any idea what?"

"No, sir."

Had Reyes received a new lead on who was responsible for shooting Keeling? "Thanks."

He pressed her cell phone number. No answer, but

hospitals didn't allow electronic devices to be turned on in certain areas because they interfered with equipment. He'd catch up with her there. Perhaps the three of them could put their heads together and crack the case.

REYES'S DARK EYES hardened. "I see you've figured it out," he said to Jill.

"Figured what out?" Keeling asked.

Her heart began to pound, but she refused to back away from Reyes's bemused sneer. "That he's the person we've been looking for, the head of the Black Hand. He's responsible for the deaths of Mack Robbins and Nita Gomez."

The words took a moment to sink in, then Keeling's tone became dismissive. "That's nonsense. He can't be. He warned me about Ronny…" His quavery voice trailed off, as a new thought struck home.

"Are you saying Ronny was not dealing drugs, that it was all a lie, that my son was telling me the truth when he said he was clean?" The full horror of what he had done drained the blood from Keeling's already pasty face.

"I called him a liar. I sent him away. He hates me, and now you're telling me it was all unnecessary?" Keeling shouted. "You son of a—" He clutched a hand to his chest, stiffened and emitted a groan of pain.

Monitors started beeping and chirping. Within seconds the door flew open. A nurse and orderly charged into the room and bulldozed their way to the side of the stricken patient.

"Code blue," the nurse shouted.

Reyes clamped a hand around Jill's elbow and drew

her out of the room as other people stormed in. She felt something being pressed to her side. A gun.

"Come with me if you want to live," he whispered into her ear.

GAGE SHOT INTO the hospital parking lot, saw Jill's car near the emergency room entrance and pulled up beside it. No sign of her, so he headed into the building.

A nurse was directing traffic as an orderly pushed a piece of equipment down the corridor toward where a guard was stationed.

Gage flashed his badge. "What's going on?"

She glanced at the shield without looking at him. "Judge Keeling suffered a myocardial infarction." A heart attack.

Gage strode toward the commotion, expecting to see Jill, but she wasn't in the crowded room or the hallway.

"Is Chief Manning here?" At the sentry's blank expression, Gage again showed him his badge. "The woman who runs the Customs office."

"Oh, her. She left about twenty minutes ago with a guy. Can't remember his name. Hispanic. Heavyset—"

"Victor Reyes?" Gage offered.

"That's it. Got here just about the time the judge's monitor went bonkers."

"Do you know where they went?" Perhaps the medical staff had sent them to a waiting room or lounge to get them out of the way.

"Took the emergency-room exit at the end of the hall. With everybody running around, it was the easiest way out—"

Gage hightailed it down the corridor. The E.R. was at one end of the parking lot. From there he could see Jill's Taurus and his Jeep, but not Reyes's vehicle.

Snapping open his cell phone, he punched in both their private numbers. Neither answered.

He speed-dialed the office.

"Have the chief and Reyes come back yet?" he asked Glenn.

"No, sir. I guess they're still at the hospital."

The sixth sense that had served him so well in the past had Gage's nerve endings tingling.

Something was wrong. Very wrong. If Jill was here when Keeling had his heart attack, why did she run off so fast? Had Reyes given her information she had to act on immediately? Another narcotics shipment coming through? Then why didn't she go directly to her office, or at least call in? Why hadn't she issued an alert? And where had Reyes gotten his information?

"I'm calling from the hospital," he said into the phone. "They left here twenty minutes ago."

"Maybe they stopped off someplace."

Where?

A gurney came crashing through the wide swinging door, pushed by a young man in green scrubs.

"The air evac is standing by," announced another man, a doctor by the looks of his white coat, who ran after the gurney. "Our main job will be to stabilize him."

"What's up?" Gage asked the orderly closest to him.

"Car accident victim coming in. Rolled his convertible in the desert. Turned right when he should have turned left at about a hundred miles an hour."

"Ouch. Teenager?"

"No. Guy works in Customs."

A bell went off. "You know the man's name?"

"Moreno, I think they said."

"Paco Moreno?"

In the distance Gage could hear the piercing two-tone warble of an ambulance approaching.

JILL WAS DRIVING the Suburban. Reyes had insisted on sitting in the passenger seat beside her. She toyed with notions of escaping, but it was a fantasy, at least for now. He had a gun pointed at her. This man who'd caused the deaths of at least two people, including an innocent young woman, wouldn't hesitate to shoot her.

"I miscalculated with you," Reyes said. "When I told Williams to give you the branch chief job—"

"You told him?" She'd suspected a mole in the organization, not a conspiracy involving the upper echelons of the Customs Service. It made sense, though.

"I figured you'd be easier to manipulate than Robbins."

"Sorry to disappoint you." Following directions, she turned right at the next intersection. "You've been manufacturing intelligence reports."

He snorted. "It isn't hard to do. Put words in the proper format on the right kind of paper and people take it at face value. I'm the expert. Who's going to question me? Turn left."

She followed instructions and briefly considered yanking on the wheel to throw him against the door, but he would recover faster than she could wrestle the gun from him. There'd be other opportunities. "Mack Robbins got suspicious, didn't he? That's why you killed him."

"I had no choice. He figured out why all his busts against the Black Hand were going south. I couldn't let him expose me."

"Who did your dirty work? Who sabotaged the chopper?"

He paused a moment. "Moreno. He needs money for his daughter."

Jill's jaw dropped. She would have suspected almost anyone else in the maintenance shop. Moreno had a perfect record, was well respected, a devoted family man. But, she reflected, he also had a child who would die if she didn't get a heart transplant, and that cost money. A lot of it.

Reyes chuckled. "Dixon thinks he has contacts. I have more, and better ones. About a year ago I found out Moreno was playing around with a woman in Sierra Vista. That made him a government security risk, which meant he could lose his job and with it his medical coverage. I eased him into helping me on some innocuous jobs. Then I upped the ante. I paid him handsomely for sabotaging Robbins's chopper, enough to finally get Tina on the waiting list for the operation. He really balked the second time—"

"When you tried to kill me, but injured Gage instead."

Reyes shrugged. "Take the next right to the hacienda. He threatened to go to the police. I reminded him he'd killed a federal official. The best he could hope for was life in prison. They wouldn't even let him out for his little girl's funeral."

Jill shuddered at the cold, calculating cruelty of using a father's love for his dying child to turn him into a monster. How could she have worked with this man every day and never suspected the evil in him?

"The investigators said the explosive on Nita's helicopter was remotely controlled. You pushed the button, didn't you? How could you kill her?" Jill asked, heartsick at the memory of her friend. "You said you waved to her, or was that another lie?"

For the first time Reyes showed uneasiness. "I couldn't let her return to base. The explosives would have been found with Moreno's fingerprints all over them. He's so guilt-ridden, he'd cave under questioning." He glared at Jill. "She'd still be alive if Engler had flown like I asked him to."

Was her nausea another bout of morning sickness or revulsion for this man she'd liked and trusted? Maybe she could distract him by barfing all over him.

"You made two attempts on Engler's life. Why was it so important to kill him?" she inquired. She should have caught on when he'd specifically asked Gage to pick him up at the hacienda, but she'd been so distracted by what was going on between the two of them. Gage was so prominent in her mind that hearing his name had seemed perfectly natural.

"He was on to Williams," Reyes explained, "or would have been soon enough. When he went to Tucson and threatened Williams if he didn't back off on your reprimand, Williams got scared. He knew it was only a matter of time before Engler put all the pieces together."

Jill had missed something. "Gage threatened Williams? With what? I don't understand."

"That's right. You don't know about the mission diversion." Her bafflement must have shown on her face, because he chuckled. "Williams radioed Engler while he was monitoring the rig at the rest stop and sent him off on a top-secret wild-goose chase. That's how we got the five hundred keys through. When Engler found out Williams was putting a written reprimand in your file, he caught up with Williams in Tucson that evening and threatened to blow the whistle on the flight diversion if Williams didn't back off."

"Gage did that?" Her mind was spinning. Thanks to Doug, she knew there had been a diversion. She didn't know it had been bogus, and she certainly hadn't known Gage had confronted the executive director. He had been willing to compromise his own career to save hers.

They'd reached the hacienda gate. She drove through. Ahead lay the picturesque Spanish-style house, the classic symbol of a proud culture. *Mi casa es su casa.*

"Where's Selinda?" Was she involved in all this?

"I sent her into town to run some errands. By the time she returns we'll be long gone."

"You're abandoning her?"

His face darkened and his grip on the gun tightened. For a moment Jill was afraid he was going to pull the trigger.

"I've left her well provided for," he said. "Park beside the garage. Don't block the door."

She complied, her thoughts on Selinda and what the proud woman would suffer when she learned of her adoring husband's malevolence.

"Get on your cell phone," he ordered her, "and call Engler."

The knot in Jill's stomach tightened. She knew where they were headed. The question was whether they would ever come back.

As the ambulance pulled under the emergency entrance canopy, Gage punched in Dixon's cell phone number.

"I have a question for you. Was Paco Moreno your source for the motorcycle bust that went south?"

Hesitation.

"This is important, Dixon. Moreno's just been in a serious automobile accident." Behind him, someone rattled off, "Massive hemorrhage. Heart rate tacky. He's shutting down."

"He may not live," Gage said.

Another beat. "Yeah, it was him. What's going—"

It made sense now. Moreno needed money for his daughter's heart transplant, and he was in a perfect position to sabotage the choppers.

"Thanks. I appreciate your help." He had no sooner disconnected when his cell phone warbled. "Engler."

"Gage, this is Jill. I—"

"Are you okay? I went to the hospital, but—"

"I need you to fly the chopper down to the Reyes hacienda right away."

"It's grounded, remember?"

"I'm lifting the restriction. This is a special mission. Something hot." She sounded tense, anxious. "Victor has a lead on the head of the Black Hand. I need you here to pick us up immediately."

"Okay, I'm on my way, but—"

The connection went dead.

Gage stepped on the accelerator at the same time he punched in more numbers on his cell phone. "Is the chopper ready?"

Ralph Higgins sounded hopeful. "We're not grounded anymore?"

"No. Do—"

"Good. I'm tired of sitting around. We've checked over that bird so many times—"

Gage cut him off. "Do the preflight. I'll be there in seven minutes. I want to lift off as soon as I jump aboard."

"Okay, but what's—"

Gage disconnected and made one more phone call. His tires squealed as he skidded around the next turn. By the time his Jeep screeched to a halt on the tarmac, the blades of the helicopter were spinning. Bradley was standing in the doorway of the aircraft.

Gage sprinted aboard and scrambled up to the pilot's seat. Fifteen seconds later they were airborne.

"What are you doing here?" he asked Fritz over the intercom.

"Heard Ortiz call in Moreno's car crash on the police radio. Sounded like the guy intentionally wiped out. I came by to talk to you about what it means, then you called Higgins. I'm not sure what's going on, but I thought you could use some help."

"Where are we going?" Higgins asked.

"The Reyes's hacienda. Jill is there with Victor."

"What's she doing there?" Bradley asked.

"Reyes is our man," Gage said. "He's holding her hostage."

"Holy sh—" Higgins started.

"What are you going to do?" Bradley interrupted.

"I assume he wants to bargain. Probably her life for his getaway."

A new voice broke in on the broadcast channel. Reyes's. "Engler, land your helicopter on the east side of the house if you want to see your wife alive again."

Bradley and Higgins both looked at him.

"Ex-wife," Gage clarified via intercom. "Let her go, Reyes," he said over the air. "Nothing will be gained by harming her."

"Do as I say. Land or she dies."

He'd killed Nita, a young woman he'd treated like a daughter. Gage had no doubt he'd kill Jill, too.

CHAPTER TWENTY-THREE

"I'M LANDING," Gage acknowledged.

"How do you want to handle this?" Fritz asked.

"I called for backup from my car, but we probably haven't got time to wait for them to show up," Gage said. "There are rifles in the back, and you have your sidearms. You and Ralph jump out as soon as I touch down inside the compound. You two make a break for the adobe wall. I'll try to negotiate— Oh, no."

Fritz, who was removing the rifles from the rack, peered out the window and muttered an obscenity. A highway patrol car was charging toward the residence, a huge cloud of dust in its wake.

"Ruben," Fritz said, recognizing the number painted on the vehicle roof. "What's he doing here?"

"Moreno must have confessed to him." Gage noted Reyes's Suburban parked by the garage. There was no sign of the intelligence officer or the branch chief.

The green-and-white cruiser lurched to a stop at the wall.

"Now what?" Fritz asked.

"Join Ortiz and see if you can keep him in check. The last thing we need is him provoking Reyes."

"Will Reyes kill her, do you think?" Higgins asked, his hands clasping an assault rifle.

"Only when she's served her purpose." Gage had planned to deploy the two men around the house, using the wall as cover. He hadn't counted on Ortiz showing up. The hothead could ruin everything. For the moment it was more important to keep him contained. "Reyes needs Jill alive to convince me to fly him out of here. At least, that's what I imagine his plan is."

"Where to? Aerostat surveillance will follow wherever you take him," Higgins pointed out.

"Mexico. He's undoubtedly greased enough palms down there to make himself untouchable by U.S. authorities."

Gage set down the chopper with the door facing away from the house, giving his two companions cover to exit. Making Reyes walk around the aircraft to board it might also give them an advantage.

"Should we shut down?" Higgins asked.

"Yes. We need to delay things as much as possible to give reinforcements time to arrive."

"Keep the engine going," Reyes's voice crackled over the radio a second later. He'd obviously anticipated the delaying tactic. Gage nodded to Higgins to comply.

"If you want to see your woman alive," Reyes warned, "you'll do exactly as I say."

"You harm her," Gage radioed back, "and you're a dead man."

"We're coming out, and you're flying us where I tell you."

"She's pregnant, Reyes. Without her and my baby, I have no reason to live. If anything happens to her, I'll kill you if I have to die in the process."

"Tell your friends to hold their fire," was Reyes's only reply.

Gage leaped out of the chopper behind Higgins and Bradley. Once they were clear of the helicopter, Reyes came out of the front door of the house, using Jill as a shield, a gun pressed to her temple.

Just then Ortiz jumped up from behind the low wall. "You're not going anywhere," he screamed, and unloaded the entire magazine of his assault rifle into the engine compartment of the helicopter. The engine stalled, the blades slowed. Oil dribbled down the side of the fuselage. The sweat that had been beading on the back of Gage's neck ran down his spine in cold rivulets.

REYES HELD JILL in an arm lock. She'd tried earlier to kick him, but all she'd gotten for it was a cuff across the back of the head, hard enough to make her ears ring. Now she felt the man's sweaty grip tighten. Her shoulder ached from the pressure. He was becoming more desperate. How long would it be before he lost his patience and killed her?

Until now she'd been able to hope he might keep his word and release her if Gage complied with his wishes. Ruben had made that impossible.

"Let me go," she implored, straining to sound convincing rather than terrified. "You'll have greater freedom of movement without me. We won't follow if you cross the border alone. If you take me, our forces have the right to follow in hot pursuit. You know the rules, Victor. Gage will never stop until he's found me." Fright warred with her utter confidence that the father of her baby wouldn't stop until he rescued her. "Your only chance of escape is without me."

Reyes started dragging her to the other end of the sprawling ranch house, toward the garage.

"Where are you taking me?" she asked.

"To the caliche pit."

Her head shot up and her knees weakened. Was he planning to kill her there? Then the answer stuck her. "You have a tunnel to the other side."

He grunted and must have hit a remote control she couldn't see, because the garage door rolled up, revealing an off-road vehicle. He was shoving her toward it when they heard a car approaching. As one, they turned to see Selinda drive past the crippled helicopter and stop a dozen yards away.

Jumping out of the Isuzu Rodeo, she ran toward them. "Victor—" She stared, confused.

"Go inside, Selinda," he shouted in Spanish. "Do as I say. Now. At once."

She halted and gaped at Jill in her husband's clutches. "What's going on?"

"Don't ask any questions. Just go in the house. This doesn't concern you."

Suddenly, Ruben leveled his rifle at the woman. "Release Chief Manning, Reyes, and drop your gun," he shouted, "or your wife dies."

"Victor?" She looked bewildered.

Gage and Fritz closed in on the highway patrolman.

"Stay away," Ruben warned them, "or I'll kill her. Then I'll kill Reyes. Nita's murderer is not leaving here alive."

"What is he talking about, Victor?" Selinda asked.

"It's all a mistake, a mix-up. Go inside."

"He's the head of the Black Hand," Ruben called out. "He's a drug dealer. He killed the branch chief. He killed my Nita."

"Victor?" She stared at him.

"It was an accident. I had no choice—"

Jill saw confusion and terror widen the other woman's dark eyes, then awareness transform her fear into blazing rage.

"Ruben," Jill called out. "Don't do this. It isn't what Nita would want. Killing innocent people won't bring her back. You owe it to her memory to do the right thing, the honorable thing, what she would have expected from you."

"He killed her," he screamed, his voice choked with emotion.

"He'll pay for her death," Jill assured him. "Please, let's end the bloodshed."

Selinda's breathing was labored. Jill could see she was fighting for control. "You killed Nita? Why, Victor?" She swayed on her feet. "*Madre de Dios,* you killed Cisco, too."

"Smugglers did it, Selinda. I told you."

She staggered over to the garden bench a few yards away and wilted onto it. Ruben tracked her with his rifle.

"Now they will kill me and you." She rocked her head from side to side. Her beautiful face showed no fear now, only infinite sadness. "I don't mind dying, Victor. Not now. If it is true that you killed Nita and took Francisco away from me, I have nothing left to live for. You've robbed me of my pride, my honor, my son. You've brought shame to our family. He was a good boy until you corrupted him. You killed him, whether or not you pulled the trigger."

Reyes's hold slackened, but not enough for Jill to maneuver her way out of it.

"Victor, let's make a deal. You release me in exchange for Ruben letting Selinda go. I know you love her and that you don't want anything to happen to her. Let's end this. Please."

When he didn't reject her proposal outright, she began to hope. He was evil, but he wasn't insane. He understood there was no way he could get out of this alive, no matter how many other people died.

"Ruben," she called out. Reyes tightened his grip, but he was no longer trying to hurt her. "Ruben, Victor will let me go if you promise not to hurt Selinda."

There was a long pause while Gage conferred with the highway patrolman. Jill could imagine what Gage was saying. *Make the deal. Reyes can't possibly escape. Once Jill is safe, we can move on him.*

"I want to hear it from his mouth," Ruben yelled back.

Jill turned her head and saw fear in Reyes's eyes, smelled it in his sweat. But she also sensed defeat. He knew things had come to an end. Like the eighteen-wheelers on the narrow desert road, there was no room for him to turn back. "Tell him you agree, Victor. Otherwise he'll shoot Selinda. You don't want that on your conscience."

"How do I know he won't kill me?"

"Ruben isn't a killer. He could have shot you and Selinda already, but he didn't. He doesn't want to hurt anyone. Not even you." Jill prayed she was right.

Reyes's voice fell into despair. "Leave Selinda alone," he called out. "I'm letting Manning go."

"Do it," Ruben demanded, the barrel of his rifle never wavering.

Slowly, Reyes relaxed his grip. But instead of darting away, Jill stepped forward out of his grasp, shielding him from Ruben's line of fire.

"I'm all right," she announced, her hands up, her voice tense. "Don't shoot."

She half expected Victor to make a run for it. The others would open fire and he would be dead. But he didn't. She turned her head enough to see him toss the gun into the flower bed along the path.

What she hadn't anticipated was Selinda running over and snatching it up. She held the weapon with both hands and pointed it at her husband.

"I thought we had a good life together," she said. "We could have gone into old age with pride and dignity, surrounded by loving children and grandchildren. Now I must forever hang my head in shame because you have disgraced us."

Jill froze. She glanced over and saw that, true to his word, Ruben had lowered his rifle.

"You deserve to die," Selinda said. "All I have to do is pull this trigger. You taught me how to shoot. Remember, Victor? Hold steady and just squeeze the trigger. Isn't that what you told me?"

Her finger tightened.

"Selinda," Victor implored. "I'm sorry."

She held the weapon steady as she pointed it at her husband. The report echoed off the front of the house. Jill stared as the older woman dropped the gun and walked calmly back to the bench by the door, where she sank down and wept.

Victor lay crumpled on the ground.

GAGE HELD JILL in his arms.

"Did he hurt you?" He ran his hands along her back, not sure if the trembling he felt was hers or his.

She clung to him, the woman he loved, the woman who carried his child inside her. He could feel her heart racing.

"He acted tough," she muttered, "but all along I had the feeling he was looking for a way out, a way to end it all. He's a regular Jekyll and Hyde, Gage. He did horrible things, yet I can't believe the good things he did were insincere."

Gage tightened his embrace, nuzzled her neck. "All that matters is that you're safe now. It's over."

"We have to talk. He told me—" She became aware of eyes on them and pulled away. "How is she?" she asked Bradley, who was standing over Victor. At the last moment Selinda had fired above her husband's head. The man had collapsed in shock.

"Ruben is with her." Higgins nodded to the garden bench. The trooper was on his knees in front of her, his head bowed. She had her hand on his cheek the way a mother would console a frightened child. "He's begging her forgiveness."

"He would never have shot her," Jill insisted.

"No," Higgins agreed, "but he's ashamed of having used a woman that way."

Jill smiled. "I'd say she's pardoned him."

"The sheriff's department is on its way," Bradley announced.

Gage approached Reyes, who was sitting on the ground, his hands cuffed behind his back.

"What I want to know is why," he said.

"She's right. I've destroyed my family, my honor, my life," Reyes muttered. "Secrets aren't important anymore."

The story that emerged was a tale of bitterness, greed

and tragedy. Selinda came from one of the old, noble
Spanish families who had once owned immense tracts
of land on both sides of the border that now separated
Mexico from the United States. Victor, in contrast, was
of mixed heritage from the lowest peasant class. His af-
fair with Selinda in college had nearly cost him his
manhood when her father found out about it, but Selinda had threatened to kill herself if she wasn't allowed
to marry him. The matter was resolved when he signed
a prenuptial agreement in which he gave up any claim
to Peralta land and wealth for himself or his children.
Even the hacienda, given in a deed of trust, would re-
vert to her family when she died.

During his adolescent years in northern Mexico,
Reyes had been a mule in the drug trade to help support his impoverished family. When he fell in love with
Selinda, he thought he had found a way out of the business—until her family severed their ties with her and
he realized the land she'd received as a grudging dowry
was as much a curse as a blessing. They couldn't sell
it or borrow money on it. Making it productive as a
ranch meant a heavy investment in livestock and equipment, neither of which he could afford, and the long-
neglected house was a money pit.

Rather than see his wife ground down by the kind
of crushing poverty his mother had had to endure, he'd
become more deeply involved in drug trafficking after
his marriage.

Latching onto an intelligence job with the Customs
Service had allowed him to manipulate both sides of the
narcotics trade. Eventually he'd taken over the Black
Hand cartel. To explain the large quantities of money
he was accumulating, he told Selinda he had invested

in the stock market. Having come from a sheltered environment, she believed him. Their friends assumed he was living high off his wife's money. The insult intensified his hunger for power.

Above all, he wanted respectability. His elder son showed promise as a classical musician. Victor took great pride in his achievements. His daughter married well and moved away, to Selinda's great sorrow. That left the youngest, Francisco.

Gregarious and cheerful, Cisco wasn't an intellectual like his big brother, but he was smart and inquisitive. He spied on his father and figured out what he was doing. At first Victor claimed he was working undercover, but the streetwise teenager wasn't fooled. Instead of turning his old man in to the authorities, he'd threatened to reveal the dirty secret to Selinda.

For all his vanity and ambition, Reyes truly loved his wife. The thought of being disgraced in her eyes was unbearable. Reluctantly he'd let his son in on the business.

The boy turned out to be more cold-blooded than his father had ever imagined—so ruthless, in fact, that Victor began to fear him. Cisco had been transporting illegal aliens across the border through the tunnel that terminated at the caliche pit. The night he was killed, he'd gone there to shake down the latest group, when one of them pulled a gun and executed him. Apparently, Cisco had left the guy's cousin out in the desert to die when the man had failed to come up with the additional fee Cisco had demanded for smuggling him in.

Because Victor hadn't wanted the authorities to know about the tunnel, he'd relocated his son's body to the border fence and made it appear as if he'd been shot from the Mexican side, knowing an effective follow-up investigation was unlikely.

Jill sagged against Gage, tears stinging her eyes. She glanced over at Selinda. Ruben was sitting next to her now; they were talking quietly. Did she ever have any notion of the monster she'd married?

And what about Moreno's wife and daughter? What agony would they suffer when they learned the man they'd been counting on had turned into a murderer? Would Tina ever get her new heart? How would she handle it, knowing the price so many innocent people had paid for it?

After the sheriff took Reyes away, Ruben's supervisor showed up and relieved him of duty. An administrative review was standard procedure when an officer discharged a firearm. In this case, he had unloaded it into a government helicopter. The investigation would be intense, and there was a good chance Ruben would face disciplinary action. To his credit, he volunteered his sidearm before it was even requested.

Selinda called a friend, who came and picked her up after her husband was placed under arrest and driven away. Because the house was a crime scene, she was permitted to take only a few personal items with her. Dry-eyed, the woman bore with grace and dignity the humiliation of having them scrutinized.

A few minutes later, Gage and Jill drove back to the Customs station in his Jeep.

"Why didn't you tell me Williams diverted you from surveillance of the rig at the rest stop?" she asked from the passenger seat.

He ran his fingers through his hair and concentrated

on the road. "Aside from the fact that I couldn't because it was classified, would you have believed me if I had?"

She had to admit he had a point. Under the circumstances, she probably would have regarded it as an excuse. "Maybe not," she admitted, "but that would have been my fault, not yours. How can I ever trust you, Gage, when you repeatedly deceived me with half-truths and in this case an outright lie?"

Chastised, he took a ragged breath and stared straight ahead. "How did you find out?"

"After I calmed down, I realized your explanation didn't make sense, so I had Doug do some checking for me."

"I'm sorry, Jill. I thought I was doing the right thing."

"I learned a couple of other things today from Victor. Did you know the mission you were sent on was phony?"

"I found out about it just before I got here. Williams told me it was an Al Qaeda summit. In fact, it was a bust at a crack house."

"I also understand you went up to Tucson and confronted Williams, made him back off on giving me a reprimand," she said.

"I couldn't let you take the blame for what I had done."

"You threatened to expose him. Would you really have sacrificed your career for me?"

He didn't hesitate. "Yes."

She shook her head. "I don't understand you."

"It's not very complicated, Jill. I love you. I'll do whatever it takes to help and protect you."

They arrived at the station. The first order of business was a secure telephone call to the commissioner's office. Together Gage and Jill delivered a verbal report on the situation and reported Brent Williams's involvement in the elaborate drug-dealing conspiracy. Sid phoned Gage later to tell him Williams had been escorted from his office under heavy guard.

Jill called a special meeting of the entire staff in the conference room and explained what she could of the day's events. They already knew Moreno was dead. Now they understood why and the role Reyes had played in the station's misfortunes. She also cautioned the shocked audience not to discuss the case outside the station and definitely not with members of the media. All questions were to be referred to the public affairs office.

From there, she and Gage drove to the district attorney's office in Tucson, where they made formal written statements recounting the day's events. It only made sense to stop by on the way home to fill Doug in on all the gory details.

It was nearly midnight by the time they arrived back in Tombstone.

"Ready for dessert?" Gage asked. They had shared a meal with Doug at the rehab center, but that had been hours ago. With both arms free, Doug was now able to wheel himself around and was in good spirits. They'd stayed longer than they'd intended, reminiscing and laughing. "I have pineapple sherbet and chocolate sauce."

He'd stocked the treats right after she'd told him she was pregnant. The combination had been her favorite when she'd been carrying Rickie. He reached over, clasped her hand and gave her a grin.

Fifteen minutes later he pulled up in front of his

apartment house. They went through the bedroom to the balcony, stopping in the kitchen just long enough for him to serve up dessert. Stars filled the sky, a twinkling blanket of shiny crystals.

They ate in silence, each lost in thought. Gage put his bowl down beside his chair, climbed to his feet and stood at the railing.

"I'm tired of the lies and deception," he said. "I want to move on, do something else." He turned to face her. "I've been giving some thought to starting a helicopter charter service and asking Doug to join me, as a pilot, if he's able to fly again, or as a dispatcher and business manager if he can't. I haven't talked to him about it yet, and he may not go along with it—"

"You mean it?" This man was still able to surprise her.

"Marry me, Jill." He placed his hands on her shoulders. "I'll get this business on its feet, and you can return to the Customs Service after your maternity leave, if that's what you want. They need good branch chiefs, and you're the best."

She threw her arms around his neck. "I love you, Gage Engler. I should never have let you go."

He chuckled. "I tried to tell you that." His mouth found hers. He deepened the kiss and felt her respond, pressing her body to his. He led her into his dark bedroom. Before they began the ritual of undressing each other, he switched on the lamp by the bed.

"I want to see you," he murmured as he nuzzled the crook of her neck.

She squirmed with delight, then let out a cry.

He stopped. "What—"

"The toy box," she exclaimed. "You finished it."

She separated herself from him. He followed her to the corner where the chest sat, its satiny finish gleaming in the dim light. "I figured it was time."

"Oh, Gage, it's beautiful." Tears threatened when she gazed up at him, her arms circling his waist. "I love you. I always have. I always will."

ON THE DAY Victor Reyes was indicted for murder, drug trafficking, racketeering and a long list of other offenses, Selinda Peralta-Rodriguez Reyes returned to *La Hacienda Dolosa* for the first time since his arrest. Her daughter by her side, she walked slowly through the rooms, her mind conjuring up images of the events that had filled the nearly thirty years since she'd come here as a bride. The births of her children. Their first communions and confirmations. The wedding of her daughter. So many holiday parties and family celebrations. Happy memories she had stored away for her old age, memories forever tarnished by the man who had made their life together a fraud.

She'd loved this place, this home where she had spent most of her life and where she'd expected to die. But she was already dead. Victor had killed the life in her as truly as if he had stabbed her through the heart with a knife.

The government had confiscated the vast quantities of cash and possessions Victor had accumulated over the years. This house alone was left because he didn't own it. But then, under the harsh terms her father had exacted, neither did she. The only thing she'd brought with her from Mexico, her heirloom jewelry, she'd sold, and given the money to the Moreno family. Selinda was now destitute.

She marched to a painting on the wall, swung the frame out on its hinges to reveal a safe, and dialed the combination. Reaching inside, she removed a thick, yellowed folder and carried it to the writing table in front of the window overlooking her beloved garden, overgrown now with weeds. From the table's center drawer she extracted a single piece of vellum paper with the hacienda's letterhead. Using an old-fashioned fountain pen, she wrote in her beautiful, flowing script.

To the Family Peralta: Herewith enclosed is the deed of trust to *La Hacienda Dolosa*. I return it to the proud family of my birth with a curse that whoever inhabits this land shall gain enormous wealth at the cost of what is most dear.

With steady fingers she signed her formal name, slipped the letter and the legal document into a large preaddressed envelope, licked the flap and sealed it with hot wax. She rose with it in her hand.

"There is nothing more for us here," she said to her daughter. "Let us be on our way."

She walked out the door, not even bothering to close it behind her.

EPILOGUE

One year later

WHEN THE DOORBELL RANG, Jill was in the bedroom nursing her daughter. Doug was in the kitchen slicing hard-cooked eggs to top the potato salad she'd made.

"I'll get it," Gage called out from the living room where he was cueing up CDs. He threw the door open wide. "Hi, Kim, kids. I'm glad you could all make it."

Kim Oliver and her three children stepped into the spacious living room.

"What's this?" Gage asked, eyeing a festively wrapped present one of the kids was carrying.

"I know you said no gifts for your anniversary," Kim said. "This is for the baby."

"You're going to spoil her," he complained without an ounce of sincerity.

"Yeah, right." Kim laughed and deposited the gift in the toy box by the fireplace.

Jill appeared in the bedroom door, the baby in her arms.

"Can I hold her?" begged Kim's sixteen-year-old daughter. "P-l-e-a-s-e?"

While the teenager sat on the couch with the infant cradled in her arms, the sound of an approaching motorcycle drew the others to the patio. Fritz Bradley pulled up the driveway, stopped in front of the detached garage behind the house and climbed off his Harley. After waving a greeting, he dug into a saddlebag and produced a gift-wrapped package.

"This isn't for you," he said. "Lead me to the toy box. Then I'm ready for a cold one."

He added his contribution to the collection, and Gage handed him a frosty root beer.

Ruben Ortiz arrived a few minutes later, clutching a red-velvet bag with a gold drawstring, which he, too, set in the toy box.

Honoring Nita's wish that he get help, Ruben had been seeing a counselor for several months, while claiming it was a complete waste of time. He wasn't dating, though he admitted to going to lunch a couple of times with Crystal, the bar waitress who'd driven him home the night of Nita's death.

"Hey, Ruben," Fritz called out, "what's this I hear about you planning to quit the highway patrol?"

He shrugged. "Just talk."

Serious talk, from what Jill had heard. She sensed a kind of wanderlust in the handsome bachelor, a need to get away from familiar surroundings and explore new opportunities. It would probably do him good.

Over the next hour all the pilots and flight mechanics showed up, except the ones stuck with weekend duty. Those who were married came with their wives and kids with them. Several of the single people brought dates. Fortunately, the house Gage and Jill had bought on the outskirts of Tombstone was on an acre of land.

The last to arrive was Pratt Dixon. Despite their earlier rocky relationship, Jill and Pratt had "connected" after Reyes's arrest and the death of Paco Moreno. On her recommendation, Dixon was appointed acting branch chief when she began her maternity leave. There was talk now of his being reassigned to a permanent post as chief at another Customs station.

"Are Ellen Moreno and her kids coming over?" Kim asked.

"I invited them," Jill replied, "and Ellen sent a present, but they had already made plans to visit her mother and brother in Flagstaff this weekend. I think they're considering moving up there."

"That might be the best thing for them," Gage said.

Thanks to Reyes's pleading guilty to all charges against him and thus avoiding a public trial, the extent of Paco's involvement in the deaths of Mack Robbins and Nita Gomez was never fully disclosed. Sparing the dead flight mechanic's family was probably the one thing Reyes did right. Ellen, Paco's wife, had been informed, but she kept it from her children, especially Tina. The fourteen-year-old had undergone a heart transplant two months after her father's death and was doing well.

"I heard Brent Williams was sentenced to life in prison the other day," the husband of the new intelligence officer commented.

"Convicted on all charges," Gage confirmed. "Racketeering, drug dealing, conspiracy and accessory to two counts of murder and one of attempted murder."

"Is it true," asked the wife of one of the pilots, "that Reyes is in permanent solitary confinement?"

The former intelligence officer had been given a life sentence without the possibility of parole. His wife and children never visited or communicated with him. He'd also agreed to be a government witness against other drug lords and was helping to dismantle the cartel he'd been instrumental in creating.

"Technically he's being protected," Bradley explained. "As a snitch, he wouldn't last very long in the general prison population."

"Hey, folks, not everything this year has been bad," Gage pointed out. "Doug will be recertified as a helicopter pilot in a few months."

Hearty congratulations were extended.

Doug had gradually recovered sensation in his lower extremities and was again walking, though with a slight hitch in his stride. He took physical therapy three times a week and hoped to be declared physically fit to fly soon. In the meantime, he was working as the dispatcher and business manager of the fledgling charter service he and Gage had started after Gage resigned from the Customs Service. Neither of them was getting rich, but they were getting by.

"Let's not forget the best news of all this past year," Doug announced as he took the baby from Jill. "My goddaughter."

Gage smiled. "For a confirmed bachelor, you seem to have discovered a soft spot for kids."

"Just this one," his friend insisted. "When are you going to open her presents?"

"I believe you're more excited about them than Annie is." Jill gazed at her sleeping daughter. "In fact, I know you are."

Doug had the grace to blush.

"He's right," Gage said in a vain attempt to help out his buddy. "Let's open them."

An hour later the toy box resembled a treasure chest. Colorful ribbons and beaded necklaces festooned the edge of the box, while clothes and a cashmere-soft pink blanket hung on the opened lid. Inside sat a tea set, a Cinderella doll in a gold-and-white gown, noisy pull-toys and sets of blocks, bricks and logs. Propped against the front were a doll in a yellow dress, a multicolored rag doll and a pair of hand puppets. Shiny and femininely patterned paper littered the floor.

"Jill, when are you going back to work?" a pilot's wife asked a few minutes later.

"I don't know," she admitted. She'd been granted a leave of absence after her maternity leave ran out. She wanted to spend more time with her baby and her husband. "I've been holding down the office here when Doug goes to therapy, and I'm considering taking over the job after he returns to the cockpit."

"That decision is still a couple of months off," Gage said. He gazed at his wife. "And it'll be up to Jill."

A little while later Gage followed his wife into the nursery, where she'd gone to check on the baby. He looked down at his tiny daughter and ran the side of his forefinger along her chubby cheek. Still touching the infant, he gazed at Jill. "I love you."

She smiled.

"I just thought I'd remind you."

In fact, he'd said those very words only a few hours earlier, when they'd made love just before their guests arrived.

They'd been married in a small ceremony with Doug as best man and Kim as maid of honor. Seven months later Jill gave birth to a healthy, blue-eyed girl. They named her Anita, after Nita Gomez, but they called her

Annie. Jill's new obstetrician saw no reason Jill couldn't have more children.

She raised her hand and touched Gage's face. "I love you, too." She kissed him on the lips. "Now why don't you go back to our guests, while I nurse Annie?"

"I'd rather stay here with you."

"Gage…" She pushed him playfully away.

"Okay, I'll go. But later…"

She grinned at him. "Definitely later."

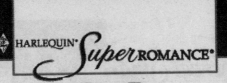

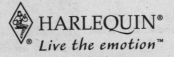

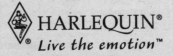

If you enjoyed what you just read,
then we've got an offer you can't resist!

Take 2 bestselling love stories FREE!

Plus get a FREE surprise gift!

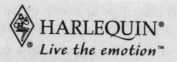